Praise for *Sing in the Morning, Cry at Night*
by Barbara J. Taylor

- A 2014 *Publishers Weekly* Best Summer Book/Pick of the Week
- Nominated for a 2014 Lime Award for Excellence in Fiction

"A profound story of how one unforeseen event may tear a family apart, but another can just as unexpectedly bring them back together again."
—*Publishers Weekly,* "Best Summer Books 2014"

"This story is at once poignant and hopeful, spiced up by such characters as Billy Sunday, the revivalist, and Grief, the specter who haunts Grace to the very edge of sanity. A rich debut."
—*Historical Novel Society*

"Taylor's careful attention to detail and her deep knowledge of the community and its people give the novel a welcome gravity."
—*Columbus Dispatch*

"An earnest, well-done historical novel that skillfully blends fact and fiction."
—*Publishers Weekly*

"A fantastic novel worthy of the greatest accolades. Writing a book about a historical event can be difficult, as is crafting a best seller, but Barbara J. Taylor is successful at both."
—*Downtown Magazine*

"An absolute gem of a book filled with beautiful characters and classical writing techniques rarely seen in modern literature."
—*Christian Manifesto,* "Top Fiction Pick of 2014"

"Like Dickens, the novel traces family tragedy, in this case the town blaming 8-year-old Violet Morgan for her older sister's death. As her parents fall victim to their own vices, Violet learns how to form her own friendships to survive."
—*Arts.Mic*

"One of the most compelling books I've ever read . . . [A] haunting story that will stay with the reader long after reading this novel."                    —*Story Circle Book Reviews*

"No one without a heart as big and warm as Barbara J. Taylor's possibly could have written a story about a family tragedy that's infused with so much hope and love, humor, mystery, and down-to-earth wisdom. This is a book I'll want to give to people. I could not put it down and can't wait to be captured again by the next book this wonderful human being writes."
—Beverly Donofrio, author of
*Astonished: A Story of Healing and Finding Grace*

"Not since reading Richard Llewellyn's *How Green Was My Valley* fifty years ago have I felt such empathy and love through fiction for a place, a time, and a people. *Sing in the Morning, Cry at Night* is a book of equal power and beauty, a bittersweet tale set in early twentieth–century Wyoming Valley, Pennsylvania, the heart and soul of America's anthracite coal mining region, a place where Grace and Grief—now, as then—walk hand in hand."
—Sara Pritchard, author of *Help Wanted: Female*

"The world of Christian miners—the core of the anthracite mining industry in northeast Pennsylvania—is beautifully evoked by Barbara J. Taylor in this remarkable novel. I found myself drawn back to its pages, living deeply in its world as I read. The sense of place—a place I know well, as I grew up there—is vividly realized. This is a lyrical, passionate novel that will hold readers in its thrall. A first-rate debut."
—Jay Parini, author of *Empire of Self*

# ALL WAITING IS LONG

# ALL WAITING IS LONG

BY BARBARA J. TAYLOR

KAYLIE JONES BOOKS

This is a work of fiction. All names, characters, places, and incidents are a product of the author's imagination. Any resemblance to real events or persons, living or dead, is entirely coincidental.

Published by Akashic Books
©2016 Barbara J. Taylor

Hardcover ISBN: 978-1-61775-471-5
Paperback ISBN: 978-1-61775-443-2
Library of Congress Control Number: 2015954207

First printing

*Kaylie Jones Books*
www.kayliejonesbooks.com

*Akashic Books*
Twitter: @AkashicBooks
Facebook: AkashicBooks
E-mail: info@akashicbooks.com
Website: www.akashicbooks.com

ALSO AVAILABLE FROM KAYLIE JONES BOOKS

*Sing in the Morning, Cry at Night*
by Barbara J. Taylor

*Unmentionables*
by Laurie Loewenstein

*Foamers*
by Justin Kassab

*Starve the Vulture*
by Jason Carney

*The Love Book*
by Nina Solomon

*We Are All Crew*
by Bill Landauer

*Little Beasts*
by Matthew McGevna

*Some Go Hungry*
by J. Patrick Redmond

*For Alice, my sister, my friend*

*Echoes of mercy,*
*Whispers of love.*
—Fanny J. Crosby

# PART ONE

*All are agreed . . . it is important that the boy be given some sex instruction . . . No such agreement exists concerning sex knowledge for the girl . . . Some say that such instruction . . . is unnecessary, because the sex instinct awakens in girls comparatively late, and it is time enough for them to learn about such matters after they are married.*
—*Woman: Her Sex and Love Life,*
William J. Robinson, MD, 1929

When Izzy passed on, it seemed fitting to christen ourselves the Isabelle Lumley Bible Class. After all, she was the one who came up with the idea for our Wednesday women's scripture meetings. At least that's how she told it. Those of us who were there from the beginning remember different, but no sense beating that drum again. Let the dead rest is what we say. Besides, Izzy left enough money to Providence Christian Church to erase any hard feelings *and* repair the crumbling steeple.

A Bible verse or two and a potluck lunch make for an edifying afternoon. And a much needed one, given the moral decline we see today. Gambling. Joyriding. Bootlegging. Not to mention the goings-on in "the Alleys" downtown. A regular red-light district. Our very own Sodom and Gomorrah right here in Scranton, Pennsylvania. Surely we're glimpsing the end times.

That's why it's so comforting to have a man like Reverend Sheets in the pulpit. An optimist through and through. Somehow he always manages to come back around to Noah's ark and that rainbow promise. An uplifting sentiment, though it wouldn't hurt to hear a different Bible lesson from time to time. Maybe something from the New Testament.

Why, just the other day we were studying that verse in Matthew about pointing out a speck in your brother's eye while ignoring the beam in your own. There's folks in our congregation who could benefit from such wisdom. Hattie Goodfellow, for one, or should we say Hattie Goodfellow Hatton. Always looking down her nose at us, but who's the real sinner? Marrying that fellow from her boarding house and traipsing off to Buffalo at her age. Here we thought she ran a respectable place. And now we're told that her nieces, Violet and Lily, are headed north to help her. Can't say why, but something doesn't ring true about that story. If Hattie needs help setting up house, maybe she's too old to be a newlywed.

Not that it's any of our affair. Who are we to judge? Just wish she'd asked our opinion before leaping. Now that the deed is done, God bless and good luck. And if the marriage comes to ruin, as we fear it might, we'll welcome Hattie back with open arms.

That's the Christian way.

# C HAPTER ONE

VIOLET AND LILY TRUDGED TO THE REAR of the Good Shepherd Infant Asylum and entered through the kitchen. According to the widow Lankowski, who'd made the arrangements, only benefactors, adoptive couples, physicians, and members of the clergy were allowed to use the front door. The Sisters of the Immaculate Heart of Mary instituted this practice years earlier in order to protect the identities of the expectant mothers they served.

"Don't let the door slam!" a fireplug of a girl yelled from across the room.

Lily pressed her hand against the oak panel and eased it shut. A stripe of fresh snow spanned the length of the threshold.

"The latch catches." The girl stood at the sink with her back to the newcomers. A tangle of red curls settled just beyond her shoulders. "Don't want to lock out all of our gentlemen callers," she laughed, throaty and low. "Names?"

"Violet Morgan. And my sister Lily." Violet stepped onto a rag rug and stomped her boots. Lily remained on the bare linoleum; water puddled at her feet.

"The Protestants are here!" the girl called out as she washed the last plate in the dishpan and dried her hands. "No rest for the wicked." She turned and smiled at the pair, exposing her swollen belly. "So which one of you is in the puddin' club?" she asked. Her eyes darted across their stomachs.

"That will be all, Muriel." A tall woman robed in dark blue serge glided into the room. "If you hurry, you'll just make confession." Her brittle voice cracked on the word *confession*, as if failing to hit a note out of range.

Embarrassment ignited the girl's cheeks as she started for the doorway. "You can't tell, is all."

"Our mother carried small," Violet explained.

"Confession," the nun repeated, patting a gold crucifix that hung from a chain around her neck.

Muriel winked at Lily from behind the nun, crossed one swollen ankle behind the other, grabbed the sides of her dress, and bowed.

Without looking back, the nun added, "You might want to save that curtsy for His Holiness should he visit us here in Philadelphia."

Muriel slinked out of the room.

"I'm Mother Mary Joseph." The woman took a step forward, and the rosary beads at her waist rattled in time. "Reverend Mother. You must be the young ladies from Scranton."

"Yes ma'am." Violet let go of the two suitcases she'd carried from the train station and pulled her younger sister Lily onto the rug. Even with nine years between them, the Morgan girls shared a strong likeness. Fair Welsh complexions, small even teeth, dimpled left cheeks. Yet in spite of their similarities, people often referred to Lily as "the pretty one." Her large round eyes were blue instead of brown; her features soft, not angular like Violet's; and Lily's hair, a warm chocolate, not that unforgiving pitch. It was as if an artist had sketched the same face twice, opting for a lighter hand the second time.

"It's most unusual for us to house both a charge and her

sister." The nun poked her hand out from a fan of sleeve and motioned the visitors forward, past a pallet stacked with brushes, paint cans, and thinner. "But Father Zarnowski from St. Stanislaus in Scranton requested the arrangement." Mother Mary Joseph sat down at the head of a table in the center of the room and nodded for Violet and Lily to each take a chair on either side of her. "And then, when your friend Mrs. Lankowski made her generous donation to the Good Shepherd," the nun waved toward a freshly painted wall, "well, how could we say no?" She pressed her lips into a thin smile and reached for a small brass bell on the table. "Have you had your supper?"

"On the train." Twenty-five-year-old Violet noted the absence of wrinkles on the woman's pale skin and wondered about her age. Under the dark veil, a starched band of white fabric stretched around her forehead and another one framed her cheeks and neck. A large bib-like collar circled her chest and shoulders in that same stiff white material. This woman possessed a confidence suggestive of age, but Violet could not see it on her face.

"A cup of tea, then," the nun said, ringing the bell. "To take the chill off."

"Thank you." Violet kicked Lily's foot under the table. Lily, head bowed, fingers tracing the tablecloth's blue and red roses, seemed not to notice.

Muriel appeared in the doorway. "Everyone's at chapel."

"Not everyone," Mother Mary Joseph sighed. "Make yourself useful then, and put on the kettle."

The girl scurried halfway across the room before she seemed to remember herself and her ungainly body. She stopped for a moment, caught her breath, and took measured steps toward the sink.

"Let's see, now." The nun began pulling items from the folds of her garment: a pair of eyeglasses, which she positioned halfway down her nose; a small ledger, leather-bound in black; several pencils, newly sharpened; and two handkerchiefs embroidered with the letters *I.H.M.* She opened the ledger to the day's date, *Saturday, February 22, 1930*, licked the tip of the closest pencil, and pushed a handkerchief toward Lily. "How old are you, child?"

"Sixteen." Lily's gaze remained fixed on the tablecloth. "One week from today."

"Look at me when I speak to you." Mother Mary Joseph lifted the girl's chin and studied her swollen eyes. "That's better." She offered another flattened smile and made a notation. "It's my understanding that your confinement should be for a period of three months."

Lily glanced across the table at her sister, then back at the nun. "Yes ma'am." Her lower lip quivered.

"You're absolutely certain?" The Reverend Mother pulled back Lily's coat and studied her belly. "Six months along?"

"As near as I can figure."

Under the table, Violet pressed her right pinky against her leg. When counting off, she always started with the pinky. *March. April. May.* Her index finger and thumb remained aloft, aimed in Lily's direction.

"I've ruined everything!" Lily reached for the handkerchief and burst into tears.

Air charged from Violet's nostrils. Lily *had* ruined everything. Violet was a forgiving person, goodness knows she had to be, but enough was enough. Lily never considered the consequences of her behavior. She only thought of herself. Had she even wondered what her delicate condition would do to their nervous mother? Had she ever weighed the cost of hiding it from their ailing father? And what about the widow Lankowski? How humiliating it had been when Violet's mother dragged the woman into what should have been a family matter. The widow had practically raised

Violet, but Violet was embarrassed all the same. And then there was the matter of her promise to marry Stanley, a secret only the widow was privy to. Violet would probably still be at the Good Shepherd Infant Asylum long after Stanley returned home to Scranton, and hand to God, that was Lily Morgan's fault.

"Don't be cross with me." Lily blew her nose into the handkerchief and refolded it.

"Not now," Violet pushed both words through gritted teeth.

"Stanley will wait," Lily continued, dabbing her eyes with a dry corner of linen. "You'll see."

"Stanley?" Mother Mary Joseph tugged off her glasses and pursed her lips.

"Hush." Violet glared at Lily. "Don't drag him into this."

"The widow Lankowski's son," Lily explained. "Adopted."

"More of a son than most." Violet dug her fingernails into her thigh.

The nun picked up her glasses, curled the wires around her ears, and started to write. "So this Stanley . . ." She looked up at Lily. "He's responsible for your trouble?"

"No!" the pair responded in unison.

"He's *Violet's* intended," Lily said, as if she had an intended of her own.

Violet slapped her palms on top of the table. "You knew?" she whispered, as if saying the words too loudly would make them true.

"Stop yelling at me." Lily looked over at the Reverend Mother. "She's always yelling at me."

Violet parceled out her words quietly, evenly. "I'm . . . not . . . yelling."

"You're yelling at me in that low voice of yours." When no one came to Lily's defense, she continued: "Mother found out you were planning to run away with him."

Violet started up from her chair and leaned toward her sister. "And just how did she find out?"

The nun patted Violet's hand, encouraging her to take her seat.

Lily gulped and squeezed her eyes shut. When she finally spoke, her words charged forth on a single breath. "I heard you and the widow talking on Christmas Eve."

Violet cursed herself for being so careless. "And you couldn't wait to tell Mother."

"She made me."

"She didn't know about it!" Violet stamped both feet, rattling the table. "How could she make you?"

Lily's eyes popped open wide. "I didn't want you running away with Stanley. I didn't want to be left alone."

"Well, you got your wish. We're together now."

"It was your idea to come with me." Lily's cheeks flushed. "I certainly don't need a keeper."

"You've done a fine job so far."

"Oh, and you're so perfect." Lily turned to the nun. "Our parents don't approve of Stanley, him being Catholic and all." She cleared her throat conspiratorially. "Not to mention Polish. But that doesn't seem to matter to her." She tossed her head toward Violet.

Silence filled the room as the Reverend Mother considered the matter. When she finally spoke, her words lacked any trace of sentimentality. "Our Lord in Heaven commands us to honor thy father and thy mother." The nun pushed the second handkerchief toward Violet. "And experience cautions us against mixed marriages."

*Experience?* The word reverberated in Violet's ear like a sour note at the piano. *What experience might a nun have? How could someone married to Jesus understand real love?* Violet twisted the hanky, as if wringing it out to dry. "I've honored my parents all my life," she finally managed.

"You'll not find a more devoted daughter." She shot a look at both Lily and the nun, daring either one to dispute her claim. Lily's lips parted briefly, but without result.

"Tea's ready," Muriel said, breaking the silence. She placed the teapot, creamer, sugar bowl, and spoons next to three cups and saucers already on the tray, and carried them to the table. A fourth cup sat cooling on the stove behind her. "Don't mind me," she said. "I'm not even here."

Mother Mary Joseph emptied the tray and poured the tea. Muriel backed away from the table, hoisted herself onto a stool near the wall, and quietly sipped her drink.

"Now, in the matter of the child," the nun warmed her hands over her cup, "we seek good Christian homes, and try to consider creed and appearance when making a match. For instance, a towheaded child in a family of Turks would cause a stir." The Reverend Mother fixed her gaze on Lily, but cast her voice in Violet's direction. "We find it best to keep them with their own kind."

Though reeling from the nun's comments, Violet couldn't bring herself to argue. Truth be told, from the moment she knew Lily's baby would be adopted out, she pictured the child being raised by a family similar to her own. Welsh. Protestant. Fair-skinned. The father, a hardworking miner, and the mother, a dark-haired beauty. They'd probably be poor like most, but no matter, as long as they raised the child to fear God.

"But enough of that." Mother Mary Joseph closed her notebook and slipped it into her pocket. "The two of you must be exhausted from your trip."

"Yes ma'am," Lily answered when Violet remained silent.

"Muriel, will you show the girls to their beds after they finish their tea?" The nun turned and stared at the girl. "Since you're still so close at hand."

Muriel's cheeks reddened again, as she lowered herself from the stool. "Gladly."

"Get some rest now," the Reverend Mother said as she rose from the table. "Six thirty comes early."

"Pardon?" Lily's head snapped up.

"Mass begins promptly at seven." Before Lily had a chance to object, the nun added, "And attendance is required. Here at the Good Shepherd, we're all God's children."

# CHAPTER TWO

"IT AIN'T SO BAD HERE." Muriel led the pair out of the kitchen into a long, mahogany-paneled hallway. At the opposite end, a hand-carved staircase wound its way to the upper floors. "Dull as ditch water, though." She nodded toward an open door on their right. "Feed hall. Food's lousy," she shrugged, "but there's plenty of it. Something to be said for that."

Violet let go of the suitcases to poke her head inside but grabbed them again when a door across from them squeaked open.

An ancient woman, whose wiry white hair started halfway back on her head, raised a trembling finger to her sunken lips. "Shush. You'll wake the babies."

Muriel dropped her voice. "Sorry, Sadie. This here's the new girl, Lily, and her sister Violet." Violet nodded. "And this here's Sadie Hope."

"A pleasure," Sadie whispered, stepping out, pulling the door shut behind her. "We just now got the babies to sleep." She motioned the girls farther down the hall, past the dining room and into the parlor. "This is better," she said, dropping onto a rose-colored couch that sagged a good deal in the middle. "Sit down, Lily." She patted the cushion next to her. "Sit. Sit," she said to the other two, waving a shaky hand toward twin tapestry-covered chairs directly across from her.

Violet let go of the suitcases and perched on the edge of the first seat. Muriel lowered herself into the chair beside her.

Sadie placed her quivering palms against Lily's stomach, and Muriel piped up: "Six months along, so she says."

"You'll blossom soon enough." Sadie smiled and her lips disappeared into the space where her teeth once resided. "Plenty of time before I see you."

"Sadie delivers the babies around here." Muriel rubbed her belly. "So what do you think? Carol Kochis says I'm having a girl, but I don't believe her."

Violet stared at Sadie's hands, now folded in her lap and still. "You're a midwife?"

Sadie eyed Muriel. "And just how would Carol Kochis know such a thing?"

"Says I'm carrying all around. Says that's what happens when you're having a girl. And she should know. Had herself two already."

Violet tried again: "Does anyone help you?"

"Nothing but an old wives' tale," Sadie said. "Only the Almighty Himself knows for sure. And if you ask me, Carol Kochis has better things to do with her time than devil you about your baby." She shook her head and mumbled, "Two girls already."

"And a boy. Every last one of them farmed out," Muriel explained to the Morgan sisters.

Sadie turned to Lily, leaned in, and pushed back her upper lip. "Teeth look good. How're your bowels?"

Lily scooted up against the far end of the couch.

Sadie seemed not to notice. "Had the shakes all my life." She stretched her hands straight out and looked at Violet. "Even as a child." She tipped her trembling palms up and examined them. "Birthed hundreds of babies, though." She paused as if in thought. "Maybe thousands. Funny thing is," she picked up a tufted pillow and cradled it, turning her eyes back to Violet, "the shaking stops as soon as I take hold of something." She smiled and her lips disappeared again.

The Reverend Mother knocked lightly on the door-frame. "The doctor's asking for you, Sadie." She continued down the hallway.

"It's been a pleasure, ladies." Sadie dropped the pillow, stood to leave, and the tremors started up again.

"So there is a doctor," Violet said, once the three girls were alone in the parlor.

Muriel looked around, then leaned forward. "Only when there's trouble." She ran a finger across her stomach. "He knows how to cut them out."

Lily shivered.

"Didn't mean to scare you," Muriel said. "He has a pur-pose, is all. And besides, a healthy girl like you," she waved her hand, "piece of cake."

Lily teared up. "I want to go home."

"Well, you can't." Violet took a breath and tried again: "They'll take good care of you. I'll see to that."

"I still don't like it here."

"I wouldn't complain too loud," Muriel said, and pointed to the wall closest to the front of the building. "Mother Mary Joseph sleeps in there. Says it's so she's close to the babies, but she can't fool me." She lowered her voice to a whisper. "The woman has elephant ears under that war bonnet. Hears everything." She hooked her thumbs behind her ears and flapped her hands. Lily laughed. "Come on. I'll show you." Muriel smiled and stood up, then led the girls back into the hallway toward the staircase. "Watch." She lifted her foot onto the first step, the boards groaning under her weight. The Reverend Mother's door opened and closed so stealthily that had it not been for Muriel's warning, the sisters would have missed the event entirely. "No need to put locks on the doors," Muriel explained, cupping her ears again. "She'll hear you if you try to give her the slip."

Halfway up the steps, Muriel leaned over the banister and pointed down to a set of half-opened French doors at the front of the hallway. "Foyer's through there. *Foyer.* Ain't that a kick. Never heard of such a word, but that's nuns for you." She paused at the landing, caught her breath, and started up again. "We go through the foyer," she laughed, "to get to the chapel on the left. Hospital's to your right. Everything here's connected. Never have to go out."

"Fine by me." Lily pulled one side of her coat over the other, and held it closed at her stomach.

Muriel continued up to the next landing. "Home sweet home," she said. "The whole second floor is ours. Third floor belongs to the good sisters." She looked up. "And Sadie Hope. Been widowed for forty years. I suppose if you're going to live like a nun, you may as well live *with* them. Not that I could ever do it," she chuckled. "Washrooms are at the end of the hall." She pointed toward the back of the building, to the place just over the kitchen. "Four of 'em. Two on each side. Knock first if you know what's good for you."

Muriel opened the door closest to them and pulled the cord on a porcelain ceiling light, one of four centered down the length of the room. Eighteen steel beds, nine on either side, lined the walls. "Clean, anyways."

Violet nodded to the two suitcases. "Where do we sleep?"

"Up here on the left." Muriel waddled to the end of the room, pulling on cords, lighting the way. "Eight and nine." She waved a hand toward two unmade beds with linens piled on blue-and-white-ticked mattresses. "I'm lucky number seven," she said, lowering herself onto the nearest bed. "A pleasure to meet you." She laughed again and lay against her pillow.

"How many girls are there?" Lily asked, backing out of the way so Violet could get in to make the beds.

"We're full up." Muriel patted the edge of her mattress, inviting Lily to sit. "Everyone's off at chapel just now."

Lily half-smiled. "Not everyone."

Muriel giggled and nodded toward Lily. "I like this one," she said to no one in particular.

When Violet finished making the beds, she set the suitcases on top.

"You can stash what's yours in the dressers." Muriel motioned toward the small chests of drawers to the left of each bed. "Stow the bags underneath."

"I want to be next to Muriel." Lily grabbed hold of the brown metal footboard and pulled herself up farther. Muriel drew up her legs to give the girl more room.

"You can't always get your way." Violet ran her hand along the tops of the cowhide suitcases before unbuckling the one closest to her. Matching luggage with forest-green lining. They were supposed to have been her wedding present from the widow who had shown them to Violet the day they'd arrived. "I just couldn't wait," the widow had said. "Act surprised when Stanley sees them. We wouldn't want him to think we have secrets."

But then the widow had dragged them out again that February night, with Violet's mother and Lily in the parlor. "I thought you could use these on your holiday," she'd said, and smiled as if she'd convinced herself that the sisters really were going to their Aunt Hattie's in Buffalo, instead of an infant asylum in Philadelphia.

"It's just that Muriel understands my delicate condition," Lily explained, as Violet lifted her sister's clothes and slid them into the dresser. Lily patted her stomach. "Anyhow, you'll still be next to me, just like home."

*Not at all like home*, Violet thought. At home, Violet

slept on the left, Lily on the right. Violet had always slept on that side, even before Lily was born, back when Daisy had been alive to share the bed. Daisy, older by thirteen months. Some of the folks in Scranton used to call them Irish twins. Almost seventeen years since that tragedy, and Violet's eyes still stung with the memory of it. She reached into her sleeve and discovered Mother Mary Joseph's handkerchief tucked inside. She dabbed her eyes and turned to the girls. "I'll be back." She headed for the door, waving the hanky.

Violet made her way down the steps. Since there was no light under Mother Mary Joseph's door, she continued down the hallway to the kitchen. When she found no one there, she decided to step outside for a breath of air. The day had been long and heavy, like every day since the first of January. New Year's, a time for luck and second chances—the day Violet had finally understood Lily's predicament. No monthly rags. Sick stomach every morning. Her two good dresses, her only dresses, pulling at the bosom. Lily had been sulking for the better part of December, but until that morning, Violet had never once thought Lily could be expecting.

A sharp wind cut across Violet's face and whipped up a sudden squall of snow, slicing the stars out of the evening sky. Violet whirled around to go inside, tried the handle, and found the door locked. Gooseflesh rippled under the thin sleeves of her blouse, prompted more by fear than cold. She cradled her arms, tucked her head, and balled her body up against the fieldstone wall. Violet had been lost in the snow when she was nine years old, the night she'd helped birth Lily, and ever since, she was terrified to be alone in it. She stayed tucked for a long time before she remembered to breathe. The air raced out of her lungs so fast it seemed to push back the wind. The snow stopped falling as quickly as it had begun, and the stars repopulated the inky sky.

Violet drew in a breath and listened for the wind to circle back, but heard only the thump of her own heart. She straightened slowly and twisted the knob a second time. The door stayed put inside its frame. *Try the main entrance,* she thought, *whether the nuns like it or not.* Just as she rounded the corner, a woman, her face hidden behind a tightly drawn shawl, bolted out of the asylum's double oak doors and down the slate front steps, vanishing into the frozen night. Violet might have thought the woman an apparition if her sobs hadn't pierced the icy silence.

Violet scurried through the yard and up the steep steps to a large porch. She looked back to make certain the woman had disappeared before turning the knob and dashing across the threshold. Violet's flesh prickled in the heated air; her limbs ached from the warmth of the foyer. She stood for a moment, dripping melted snow, silently thanking God for the unlocked door, when what sounded like a baby's whimper interrupted her prayer. Violet looked around and spotted a large white cradle to her right, near the arched entrance to the chapel. A wooden sign above the cradle instructed, *Go and Sin No More.* The cries started again, full on, so Violet walked over and scooped a swaddled bundle into her arms. A note pinned to a moth-eaten blanket simply read, *Be good to my boy.* Violet offered the infant her finger to suck, and noticed his disfigurement. She'd only seen two other harelips in her life. They reminded her of a pig's notched ear. The crying stopped momentarily, and the baby looked up with his broken expression. Violet kissed her finger and lightly traced the triangular opening from the infant's nostril to his lip.

"I'm right here, Sister!" a male voice yelled from the hospital side of the entrance. "I'll see to the matter."

Violet looked to her left as a corpulent man in a blood-stained apron parted a set of pocket doors on the opposite wall.

"What is it, Dr. Peters?" Mother Mary Joseph called out.

The man stood for a moment, eyeing Violet as he would a bit of gristle on the side of his plate. "Just another whore," he answered, in a voice too low to carry into the next room. He pushed a plug of tobacco into his bearded cheek, walked over to Violet, and whispered, "Just another stinking whore."

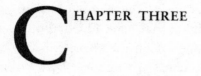

# CHAPTER THREE

As SOON AS VIOLET LEFT THE ROOM with Mother Mary Joseph's handkerchief, Lily walked to the door on Muriel's orders and looked down the hallway in both directions. "Coast is clear!"

"Not for long," Muriel called from the other end of the room, "what with all your yelling. Now, hurry up. Chapel will be over soon. And who knows when that sister of yours will get back." She reached into her top drawer, pushed aside a crumple of nightclothes, and pulled out a pile of magazines. "If the Reverend Mother catches us, we'll have to scrub floors for a month of Sundays," she said, fanning the magazines out on her bed like a winning hand of pinochle.

"Can she really make us do that?" Lily's eyes dipped toward the contraband.

Muriel grabbed her nightgown and draped it over her curly red locks, making a pious face. "With our own toothbrushes." She tied the gown's arms around her forehead, fashioning a nun's wimple for her makeshift veil. *"Here at the Good Shepherd,"* she said in Mother Mary Joseph's unsteady falsetto, *"unwholesome pursuits will not be tolerated."* Muriel lifted a pudgy thumb and started ticking off the rules. *"No tobacco. No cards. No alcohol. No profane language."* She unfolded her pinky with a flourish. *"And no suggestive literature.*" She cleared her throat and stretched her voice another octave. "*It'll rot your very soul.*"

"I'll not scrub one floor," Lily said, as she considered the consequences for the infraction she was about to commit. "And I'm not afraid to tell her that," she added, though her voice lacked conviction. She sat on the corner of Muriel's bed and fingered the magazines. *True Story*, *True Romances*, *Modern Screen*, *Movie Monthly*—all scandalous, though none very recent. Why, Gertrude Olmstead was on a November 1928 cover of *True Story*, and she hadn't been heard from since talkies became the rage.

"I'd like to be a fly on the wall when you tell her that one."

"Who?" Lily picked up the December 1929 *True Story* with a picture of Clara Bow on front.

"Mother Jesus, Mary, and Joseph." Both girls erupted into laughter. "Oh!" Muriel pressed her hands against her belly. "He's a real scrapper," she said, rubbing a tip of elbow or knee poking up.

Lily grimaced. "What was that?"

"He's kicking."

Lily looked at Muriel's belly, stunned.

"You didn't know?" Muriel swung around sidesaddle, reached for Lily's hand, and placed it against her stomach. "Here," she said. "Feel that?"

When the baby kicked again, Lily pulled her hand away and wiped it on the blanket. "How awful!"

"Awful? Happens to everybody."

"Not me!"

"You too, silly."

Lily's mouth dropped open.

"First you feel flapping inside," Muriel squinted, "but soft, like a hummingbird's wings. After that, the kicking starts."

Lily's eyebrows sprang up.

"I'm just starting my seventh month," Muriel said, "so you should be showing any day. Probably just need to put a little meat on those bones." She picked up a 1925 *Movie Monthly* with a picture of Priscilla Dean on the cover. The headline read, "Ladies in Peril." She scooped up the remaining magazines and buried them in the open drawer. "Didn't your mother teach you anything?"

Lily shook her head and moved to her own bed. Clara Bow peeked out from under her arm. "She said I'd already had *quite an education,* and that nature would take care of the rest."

"How 'bout that sister of yours? She's no spring chicken. Imagine she's been around the block a time or two."

"Violet? Hardly. She's too busy mooning over Stanley. *Stanley, Stanley,*" she singsonged. "That's all I ever hear."

"What sort of fella is he?"

"Sweet enough, I suppose. Not much taller than Violet. Educated. Finishing up law school right here in Philadelphia."

"How romantic. Will she see him?"

"No!" Lily slapped the magazine onto her lap. "He doesn't know a thing, and Violet swore it would stay that way. He thinks we're off in Buffalo visiting our relations." She picked up the *True Story* and smoothed its pages. The publication's motto, *Truth is stranger than fiction,* stared up at her. "It's bad enough the widow knows, but Mother couldn't be stopped. She said Catholics know more about worldly matters."

Muriel closed her eyes and smiled. "Is he handsome?"

"Promise you won't tell?"

Muriel nodded so vigorously that her wimple and veil slid off her head, down onto her pillow.

"I couldn't say." She leaned in and whispered, "I've never been able to get past the hand."

"What's wrong with his hand?" Muriel scooted toward the edge of her mattress, closer to Lily.

"It isn't there." Lily drew back and shivered. "For as long as I've known him, he's always just had the one."

"Born that way? I've heard of that. A woman oughtn't look at a crone or a cripple when she's in the family way. It'll mark the baby for sure."

Lily considered the warning. "It's different with Stanley. Lost his hand in the mine when he was a boy. Came *this* close to dying." She pressed a half-inch of air between her thumb and forefinger. "He swears it was Violet's voice that brought him back."

"Now there's a romance story if I ever heard one. And what about you?" Muriel rolled her copy of *Movie Monthly* and rapped it against Lily's headboard. "Do you have a sweetheart waiting for you back home?"

Lily considered the question. She loved George Sherman Jr., but that didn't make him her sweetheart. Or her his. He'd told her to come back in a few years after she'd "grown up some," but that hardly meant he was waiting for her. She'd seen him around town with those other girls. And he'd certainly never want her now if he knew she was expecting. "I can't say for sure." Her eyes teared up. "How about you? Do you have a beau?"

"Promise you won't tell?" Muriel leaned in.

"Cross my heart."

"I'm a married woman," she said, stretching out a ringless hand. "All very proper."

Lily examined Muriel's unadorned fingers out of politeness. "Why not tell?"

"Pa would kill him."

"Is he mean?"

"My pa? He's wonderful to me. Says I'm his little princess." Muriel wrapped her arms around her stomach. "I'm the only girl in a family of nine." She trembled. "So naturally he favors me."

"What're you going to do when the baby comes?"

"Take him home, of course. Raise him with his daddy."

"Or her. Could just as easily be a girl. Even Carol what's-her-name said so."

Muriel winced. "It's a boy," she directed toward her belly, as if issuing a command, "no matter what Carol Kochis says."

"What makes you so sure?"

"Just has to be, is all." Muriel shivered again.

"What's he like?" Lily asked. "This husband of yours?"

"He married me for my green eyes." Muriel tipped her head, batted her lashes, and laughed. "Men always notice my green eyes."

"Same here," Lily said, "except mine are blue."

Muriel opened her magazine to a story called "Love Bound," with a picture of a happy couple standing along-side a train. "My husband's a conductor for the D&H Rail-road." She paused, then nodded. "Yes, that's it. He travels all over the country." Muriel closed her eyes. "Said he'd take me with him. Far away where Pa can't ever hurt me again."

"But I thought—"

The sound of footsteps carried up into the room. Muriel leaned over, snatched Lily's magazine, mated it with her own, and shoved them in the drawer. "This is just between us."

Women and girls filed in from the evening service, heads still bowed in either prayer or obligation.

A thickset nun—all girth, no stature—squeezed in behind them. "Lights out in twenty minutes." She backed up into the hallway and disappeared.

"Sister Immaculata," Muriel said as she grabbed for her nightclothes. "A homely sight, even for a nun."

Lily watched as some of her roommates scurried toward the bathrooms, nightclothes in hand, while others undressed alongside their beds, Muriel among them. Lily wondered at their immodesty while she pulled her own gown out of the drawer and made her way to the washroom.

Sister Immaculata returned exactly twenty minutes later, barking, "Bed check!" She walked the length of the room, crossing off names on her clipboard. "DeLeo?" Check. "Mancini?" Check. "Kochis?" Check. "Lehman?" She looked around and called again. "Lehman?"

A rather pale-looking girl, no more than eighteen, followed her swollen belly through the doorway. She pressed one hand into her back and used the other to hold onto the footboard she passed. "Sorry, Sister." She paused one bed away from her own to catch her breath. "I slow down a little more each day."

The nun sneered as she marked off the name, and proceeded up the aisle. "Dennick?" she said in front of an empty bed. "Judith Dennick?"

"She's being delivered," someone offered from a bed in the front of the room. "Breech birth. Had to call the doctor."

Sister Immaculata made a notation on her clipboard and took a few steps forward.

"Hartwell?" Check.

At the sound of her last name, Muriel offered up a smile that tried too hard and went unnoticed.

As the nun stepped forward, Lily focused on the three fleshy chins protruding from her wimple.

"Morgan?" Check.

"Other Morgan?" She spun toward Lily and glared. "Where's your sister?"

When Lily froze, Muriel answered with that same

smile. "I believe she's with Mother Mary Joseph." The nun scratched something on her clipboard. "Besides," Muriel said, "I imagine she can come and go as she pleases, seeing it's Lily who's with child."

The many-chinned nun yanked the cord on the nearest ceiling light. "We'll see about that." She marched toward the door, pulling each of the three subsequent cords as she passed.

Muriel crawled under the covers and turned her body in Lily's direction. "So what did you mean when you said you couldn't say for sure if you had a sweetheart?"

Lily tipped her head toward the empty bed. "Where do you think Violet got to?"

"Pipe down!" someone yelped from across the aisle. "Six thirty comes early."

"Don't worry," Muriel whispered, "Mother Mary Joseph's a talker. Probably running Violet through the other nine Commandments, seeing they already covered the one about honoring your parents." She laughed lightly.

"Thanks, Muriel." Lily grabbed a handful of sleeve and soaked up tears as they sprang to her eyes.

"Good night." The words attached themselves to a yawn. Muriel rolled over on her side and nuzzled the pillow. "I'm glad you're here."

"Sweet dreams." Lily lay still, listening to the sound of the other women, a despairing dirge of prayers and whimpers. After some time, she turned toward the window and added her voice to their song.

Violet stood at the sink rinsing the infant's soapy skin with handfuls of warm water. *Stinking whore.* She shook her head to loosen the words, but each spiny syllable dug into her skull like barbed wire.

Mother Mary Joseph returned to the kitchen carrying a

gray two-piece sleeping suit. "It's a little big," she said, holding it up to the light, "but it'll do for now." The thick, sweet smell of Fels-Naptha soap wafted up from the nightclothes and filled the room.

Violet lifted the baby and wrapped him in a towel that had been warming on the radiator. "Reverend Mother, I think you should know—"

"Normally, we bathe the children in the nursery," the nun interrupted, setting the sleeping suit on the already blanketed table, next to the talcum powder, rash cream, mineral oil, diaper, and pins, "but not at this hour. No sense waking the other children."

"This Dr. Peters . . ." Violet carried the boy over to the nun and handed him in her direction.

Mother Mary Joseph walked past the pair, struck a match, and lit the front burner on the stove. "A little gruff." She warmed a bottle of milk in a shallow pot of water. "A fine man though." Nodding toward the mineral oil, she said, "Rub his head good. Nothing makes a baby look neglected more than cradle cap."

Violet poured a few drops of oil on her palm and worked it gently into the boy's yellow-crusted scalp. "Should flake off in a day or two." She creamed, powdered, diapered, and dressed the infant with a deft hand.

"You know your way around a baby."

"I practically raised Lily." Violet bent down and inhaled. "Nothing smells sweeter."

"And your mother?" The nun shook a few drops of milk onto her wrist.

"She had a hard time of it for a while." Violet settled the boy on her lap and explored the opening in the roof of his mouth with her finger. "Now, about that doctor."

Mother Mary Joseph handed the bottle to Violet, sat down, and caressed the baby's sunken cheek. "Can't be more than a month old, poor thing. He's wasting away. Probably never had a proper feeding."

Violet tipped the bottle toward the right side of his mouth, away from the cleft. He started sucking, but seemed to take in more air than milk. A moment later, the little bit of liquid he'd consumed leaked back out through his nose in a fit of sneezes. "You better do this." She lifted the bundle toward the nun.

"Sit him up," Mother Mary Joseph replied, not moving from her seat. "That's right. Now point the nipple down a little. Good."

The infant quickly fell into a satisfied rhythm of suck, swallow, breathe. In ten minutes, he'd finished the bottle and expelled a boisterous burp without any coaxing.

The Reverend Mother tickled the boy's chin and looked at Violet. "Now, keep doing that every three to four hours, and he'll get some weight on him in no time." She stood up and grabbed the washcloth to wipe his face.

"But I'm here to look after Lily," Violet said, keeping her eyes on the boy.

"A little late for that."

"If you're suggesting . . ."

"I'm sure you won't mind helping out." The nun's words rolled over Violet's. "Babies get born here." She nodded in the direction of the front entrance. "Or left in that cradle. Either way, we don't have enough hands." The infant started to fuss a little, and Mother Mary Joseph walked over to the cupboard on the wall opposite the sink. "People losing jobs every day. Can't afford another mouth to feed. It would break your heart if you let it." The earthy smell of potatoes and onions wafted up as she searched the shelves. She found a bottle of vanilla extract, tipped it onto her finger, and ran it along the baby's gums. "We're full up," the nun continued, "but God as my witness, the Good Shepherd has never refused a mother or a child, and as long as I'm alive, we never will." She turned as the doctor strolled into the kitchen.

Violet looked up. "Speak of the devil."

"Thank you again for all your help this evening, Dr. Peters. We might have lost Judith and her newborn if you hadn't come when you did." The Reverend Mother cleared a spot at the end of the table. "Sit."

"Another time. Good Shepherd babies don't arrive during bankers' hours," the doctor cackled. A bit of spittle caught at the corner of his beard and hung there. He set his medical bag on the table and put on his topcoat. "And once again," he placed his hand on Violet's shoulder and squeezed, "I apologize for any misunderstanding. When I saw you with that," he paused as if considering his next word, "*child*, I assumed . . ."

Violet bristled and opened her mouth to speak.

"No harm done." The Reverend Mother turned to Violet. "Dr. Peters has been with us for nearly ten years. And I daresay, he loves our unfortunates as much as we do."

"Happy to do the Lord's work," he said.

Just then, the infant started to cry. Violet tipped the neck of the vanilla bottle onto her finger and rubbed the liquid along the baby's gums. Glaring at the doctor, she shrugged his hand off her shoulder without another word.

Violet tiptoed through the dormitory doorway and headed down the aisle. She stopped to tuck the blanket around Lily's bared feet before continuing past her own bed to the window. Puffs of frigid air invaded the room where expectant mothers either slept or tried to. Violet pushed her thumb against a pane, melting tendrils of frost. She pressed again with her other thumb, and a heart appeared in the midst of the icy strands.

"Vi, is that you?" Lily squinted toward the moonlight.

"Go back to sleep," Violet said, flattening her palm against the window, supplanting her flimsy heart with a sturdy handprint. "It'll be morning soon enough."

Lily mumbled something incomprehensible and closed her eyes.

Shrill winds raged outside; the frosty glass shivered against its tired frame. *Stanley*, Violet thought. How was it that a person could be so close, and yet so far away?

If he'd married her early on like she'd wanted, married her before going off to law school to save the world (and her reputation, or so he'd said: "Let me prove to your father that I'm worthy of your hand"), Stanley would be with her now. He'd help her make sense of a world where mothers abandoned their babies in the name of duty, or selfishness, or God. If he'd married her before going to the University of Pennsylvania, as he used to say he would, she'd be surrounded by her own children now, and not the Good Shepherd's brood. So what if her parents spurned her? It wouldn't be the first time. She'd spent the better part of a year as an outcast after Daisy's death.

Daisy. Everyone had blamed Violet for the tragedy, except Stanley. Even her mother thought she threw that lit sparkler out of jealousy. Violet had been jealous of her sister, it was true. With one year between them, Daisy got the store-bought dress, since it was she who was being baptized that morning, while Violet wore one of her sister's hand-me-downs. But they'd made up that afternoon when they'd found the fireworks their father had bought for the evening's Fourth of July celebration. It was Daisy who told Violet to hold them while she lit the match. It was Daisy who said the first one wouldn't light. And Daisy who told her to keep a lookout for their parents and that nosey Mrs. Evans, causing Violet to turn away when the sparkler unexpectedly caught fire. She didn't throw that firework out of jealously.

She tossed it out of instinct when the flame burned her fingers. Daisy knew that. Violet saw forgiveness in those blue eyes the moment the sparkler touched the hem of her sister's dress. Folks around Scranton still talked about Daisy—the little Morgan girl who sang hymns for three days as she lay dying. *God called home an angel*, they'd concluded, as if they knew God's ways. Yet, for months, many of those same good Christians assumed Violet had hurt Daisy on purpose. Assumed an eight-year-old girl could kill her sister. Was that God's way?

Violet had spent the rest of that year looking in from the outside. As awful as it was, she learned early on she could endure it, endure almost anything with Stanley close by. How ironic that Stanley should be so near, as Violet stood in the mothers' ward of an infant asylum, sworn to secrecy.

# C HAPTER FOUR

FEBRUARY WINDS KICKED UP A FRESH DUSTING of winter outside Stanley's bedroom window. Triangles of snow pressed into the ledge's corners, as if taking refuge from the punishing squall. Inside his rented room, Stanley rubbed his stinging eyes with thumb and forefinger. He'd spent his entire Saturday studying, and still felt ill-prepared for Monday's exam. Mining law. His most difficult class, and the most important one, if he intended to make a go of it in Scranton where politics and coal were a dirty business. *Scranton.* The word swelled inside Stanley's brain, squeezing out the likes of *Pennsylvania Coal Company v. Mahon* and *The Anthracite Coal Strike Commission of 1902.*

*Scranton. Home. Violet.*

And there he was again, imagining her in that red dress on New Year's Eve. The neckline dipped in the middle and curved up and around her breasts. A channel between two seas he ached to explore.

Stanley shook his head to loosen the vision. He couldn't afford to get lost in her. Not tonight. He looked at the open textbook on his desk in front of the window. Clarence Darrow stared back at him in a photo taken at the Lackawanna County Courthouse in downtown Scranton. Someone had snapped it the day Darrow gave his closing argument to the Anthracite Commission in support of the striking miners.

Stanley eyed the speech included on the page. *We are working for democracy, for humanity, for the future . . .*

Darrow's words usually bolstered Stanley, especially when he flagged in his resolve to finish school before marrying. Violet would wait, he'd tell himself in the darkest part of night when longing took its shot at reason. With a law degree, he'd be able to feed his family *and* fight for the miners, who deserved better working conditions and higher wages. His own father had died in the mines, and though he had mostly been known for his cruel ways, Stanley still wanted to honor him and all the men who'd lost their lives to coal. Yes, he missed Violet. But what of it? There were families back home who'd never see their loved ones' faces again. Stanley simply had to hold out for three more months. A small price to pay for their future. Violet knew that, even if she had been sulking when they'd said their goodbyes at the train station on New Year's Day.

She would wait. She'd promised.

It was no use. The thought of her in that red dress washed over him again. Stanley shut his eyes and pictured Violet standing across the street on her porch just before midnight on New Year's Eve. There she'd stood in that dress (oh, how he loved her in red), no coat, laughing, waiting for someone to open the door. "It's my turn to be the first-footer," she'd called out, rubbing her arms for warmth. According to Welsh tradition, the first foot to cross the threshold in the New Year should belong to someone with dark hair. "I almost forgot," she'd said, grabbing the coal bucket from the steps. Fuel in the hand of the first-footer symbolized work and warmth, two gifts all mining families needed.

Violet hadn't waved Stanley over that night. Her parents didn't approve of their relationship. Owen, her father, had loved Stanley for as long as he'd known him; he'd carried the boy out of the mine the day he'd lost his hand, but even he couldn't abide a mixed marriage. "Unevenly yoked," her father had said. "Protestants should marry Protestants. Catholics, Catholics. Says so in the Bible."

After Stanley's father died, the widow Lankowski raised the ten-year-old as her own son. She brought him to live in the only Polish home on Spring Street, across from Violet and her family, so Stanley understood Owen's way of thinking. Most Catholics from up at St. Stanislaus felt the same way.

That's why Stanley had to finish school before asking Violet's father for her hand. The lot of a lawyer's wife was far better than that of a miner's, and Owen Morgan knew it. Would he rather she end up with someone poor just because he was Protestant? Someone like Tommy Davies? A nice enough fellow who'd lived next door to Violet all her life, baptized in the Providence Christian Church. But what did any of that matter if Tommy Davies would never be able to give her the life she deserved on a miner's wages, or worse yet, make a widow of her before her time? Owen understood the dangers of that life, and Stanley was convinced that like most fathers, he wanted better for his daughter.

His purpose renewed, Stanley turned his attention back to his textbook and began reading.

"Don't shoot!" The door inched open, and a pasty arm poked into the room, waving an envelope like a flag of surrender.

Stanley watched as Evan Evans stepped inside, laughing good-naturedly as though they'd shared in the joke.

Evan Evans had been the neighborhood bully as far back as Stanley could remember. Bad enough they'd grown up one block away from one another, but fate had somehow thrown them together in the same rooming house a few months earlier, when Evan took a job with the railroad.

"I'm trying to study."

"My mistake." Evan held the envelope to his nose and inhaled loudly. "I thought you'd want to hear from . . ." He paused. "Now that's odd. It's the widow's return address," he held the letter up to the light and squinted, "but the signature reads, *Your Violet.*"

"Where did you . . . ?" Stanley jumped up and grabbed the envelope.

Evan shrugged. "Someone must've seen the Scranton postmark and put it in my box."

"I'll bet." Stanley sat back down with the letter in hand and turned toward his books. He'd had it with Evan Evans and his dirty tricks—in grade school he'd tell on classmates any chance he got, running his mouth about the gossip his no-good mother concocted, and worst of all, picking on Violet after her sister died.

Sniffing the air, Evan remarked, "You can still smell the perfume." He snickered. "I'd say she's sweet on you."

"Stay out of it. I'm warning you."

"Whoa! I'm just the messenger." He pivoted his foot as if to leave but continued facing forward. "Of course, I have to wonder what her parents would think if they found out."

Stanley shot up from his chair and the letter fell to the floor. He pinned Evan against the wall with his handless arm and gripped his throat with the good one. The fact that Evan stood a head taller made no difference. "Tell anyone about this," Stanley paused to give his words weight, "and, swear to God, I'll kill you." He held Evan a moment longer before letting go.

Evan smoothed his shirt, adjusted his collar, and finger-combed his hair. "Nice way to treat an old friend," he said.

"We were never friends." Stanley picked up the letter and sat down on his bed. "Now get the hell out."

"I won't forget this," Evan said, and he skulked out of the room.

Fifteen minutes passed before Stanley finally began to simmer down. He held the envelope the whole time, but chose not to open it in his agitated state. Violet deserved his full attention.

Threat or no threat, by Monday morning, Evan Evans would have a letter in the mail to his mother Myrtle who would claim it was her Christian duty to call on Violet's mother, Grace.

The news would upset Mrs. Morgan, but it probably wouldn't shock her, or Owen. They'd spent a considerable amount of time over the years trying to thwart the most steadfast kind of love—that which is rooted in friendship. Stanley and Violet had been playmates in childhood, fishing up at Leggett's Creek, calling birds in the woods alongside the dairy. But when adolescence struck, society's mores and a newfound self-consciousness created a natural distance between them. Mrs. Morgan seized her chance, nudging Violet toward more feminine pursuits such as painting, needlework, and Bible study with the girls from Sunday school. On the occasions when Stanley did stop by, Mr. Morgan would say, "It's too nice a day to be cooped up inside," or, "Go have fun with your buddies," before sending him on his way.

Fortunately for Stanley and Violet, the widow Lankowski favored romance over practicality. "You were destined to be together," she often said when recounting her part in their courtship. "I knew it the day I caught the pair of you playing hooky down at Murray's store. You couldn't have been more than eight or nine. There you both were, trembling in your boots over getting caught. But neither one of you turned against the other. You faced what you had coming together. God's hand is in that kind of love." Just to be sure, the widow had explained, she decided to put her hand in as well.

"I hear Violet's been working over at Walsh's," she said on the Saturday Stanley returned home from his freshman year in college. When he didn't bite, she added, "The studio," then another pause, "on Lackawanna Avenue."

"I know where it is." When had Violet taken an interest in photography? For some reason this irritated Stanley.

"She's coloring the portraits."

At least that part made sense. Violet had always had a steady hand. "I know what you're doing, Babcia." He called her grandmother in Polish. Although the widow wasn't related to Stanley by blood, he'd started using the name soon after she'd taken him in. It seemed fitting, given her age and importance in his life.

"I'm telling you about an old friend. That's what I'm doing," she'd said, peeling a lace tablecloth off a pile of linens and handing one corner to Stanley. "An old friend." She searched the outstretched lace for the portion in need of repair. "With a new job."

"There." Stanley used his stump to point to a small tear near the center of the fabric.

"Who works most Saturdays." The widow sat down in a chair next to her sewing table and draped the cloth across her lap. "Perfect for an unmarried girl." She examined several spools of thread before selecting the closest match. "Almost as good as lace work."

Stanley ignored the widow's obvious attempt at matchmaking. For one thing, he had no interest in courting Violet. And for another, he'd purposely taken the early train back from school so he'd be home in time to see the debut of Queenie the baby elephant up at Nay Aug Zoo. Queenie, Scranton's first elephant, had been purchased with donations from children all over the city. Stanley had always had a soft spot for animals. As a boy, he'd even had a pet mule named Sophie. A beautiful creature, white as snow. She'd met her maker some years earlier, but every time Stanley passed the Harrises' barn where he'd kept her, he liked to pretend she was still inside, sleeping or munching on an apple.

"I'll be back in a few hours," he called out to the widow. June 14, 1924—a day so beautiful, he decided to walk the four miles to Nay Aug. It would give him a chance to clear his head.

*Violet.* Although he was no longer interested in her, he did find it funny that she was working for an Irishman, a Catholic no less. What would her father think of that? *I suppose he has no qualms about Catholic money*, Stanley thought, *just Catholic suitors.*

He walked over to Providence Square and continued down North Main Avenue, toward town. But Stanley liked Owen. He'd always been kind to him. They just happened to disagree about what was best for Violet. Not that it mattered now. Yes, Stanley had carried a torch for her in high school, but he'd moved on. He'd taken Lorraine Day to the St. Valentine's Day formal. Hadn't seen her since, but Violet certainly didn't figure into that.

Stanley walked on, past Scranton Central High School, their alma mater. For a moment he remembered standing outside the boys' entrance, trying to catch a glimpse of Violet as she entered on the girls' side.

Instead of turning up Vine Street to get to Nay Aug, he headed toward town. Toward Lackawanna Avenue. Was there a law against a fellow stopping by to say hello to an old friend? For that's what she was, an old friend. He continued this line of reasoning as he passed the post office, the courthouse, and another block of storefronts.

He stopped and looked across the street at a moss-green awning proclaiming, *Walsh's Portrait Studio,* in bright white letters. Stanley considered his greeting. Keep it cheerful, he

thought, as you would with any friend. *So good to see you.*
No need to fawn over her. Wouldn't want to give the girl the
wrong idea.

He glanced at his reflection in a shoemaker's window,
pushed down a cowlick at the part in his hair, and crossed
the intersection. Maybe he'd tell her how well she looked.
To do less would be impolite.

As soon as he arrived on the other side of the street,
his heart fell. A sign, posted on the front door, read, *Closed
early*. Tacked next to it, a newspaper clipping announced,
"See Queenie, the Kiddies' Own Elephant, All Day Saturday." Someone, Mr. Walsh most likely, had also put a basket
of peanuts out for anyone heading up to the zoo.

Well, if that didn't take the cake. It wasn't her fault, of
course, but he was annoyed with her just the same. And
with Babcia for wasting his time. And with himself for be-
having so foolishly. He grabbed a peanut out of the basket,
cracked the shell with one hand, and popped its contents
into his mouth.

The door swung open. "They're for the elephant." Violet
laughed, stepping outside.

"I thought you . . ." Stanley's cheeks burned.

She pulled the door shut, locked it, and turned toward
him. "What a wonderful surprise." She squeezed his arm
and stepped back to look at him. "College suits you."

Stunned, Stanley stood in silence another moment before saying, "You're still . . ." he paused to gaze, "so beautiful." As soon as he said the words, an awkwardness settled
over them, the sort of awkwardness that comes when two
people suddenly and simultaneously understand the stakes.

"Queenie awaits," Violet finally said, looping her arm
through Stanley's handless one and pulling him toward Nay
Aug.

* * *

Thousands of people turned out for a chance to see a real elephant, so the line stretched beyond the limits of the zoo, into the picnic grove.

"All waiting is long," Violet said after they'd been standing for half an hour.

Stanley could be impatient at times, even stubborn, but not today, not with Violet so near, so beautiful. "Didn't your mother used to say that?" He studied her dress, that face, those eyes, committing all of it to memory.

She nodded. "And her mother before her."

"All depends on who you're waiting with, I say." He smiled and thought for a moment he might kiss her.

"Get your souvenirs here!" a vendor called out from behind a wheeled cart. He stopped alongside Stanley and motioned to a herd of button-eyed elephants with colorful chintz hides. "A remembrance for the lady?"

Coins changed hands before Violet could object. Stanley studied the pile and selected the floppy-legged version whose loaf-shaped body suggested a permanent state of repose. "Violets," he said, pointing out the delicate flowers on the fabric. He handed her the keepsake, adding, "For you."

Twenty minutes later they took their turn in front of Queenie, a footnote now in Stanley's memory. His wait with Violet, her sunburned nose, her licorice breath, was what remained indelible in his mind.

They were holding hands by the time they left the zoo. The kiss took another two days and a good deal of courage on both their parts. When Stanley finally asked if that had been her first, Violet simply said, "It's the only one that matters." She'd meant to reassure him, he was convinced, but her words rankled him. Someone else had tasted those lips. Tommy Davies, most likely, though Violet refused to discuss the matter. She didn't have to. Stanley had seen the way Tommy looked at her.

\* \* \*

Stanley lifted the letter to his face, savoring the scent of lilacs. Violet had waited long enough. Come graduation, he
was going to marry her. He wouldn't even unpack his bag.
He'd go over to her house and ask her father for her hand,
as a gesture of respect. If Mr. Morgan said no, he'd take Violet and leave as planned. He knew of a justice of the peace
in Philadelphia who would marry them, and before the end
of May, they'd be Mr. and Mrs. Stanley Adamski.

# CHAPTER FIVE

"FOLLOW ME." Muriel signaled for Lily to grab her coat from the hall closet and head toward the kitchen where the two workmen, who had finished painting the last room that morning, were cleaning their brushes and packing up for good. "Say it ain't so, Joe." Muriel winked at a stocky fellow, wiping excess paint off a can.

"Yes, kid," he said, picking up on her reference to the Shoeless Joe Jackson scandal and playing along, "I'm afraid it is."

"No more foxes in the henhouse," the other man chimed in, either unaware of the baseball banter or unable to add to it.

"We'll miss you, boys." Muriel linked arms with Lily and the two girls slipped sideways out the back door.

"Where are we going?" Lily asked, trying to button her coat one-handed.

"You'll see." Muriel let go of Lily's arm and the two walked single file along the chapel side of the building.

"What if we get caught?" It had only been three days since Lily's arrival, yet she found herself struggling with the button at her belly.

"I haven't gotten caught yet." Muriel pulled Lily into a natural alcove behind some overgrown forsythia bushes that ran the length of the wall. "Anyhow, Mother Mary Joseph is meeting with some of the benefactors. She'll never miss us."

"But what if Sister Immaculata . . . ?"

Muriel silenced Lily with her eyes. "We can go back in as soon as I have a smoke." She reached into her pocket and pulled out a cigarette and a matchbook. "I don't know about you," Muriel said, "but I'm in no hurry to get back. Who needs lessons in needlepoint, anyway?"

"I embroidered two pillowcases once, and Mother put them in my hope chest. *Her* hope chest, really, but she said it'll be mine someday."

"Well, if that don't beat all." Muriel cocked her head and laughed. "Are you rich or something?"

"Hardly."

Muriel glanced at Lily's threadbare coat. "You don't look rich," Muriel said, "but you sound it. *Hope chest.* That's almost as funny as *foyer.*"

"I'm going to be rich," Lily said, as confidently as if she'd said, *I'm going to the store*, or, *I'm going to have a birthday.*

"*Hope chest.*" Muriel shook her head and laughed again. Just as she was about to strike a match, a maroon Model T started up the driveway and stopped at the foot of the main entrance. Instinctively, she stepped farther into the bushes, pressed her back against the wall, and put a finger to her lips. Both girls watched as the driver emerged from the car, feet and head first, unfolding himself to a height of six and a half feet. "Jack Barrett," Muriel whispered. "A benefactor." With legs almost as long as the car was wide, the man climbed the steps, crossed the porch, and entered the building in under ten seconds.

Lily broke out in a fit of giggles. "I don't think you'll be winning at hide-and-seek anytime soon." She glanced at Muriel's stomach poking through the branches, and they both started laughing.

"That was a close call," Muriel finally said, still smiling as she struck the match and lit her cigarette.

Lily sobered and pointed to the passenger side of the car where a pudgy woman stared straight ahead and fidgeted with her uncombed hair. *What do we do?* Lily mouthed.

Muriel started laughing again. *"Jack Sprat could eat no fat,"* she singsonged. *"His wife could eat no lean."*

"What is wrong with you?" Lily whispered as she eyed the wall to see if she could sneak back in, staying hidden behind the forsythia bushes.

*"And so betwixt them both, they licked the platter clean."* Muriel took a drag on her cigarette, and for that moment she was a study in contentment. "That's just Mamie," she said, blowing a smoke ring, then erasing it with her hand. "Crazy as a bed bug. Never says a word. Just stays put when her husband comes by."

"How sad." The bushes were too thick farther up, so Lily decided to stay and wait the Barretts out.

Muriel licked the ends of her thumb and index finger and extinguished her smoke. "For another day," she said, her tone reverential, as she tucked the cigarette back into her pocket.

Lily kept her eyes on the car.

Muriel peered through the bushes for a better look. "I heard talk about how Mamie lost a baby girl and can't have any more. Never been right since."

"That happened to my mother," Lily said. "Had a nervous breakdown after she lost my other sister." When Muriel didn't say anything, Lily added, "That was a long time ago, before I was born."

"You just never know," Muriel finally said. "Here I thought you had the perfect life."

"I do. I mean, she's better now. I never knew her that way. She still has sad spells, now and again. Not often."

"How'd she get better?"

"Me." Lily stood straighter, momentarily prideful. "At least that's what everyone says. I was a miracle baby, and that got her living again."

"I wonder if a baby could cure Mamie." Muriel pulled back a few branches to get a better look. "Nah," she said, watching the woman who was now as still as a statue, "she's too far gone." She let go of the branches and turned back. "So life is perfect." Muriel noticed that Lily's coat was unbuttoned at the belly. "Almost perfect."

"Everyone was always worried. They never let me out of their sight. It's unnatural to be brought up that way. If they could've wrapped me in cotton and locked me in a room, they would have, just to keep me safe. What if something happened to me? That kind of love suffocates a person."

"I don't know. I think I could use a little suffocating." This time Muriel's laugh sounded hollow. She stepped out of the bushes, pulling Lily along with her, and started back.

"They always tell me I'm special, but if I'm so special, why am I poor?" Lily turned to Muriel for an answer.

"Don't look at me. I've accepted my lot." Muriel eyed Lily up and down. "But you? I see you in a mansion someday, high on a hill."

"Married to a benefactor," Lily said. "A man who can afford to give his money away because there's always more to be had."

"And I'll swing by for a visit sometime, and we'll needlepoint pillowcases all day long." They both giggled now, and Muriel added, "You're spoiled, but I don't mind."

"I *am* spoiled," Lily said, glancing at her disappearing waistline. *Spoiled for George,* she thought, but didn't say it.

Mother Mary Joseph shared the couch with Thelma Powell, the railroad magnate's wife, whose plumed hat molted as she spoke. "I truly believe the worst of it is behind us," she said, fanning a feather away from her nose.

In a chair opposite, Stephen Francis Poklemba looked more serious than usual. "Harder times are coming, I'm afraid." As the business school dean at Villanova, his opinion usually carried weight.

"I disagree," Thelma said. "Did you read today's paper?" She pulled the *Public Ledger* out of her handbag and read the headline. *"Effects of the Stock Market Crash Have Disappeared.* They wouldn't print it if it weren't true." She scanned the article. "Says it'll all be over," she swatted another feather, "in thirty to sixty days."

"With all due respect . . ." Stephen began.

Thelma handed the paper over to him. "Read it for yourself. They don't make these things up."

As usual, throughout the meeting Jack Barrett stood behind a tapestry-covered chair, tipping it back and forth. He had energy to spare and could never sit for very long. "The point is," he now interjected, "we're all committed to the Good Shepherd, and whatever the future holds, we'll continue to lend our financial support."

"That's comforting," Mother Mary Joseph said.

"Enough of the doom and gloom. Have you had a chance to try the new machine?" Jack asked, referring to the incubator he and Mamie had donated a month earlier. "My friend Couney swears by them." Dr. Martin A. Couney, the world's foremost expert on incubators, had delivered the machine in person. "He traveled all over the country setting up what he called *incubator hospitals.* State fairs, Coney Island, you name it."

"We haven't had to yet," the Reverend Mother said.

"That's too bad," Jack replied, then corrected himself: "It's good you haven't needed it. I'm just anxious to see how it works." He stopped tipping the chair and walked over to the doorway. "I have to wonder if a machine like that would have made any difference when our Nellie was born. Guess we'll never know," he murmured.

Mother Mary Joseph stood up, signaling an end to the formal portion of the meeting. "How is Mamie?" she asked.

"About the same."

"She's in our prayers," Thelma offered, collecting her newspaper and adjusting her hat.

Jack nodded his thanks. "Yes, indeed," he said. Still not finished with the topic of the incubator, he added, "Couney says you're lucky to have such a modern piece of equipment in your hospital."

"We're very blessed," Mother Mary Joseph said, keeping whatever reservations she still harbored on the matter to herself.

## REASONS WHY A MISSTEP IN A GIRL HAS MORE SERIOUS CONSEQUENCES THAN A MISSTEP IN A BOY

*If a girl makes a misstep . . . she has for the rest of her life a Damocles's sword hanging over her head, and she is in constant terror lest her sin be found out . . . even if the girl escaped pregnancy, the mere finding out that she had an illicit experience deprives her of social standing, or makes her a social outcast and entirely destroys or greatly minimizes her chances of ever marrying and establishing a home of her own. She must remain a lonely wanderer to the end of her days.*
—*Woman: Her Sex and Love Life,*
William J. Robinson, MD, 1929

Caught on the horns of a dilemma. That's how Myrtle Evans put it after Evan told her about that perfumed letter from Violet to Stanley. If it were our daughter, we'd want to know, but Grace is another story. The most innocent remark can set her off. Only last month, she huffed out of church after someone suggested Grace might want to keep a closer eye on Lily. Such a pretty girl. Beauty like that can lead to trouble. Better sure than sorry.

In the end, Myrtle decided she was obliged to tell Grace, but not until after March 1. No sense ruining St. David's Day for her and Owen. This year's banquet is being held at the new Masonic Temple on North Washington Avenue. What a thrill. We're eager to see if it's as magnificent inside as out. A real jewel in Scranton's crown, designed by a fellow named Raymond Hood, according to the paper. It promises to be a wonderful time, though we could do without the dancing later in the evening. That sort of cavorting might seem innocent to some, but as the saying goes, *A great sin can enter through a small door.*

Or a perfumed letter. That's why Grace needs to put a stop to Violet's antics before she gets carried away and disgraces the whole family by marrying a Catholic. And a communist, if Evan has his story straight.

We can't imagine a worse fate for one of our own, and goodness knows we've tried.

## CHAPTER SIX

ONE WEEK AFTER ARRIVING at the Good Shepherd Infant Asylum, Lily felt her baby kick for the first time. It was Saturday, the first of March, the morning of her sixteenth birthday. Although it was too dark to see, Lily knew all of the girls would still be asleep at that hour. Even the most troubled ones succumbed to exhaustion by early dawn. The baby kicked again, and Lily couldn't decide how to feel about this startling sensation. Until that moment, she'd managed to convince herself that everyone around her must be mistaken. Perhaps her recently blossomed belly would turn out to be too much fried chicken and applesauce cake like Alice Harris next door, or better yet, stomach cancer like Mrs. Manley down the street. Lily often imagined herself lying on her deathbed with an inoperable tumor while her mother and sister begged for forgiveness. She'd absolve them with her dying breath, and they'd collapse in tears over her cold body.

But now, as the baby kicked, Lily could no longer deny its existence. She had a life growing inside her. And all because she wanted to prove to George Sherman that she was no longer a child.

George Sherman Jr., the most handsome fellow in Scranton, lived in a sprawling house in the neighborhood of Green

Ridge, where the moneyed people laid their heads at night. His father, George Sr., owned several company houses and the Sherman Colliery, an anthracite mine a few streets over in the Providence section of Scranton. It had some of the richest veins of coal in Pennsylvania. Even with the recent decrease in demand, Sherman's mine continued to operate at full capacity. Almost everyone in Providence had family at the Sherman, including Lily. Her father worked there as a miner and had for the better part of thirty years, and even though the family struggled to survive on such low wages, they were still better off than so many others who'd lost their livelihoods outright in the months after the stock market crashed.

George Jr., who attended the Providence Christian Church with his parents and siblings, never took particular notice of Lily until Easter of '29. Prior to that day, if he paid her any mind at all, it was due to her incessant fidgeting in the pew ahead of him. George had four years on Lily, and by that fateful Easter Sunday, almost a full year of college behind him. Later that summer, while trying to steal a kiss, he would tell her that on Easter Sunday, when the entire congregation stood for the invocation, she turned to borrow a hymnal, and he saw her as if for the first time. She'd suddenly transformed into a woman, with ringlets of thick dark hair, lovely curves, and those sapphire eyes.

When George showed up a few days later at the Morgan house on Spring Street, Lily had to pull her mother's hand off the curtains. "You're embarrassing me."

"He has his own automobile." Her mother stayed planted at the window.

"No daughter of mine is going out in a car with a boy." A fit of coughing rolled through Owen with the intensity of a freight train. "I don't care what his last name is." To catch his breath, he leaned against the Tom Thumb piano in the front parlor—the only parlor in their four-room company house.

"Making him pay for the sins of his father, is that it?" Her mother crossed the room and dragged the piano stool out.

"The man may own my house," Owen said, dropping onto the seat, "but he doesn't own me."

Lily looked pleadingly at her parents as George walked up the front steps.

Her father pulled out a handkerchief and wiped his mouth. "Let the boy in," he said with a wave of the blood-speckled hanky.

Most of that evening, George and Lily sat on the porch steps, talking and drinking lemonade. Around nine, Lily's father opened the screen door and barked, "Time for all good souls to say good night." The screen door snapped shut behind him.

"Yes sir," George called back, but he didn't budge. Instead, he slid closer to Lily and started to play with a rebellious curl at the nape of her neck. "I'd sure like to make you my girl this summer," he said, "but I'm afraid you still have some growing up to do."

When Lily tried to object, he pressed a finger to her lips. "I'm a Yale man. I need a girl who can ride around with me." He nodded toward the front door. "Someone without a bedtime." He stood up to leave. "Maybe we should try this again when you're a little older."

Lily hopped up from the step, grabbed George by the shirt, and set her mouth against his ear. "I'm old enough to do as I please."

"That's what I wanted to hear," he said, and whistled all the way to his car.

After that night, George would send Little Frankie over to the Morgans' house when he wanted to be with Lily.

Seventeen-year-old Franco Colangelo, a runt of a kid with oversized ears and slicked-back hair, looked closer to thirteen, so as George explained to Lily, her father would see him as less of a threat. Frankie lived over in Bull's Head, a predominantly Italian neighborhood in Scranton where his uncle ran a numbers racket out of a speakeasy behind the barbershop. Since Frankie supplied the Green Ridge boys with homemade *vino* and directions to the occasional game of chance, they allowed him to pal around with them, as long as he kept his hands off their sisters.

When George wanted to see Lily, he'd have Little Frankie go over to her house with enough pocket change for both of them to take the Northern Electric Streetcar to Lake Winola. George's family had a cottage up there, and he and his friends spent the better part of their summers at the lake, unchaperoned.

The plan worked well for most of July. Frankie had a crippled sister whom Lily sometimes visited, so no one thought it odd when he came by the house to pick her up. Lily was thankful that George was willing to go to such lengths on her account, and George seemed happy to have her on his arm without the watchful eye of her father.

George couldn't live without Lily, he told her the afternoon he kissed her in the front seat of his Nash. They'd gone alone to pick up corn for the roast that night, and on the way back, ended up necking on the side of the road. Lily wanted to yell *Stop!*; she tried to yell *Stop!* but the word melted in the heat and slid off her tongue.

"I think I'm falling in love with you," he said, placing a hand behind her head, pressing his weight on top of her.

A whispered "No" slipped past her lips like steam from a kettle.

His fingers searched for the hem of her skirt, and he

pushed it past her garter. "I thought you wanted to be my girl."

"No!" Lily stretched her arm and pointed out the window.

George shot up. There, on the driver's side, Little Frankie stood with his face pressed against the glass.

"Get the hell out of here, you greasy Guinea." George slammed his hands onto the steering wheel.

"Everyone's out looking for you." Frankie watched as Lily tugged her skirt down past her knees and adjusted her blouse before dropping his eyes. "Thought maybe you was wrecked somewheres." Frankie blushed, stepped back from the car, and raised his hands. "My mistake." He turned and started to walk away.

George lunged from the car and took a swipe at Frankie's head. "What do I always tell you?" He glanced back at Lily hunched over, crying in her seat. "Never come looking for me!" He climbed back into the car and started the engine.

Lily made George drop her off at the Northern Electric stop, a mile over from the lake. After trying to placate her with words of affection and consolation, he yelled something about seeing her when she grew up, and disappeared in a cloud of dust. Sweat trickled down her face as she stood waiting for the streetcar in the late-afternoon sun. What had she done? What had she *almost* done? The streetcar finally arrived, and she took a seat in the rear, away from the handful of passengers who boarded with her. She closed her eyes and felt the burn of his hand on her thigh. Even with the windows open, the smell of him clung to her skin and stirred some unnamed feeling within her.

Little Frankie showed up at Lily's house the next day to apologize. He said he hadn't thought George would try that—not with a girl like her. He was just worried when they didn't come right back. He felt responsible for her since he'd brought her to the lake in the first place. Lily thanked him, said she understood, but told him she needed to be alone.

For the rest of the week, Lily thought about what had happened that afternoon. She'd been embarrassed, but that didn't mean she had to run home like a child. Now she'd ruined everything. George hated her, she was sure of it. He'd find another sweetheart, someone older, like Debbie Tomasetti, the lanky blonde who always showed up at the lake uninvited. Or worldlier, like Janetta Baugess, the voluptuous one with the big eyes. Lily needed to talk to George, but what would she say? That she was sorry? That she loved him? No matter. Seeing him was out of the question. She knew if she spoke to him, smelled the sweetness of his breath, she'd surrender to the dangerous longing she'd felt every minute since he'd pulled her into his arms.

When Frankie came by a few days later, Lily's heart raced. She was sure George had sent him, that he wanted a chance to make things right. What would she do? Resist? Succumb? But Lily didn't have to worry. Frankie had stopped by out of concern for her. And no, he hadn't seen George for days.

By the end of the summer, Lily returned to high school and George to college. Though the longing continued, it started to burn more slowly. She tried to convince herself that she was over him, and she succeeded for the most part—until the hayride.

Lily hadn't expected to see George that day. He was supposed to be off at college that first full weekend in September. She'd gone to Grayce Farms with Little Frankie, in part due to her mother's prodding. "Get outside and blow some of the stink off you"—her way of telling Lily to stop sulking. She noticed George at the far side of the wagon, but just as she started toward him, Janetta Baugess, the most buxom girl in Lily's grade, pushed past her, settled next to George, and took his hand. "Stop teasing," the girl was saying. "You know very well how to say my name." She held up a finger as if to chide him. "It's *Jane*," she paused, "and *etta*." She laughed. "My mother knew I'd never be a plain Jane."

Lily dropped onto the bench across from them, pressing her palms into her lap to stop them from shaking. As Janetta prattled on, Lily learned that George had come home for his sister's birthday, and intended to return to school on Sunday. Until then, the couple planned to spend every moment together. Lily looked up at George, trying to see the truth of the situation in his eyes, but he turned away from her and watched the horses. *Being ignored is worse than being hated.*

When the driver pulled up alongside a table of cider and doughnuts put out by the ladies of the church, Lily allowed Frankie to take her hand to help her down from the wagon. "Why, you're the sweetest boy I know," she said, at a volume that rivaled Janetta's. Frankie grinned. Once on the ground, she held his hand for another minute or two, long enough for people to notice.

"Little Frankie," George called, patting the pocket of his coat, "my turn to provide the hooch." George motioned toward a line of white birch trees at the edge of the pasture. When Frankie nodded toward Lily, irritation registered on George's face. "She can come, I suppose." His eyes slowly traveled up and down her body. "Providing she's grown up some."

"Let's go," Janetta said, already facing the woods. "What are you bothering with them for?"

"Frankie here's an old friend. A man always sticks by his friends." George shot an elbow into the boy's side. "Even the I-talians," he said, chuckling.

"So why are we standing around?" Lily said, as if George

had been addressing his comments to her all along. "Last one across the field is a rotten egg!" She sprinted ahead of them, hoping the blush of her cheeks would be mistaken for exertion, but slowed soon enough with a stitch in her side.

George pulled Janetta by the arm, and the two took the lead. Little Frankie hung back initially, but quickly caught up with Lily. "I'm not sure this is a good idea," he said. "No telling what George has in mind."

"Don't worry," was all she could think to say, as they made their way past the birches, into a forest of golden ash trees whose leaves had already changed.

Frankie walked ahead of Lily, lifting fallen branches, clearing a path. "Watch where you're walking," he said.

"Over here!" George's voice thundered from up ahead.

Lily noticed a wooden structure about twenty feet in front of her, too small for the four of them to share. The roof rose to the height of a full-grown man, but the walls only reached the halfway point. George entered through what could be described as more of a gate than door, and handed items out to Janetta.

"Never knew there was a turkey blind out here till my brother mentioned it." He grabbed a quilt and stepped back outside. "He found it hunting with a buddy of his. Makes a pretty good hiding place." He snapped the cover across the ground and looked at Janetta. "It's going to get chilly," he said to her. "I have a couple more blankets in the car. Would you mind?" Before Janetta could object, he kissed her cheek. "I thought you wanted to spoon in the moonlight."

"Don't start without me," she said, winking.

"Wouldn't think of it." George kissed her on the nose and squeezed her behind. "We'll wait right here." He motioned for Lily and Frankie to sit as Janetta walked away. "And grab a plate of those doughnuts if there's any left."

As soon as Janetta disappeared, George unwrapped

newspaper from around three of the four quarts of homemade beer he'd stashed in the turkey blind. "Down the
hatch," he said, passing two of the bottles to his companions. George watched as Lily touched the beer to her lips
without drinking. "Still yellow, I see."

Lily looked at him straight on, took three large gulps,
and wiped her mouth with the back of her hand. She closed
her eyes to keep them from tearing as the beer burned its
way down her throat. When she raised the bottle again,
Frankie pried it from her fingers.

"Give the lady what she wants," George said, offering
his beer to Lily with one hand while removing a flask from
inside his coat.

"She's had enough." Frankie grabbed Lily's arm.

"Let go!" She pulled away and took a generous swig.
"I'm not leaving till I talk to George."

"You have to drink a little more first." George tipped
the bottle up to her lips and held it there.

Frankie stood. "You told me to bring her here so you
could apologize. That was it."

"I'll apologize," George said evenly.

Lily looked up, and pointed at Frankie with the bottle.
"You brought me here for him?" She turned to George.
"This wasn't a . . ." she stopped to think of the word and
giggled at her momentary lapse, "coincidence?"

"I'm taking you home," Frankie said. When Lily didn't
budge, he added, "You don't need him. He looked down at
his shoes. "A girl like you could have her pick of guys."

"Well, I'll be." George squinted up. "The Guinea's
in love." He slapped his leg. "That deserves a drink." He
pushed Lily's beer to her mouth again. They both laughed
and the foam dribbled down her chin.

"Don't be silly," she said to Frankie. "George is trying to
make up with me."

George draped his arm around Lily and pulled her into his chest. "Get outta here," he said to Frankie. "I like to say my sorrys in private." He winked and tossed the flask to him. "Compliments of the house." He leaned into Lily and nuzzled her neck. "Now go find Janetta before she comes back," he said to the boy, "and keep her company for a while." He winked again.

"You're too good for him." Frankie stretched his arm toward Lily once more. She put down her beer and waved him away as George pulled her in for a kiss.

Frankie stood for a moment longer, watching as George lowered Lily onto the blanket, their lips locked throughout the descent. "Son of a bitch," Frankie mumbled. He unscrewed the flask, poured its contents down his throat, tossed the empty container aside, and walked away.

George stretched toward one of the bottles and placed it in Lily's open hand.

Lily caught her breath and half sat up. "I need to say something."

"Sure," George replied, taking a swig from the beer she held. His fingers trailed the length of her neck, lingering at the top curve of her breast. He pushed her back down, rolled on top of her, and kissed her hard.

She shivered underneath his weight. "I'm scared," she said weakly.

"That's how love feels."

"Tell me you love me."

"I love you, baby."

She pushed his head back a little so she could see into his eyes. "Who else do you love?"

"Nobody. Just you. Just my beautiful baby."

"I'll *baby* you." Janetta stepped onto the blanket and threw a napkin filled with doughnuts at George's head.

George jumped up, shaking powered sugar out of his hair.

"Send me on a wild goose chase!" She kicked over a half-empty bottle. "For Little Miss Goody Two Shoes over there?" Her foot landed in George's shin and he buckled slightly. "Nothing but a dirty two-timer, that's what you are."

Lily sat up, pulled herself over to a tree, and leaned against it, a safe distance from the scuffle.

George took Janetta's arm and leaned in close. "Let me explain." He looked at Lily again. "Later."

"Never you mind, George Sherman." Janetta wriggled out of his grip. "You told me I was your girl." She spit in Lily's direction. "Just remember," she leaned in close to George and lowered her voice, "she'll never do for you like I done. We both know it." Janetta kicked over the second bottle of beer and stormed away.

As soon as Janetta had disappeared into the trees, George turned back to Lily and sat down. "Now where were we?" His pressed his palm against her thigh and circled the flesh with his thumb.

"Everything's ruined!" Lily burst into tears. "It's not supposed to be this way." She pushed his hand away and pulled her legs up to her chest.

George inhaled deeply. "Come on, baby."

"You said you loved me!"

"And I do, baby. I do." He dabbed Lily's tears with sleeve. "Only you," he said, pushing her hair back from her face. "She's nobody. I brought her here to make you jealous." He dropped his eyes and kicked at the ground with the toe of his shoe. "Stupid, I know, but I get crazy when it comes to you."

Lily's shoulders relaxed, and she stretched her legs out.

"All the other girls give me what I want." George reached up and stroked Lily's cheek. "But not you." He looked at her straight on as if seeing her for the first time. "I've never known anyone like you."

She rested her head inside his palm. Pulling himself closer, George slid his free hand between Lily's calves, slicing his way past her knees to her trembling thighs.

"Stop," Lily said, pushing his hand away. "I can't think."

"Don't think. Just trust me, baby." His hand found its way to her thigh again. "I love you."

"I need time," she said, and drew her legs up to her chest once more.

"Time?" He tried to rest his hand on Lily's knee, but she pushed him away. "Don't make me beg."

"I mean it," she said, and twisted away from him.

George stood up, slammed his foot into the trunk of the tree, walked over to the blanket, and knocked over the third quart of beer. "Janetta!" he yelled as he started to sprint. "Wait up!"

Frankie came back and found Lily sitting on the blanket, crying.

"He said I'm not grown up enough for him."

"A girl like you deserves better." Frankie knelt on the ground and handed her his hankie.

She blew her nose and wiped her face. "He'd rather spend his time with girls like Janetta."

Frankie reached over for the last quart of beer, peeled back the newspaper, and took a long swig. "Janetta can't hold a candle to you."

"You're sweet, Frankie." Lily grabbed the beer and sipped. "Why can't George be sweet like you?" She started crying again.

"He's a damn fool." Frankie scooted in next to Lily and held her in his arms. "You're the most beautiful girl in Scranton," he said, caressing her cheek.

"You really think so?" Lily looked up at him. Dizzy, she fell back onto the blanket, pulling Frankie on top of her.

They bumped noses hard as they landed, setting off a fit of tears and giggles. And kisses. Awkward at first, but rhythmic in short time, and soon enough, Lily gave herself over to him, thinking of George and Janetta. She lifted her hips as Frankie fumbled with his trousers, groped for her bloomers, and pressed his body into hers.

Lily felt the baby kick again, just as Sister Immaculata charged through the door and turned on the first light. "This is the day that the Lord hath made." She stopped as she did every morning and waited for the women to respond from their beds.

"Let us rejoice," Lily said, blinking tears from her eyes, "and be glad in it." She turned her head toward Violet's bed and saw that it hadn't been slept in. "Must be down with that baby again," she whispered to her belly. She turned back toward Muriel's bed. It too was empty. Lily rolled onto her side and dropped her feet to the floor before standing. "Birthdays are supposed to be happy," she mumbled on her way to the washroom.

# C HAPTER SEVEN

STANDING AT THE KITCHEN WINDOW, Violet watched the breaking sun lap up the last edges of the night. In the next half hour, all the girls at the Good Shepherd, including Lily, would be congregating in the dining room for a breakfast of creamed wheat topped with a little butter and sugar. Violet closed her eyes and imagined *pice ar y maen,* the little currant-filled Welsh cakes her mother would have made had they been home for Lily's birthday. Whatever troubles her mother had, she always tried to make their birthdays special, and Violet would do the same, though she doubted the Reverend Mother would approve.

On top of the stove, an open glass bottle shivered inside a small pot of water. Violet grabbed the bottle, stretched a rubber nipple over its mouth, and tipped it onto her left wrist. The temperature was right, but a sour smell invaded Violet's nose. Buttermilk. Extra nourishment for the harelipped infant now called Michael.

Mother Mary Joseph had named him. All of the asylum's abandoned babies were named for saints. The day after the baby arrived, the Reverend Mother had asked Sister Immaculata to check her records.

"We haven't had a Michael for some time," the rotund nun had said without looking up from her paperwork.

Mother Mary Joseph had examined the child, bottom

to top, holding her gaze on his crooked expression. "After the archangel. *The great prince which standeth for the children.*"

Violet carried the bottle back to the infant nursery and took Michael out of the crib. The Reverend Mother had been right about the buttermilk. Michael felt heavier in just a week's time. After ten minutes, Violet draped a clean diaper over her shoulder and patted the baby's back to coax a burp. He obliged almost immediately, with a sound usually reserved for bullfrogs. "Well, excuse me," she said, her eyelids widening in feigned shock.

"He's taken to you," the Reverend Mother said, walking into the room and lifting the child from Violet's lap. The nun gently placed the baby onto the white-enameled platform of an old spring scale that hung from the ceiling. A local grocer, who'd once used the device for cuts of meat, had donated it to the Good Shepherd after buying a newer model. "Weighs about . . ." Mother Mary Joseph waited for the needle on the dial to settle, "six and three-quarters. Up a pound and a half." She handed the infant back to Violet. "Thanks be to God."

For almost an hour, the Reverend Mother and Violet fed, bathed, and dressed twelve babies, one for each ivory-colored crib in the room. At five minutes to seven, the nun looked up at the clock. "Time for Mass." She laid Judith Dennick's infant in his crib, rubbed his belly, and turned to Violet. "I had hoped Sadie would be in to help you," she said, glancing at the clock a second time. "But not today. I trust you'll be fine without us this morning."

Violet looked up and down three rows of cribs, four deep, with just enough space in between for one person to pass. "I'll manage." She tacked a smile onto her words, hoping to cover at least some of the indignation in her voice. Violet was annoyed with the nun for being so presumptuous with her time, but then again, she liked not having to go to Mass. All of that kneeling and bowing seemed undignified somehow. Protestants kneeled too, but in the privacy of their own homes.

"We'll be offering up a prayer for the Hartwell girl."

Violet looked up. "Muriel?"

"Started her pains in the middle of the night."

Picturing the midwife's hands, Violet asked, "Did someone go for the doctor?"

"No need for that. Sadie Hope is in with her." Mother Mary Joseph stopped at the doorway and plucked a set of silver rosary beads from a nail on the wall. "Trust in the Lord and let nature take its course," she said and walked out of the room.

Alone, with only infant witnesses, Violet dropped to her knees and prayed.

Mother Mary Joseph returned to the nursery at half past eleven.

"Any word on Muriel?" Violet asked.

"No change, but that's not unusual." The Reverend Mother walked across the room, pushed back the curtains over three identical windows, and peered out at the cheerless March day. "I had hoped for a little sun this afternoon . . ." She turned to the closest crib and scooped a baby girl into her arms. "Let's get the little ones bundled up."

The Reverend Mother believed in fresh air, no matter the weather. Each afternoon, the babies were swaddled in thick blankets, paired off in carriages, and placed on the front porch for two-hour naps. Mother Mary Joseph claimed that time outdoors kept children healthy—good advice, considering how robust her charges seemed to be.

"I need to run an errand," Violet said. "I'll wait till the children are napping." She placed a bundled Michael into a wicker buggy, stepped over to the next crib, and started dressing a two-month-old named Bernadette. When Mother Mary Joseph didn't respond, Violet added, "It's Lily's birthday, I'd like her to have something to open."

"We don't allow the girls—"

"With all due respect," Violet interrupted, "I'm not one of the girls."

The nun paused, as if to consider the point. "Well, we still have to dress the toddlers." She nodded toward the room next door. "Sister Teresa is still in bed with a cold."

"Yes," Violet said, "but after that."

"If you think it's wise to reward her." The Reverend Mother pushed a carriage to the doorway, and a waiting nun pulled it out of the room and onto the front porch. "Personally . . ."

"I wouldn't have mentioned it otherwise," Violet said, her curt tone putting an end to the discussion.

Once all of the children were dressed and in their carriages, Violet left through the kitchen door and headed around front. When she reached the sidewalk, she turned back, examining the grounds in the daylight. A tall iron fence lined the tar-and-chip driveway leading up to the Good Shepherd Infant Asylum. Short but wide, the road stayed to the right, where a redbrick chapel stood, low and broad. According to Sadie, who loved a good story, the church had been erected in 1880 and was the first structure on the property. The adjoining three-story convent had been added a decade later, at the urging of Bishop McGoff, who thought a contingent of nuns would bolster the flagging morality of the women in Philadelphia. The convent appeared so grand with its tiled arches and rounded windows that the workmen added a twenty-foot steeple to the unadorned chapel free of charge. Almost immediately, and much to the bishop's dismay, the Sisters of the Immaculate Heart of Mary started sheltering unmarried women who found themselves in the family way. By the turn of the century, the nuns had raised enough money to add a small maternity hospital onto the left side of the convent, where the women could be delivered within the walls of the Good Shepherd.

Violet gave the asylum one last look before heading toward the millinery on the corner of Market and Broad, across the street from the train station. She'd noticed the shop the night she and Lily arrived. Considering Lily's burgeoning form, a hat would make a sensible gift. *Nothing too fussy*, Violet thought. *Nothing that would draw unwanted attention.* She looked up at a street sign to get her bearings, and after a moment she turned left onto Market Street and followed it for six more blocks.

Gold letters on the store's red sign announced, *Widenor's Hats. James Widenor, Proprietor.* Violet eyed the merchandise in the window, wondering if Mr. Widenor would be willing to barter. She reached into her coat pocket and fingered the gold medallion awarded to her at graduation. The raised letters on front read:

*Scranton Central High School*
*Valedictorian*
*Class of 1923*

Violet's parents had been so proud of her when she'd received the medal and delivered the valedictory address. She'd been honored with a scholarship to Bloomsburg Teacher's College, and she might have gone too, if Lily had been a little older. Lily was only nine, and given their mother's nervous episodes, Violet felt obligated to stay.

"I'm sorry," was all her father had said. But the morning after graduation, she watched unseen as he placed the scholarship letter between the gilded pages of the family Bible.

Now Violet entered the milliner's shop. Inside, she zig-zagged around hat-covered trees in search of the shopkeeper or one of his assistants. At the rear of the store, she discovered a high counter with a cash register and silver desk bell. A note alongside the bell read, *Ring once for service.* Violet tapped the bell on top, releasing a tinny note.

"Be there in a minute!" a man called out.

"I'm in no hurry." Violet meandered through a forest of tams, berets, and Panamas, in search of something quiet and sensible. Instead, she found herself staring at one of those modern, felt, creased-crown hats, trimmed with a periwinkle ribbon and matching silk forget-me-nots.

"A lovely choice."

Violet jumped.

A pudgy gentleman was standing behind her. "What can I do you for?" He reached past Violet to the hat. "I own the place." He took the hat and evened out the crease before placing it on her head.

"It's not for me." She snatched the hat and hung it on the bare limb before her. "I'm here to buy a present for my sister."

"Just the same." Mr. Widenor pulled a handheld mirror from a nearby shelf. "Indulge me." He took the hat once again and pushed it down over her curls. "Lovely." He handed her the mirror.

She looked at her reflection and fingered the periwinkle ribbon. "My favorite color." She smiled, surprised that such a daring headpiece would flatter her face.

"Wear that and you'll not want for suitors."

"I haven't any money."

"I'm sorry, miss." Mr. Widenor took the hat back and placed it on the tree. "I wish I could help you, but I have five mouths to feed at home, and a sixth on the way." He fluffed a beret at the top of the stand. "We're hoping for a girl this time." He turned back, smiling sheepishly.

Violet pulled the medallion out of her pocket and felt the weight of it in her palm. *Lay up not for yourselves treasures upon earth*, she reminded herself, and handed it to the proprietor. "I thought we might barter."

He flipped it over and read its message. "You?"

She nodded.

"I can't take this." He tried to return the award. "You earned it."

*And it wasn't easy,* she thought. If only their mother hadn't taken to her bed so often in the years following Daisy's death.

Violet slipped her empty hand into her coat pocket. "What can I get for it?" she asked.

Mr. Widenor bit down on the medallion. "Gold-plated." He tipped it to the light. "Ten carat, no more."

Violet didn't budge.

"Wait here." A minute or two later he returned with something sturdy but unremarkable, the kind of straw bonnet every miner's wife in Scranton owned.

Violet tried it on. Her face fell.

"Best I can do," he said. "I'm sorry." He offered the medallion back to her. "Just as well. A person should hold onto something this special."

Violet shook her head at the coin and handed the straw hat over to the shop owner. "This one will have to do. Box it for me, please." She walked to the front of the store, took a seat in a straight-backed chair, and waited.

Several minutes later, Mr. Widenor returned from the back room with a bright red hatbox, exclusive to his store. "I tied it good and tight," he said, handing it over. "With a sister like you, she's a lucky girl. God bless, miss."

Violet forced a smile and a "Thank you," but they didn't match up. She threaded her fingers through the string and headed for the door.

As soon as her foot crossed the threshold, a nearby mill whistled its workers back from lunch. It was a familiar sound. The Lace Works, a factory in the Providence neighborhood of Scranton, used the same method. On weekdays, Lace Works employees and schoolchildren within earshot eagerly awaited the first whistle, a signal for lunch. An hour later, the whistle would sound again, urging everyone back to their duties.

Since Violet had left the asylum at half past twelve, she knew that must have been the one o'clock whistle. She was surprised at how quickly she'd managed her errand. The suitcases must have slowed her the last time she'd walked these streets. No one expected her back before two o'clock, so she decided to savor her solitude. Violet settled herself on a nearby bench to watch the bustle of the large city. For the first time in the two weeks since her arrival, she noticed the gray air. The smoke, expelled from countless trains and automobiles, hung in front of her like gossamer curtains. Pedestrians hurried through the haze, eyes downcast, coats drawn up toward their faces. Tracks cut through the middle of the street, where fast-moving cars and crowded trolleys shared the road. Across the way, arched windows and Gothic spires graced the massive train station.

Violet wondered if she could ever make a life in such a place. One of Stanley's letters had suggested getting married in Philadelphia. What if he decided to move them here? She found the anonymity of a big city inviting. If she were sitting alone on a bench in Scranton, half the congregation of the Providence Christian Church would know about it, and what's more, have shared their opinions on it before she ever made it back to her own front porch. And a predicament like Lily's wouldn't be tolerated back home, though Violet hoped never to be compromised by such troubles again.

Yet, there was also comfort to be had in a place like Scranton. Last winter, when Mr. Harris was laid up with the gout, the men on Spring Street took turns cleaning the ashes out of his furnace and spreading them on the icy sidewalks. And when Susie Hopkins lost her husband in that mine fire, the ladies of Providence stepped in, providing enough staples and canned goods to feed Susie and her three children through the winter.

A sudden gust of March air stirred the dust, and Violet's hands flew to her eyes. An instant later, when the wind subsided, she saw the red hatbox tumbling toward the trolley tracks. Without thinking, she ran into the street and snatched Lily's present just as a streetcar approached. Violet looked up, and for a moment time faltered, unable or unwilling to move along.

Stanley stood in the middle of the overcrowded trolley, gripping a leather handhold, facing the motorman up front. Reason demanded that Violet run away, but Stanley's sudden presence pinned her in place. She studied his profile, his lips, his nose, and found solace in the familiar. It was as if she'd been in foreign lands for untold years and awakened one day to the sound of her native tongue. She was home.

Time lurched forward. Violet's fingers started throbbing from the too-tight string on the hatbox. *The hat. Lily!*

She lingered another second, not long at all, yet long enough for Stanley to turn and glance out the window as the streetcar passed by her. Uncertainty seemed to tug at the corners of his eyes as he yelled, "Stop!" either to her or the conductor.

Fear propelled Violet in the opposite direction, away from the trolley, away from the man she loved.

# CHAPTER EIGHT

"WHERE HAVE YOU BEEN ALL DAY?" Lily asked when Violet walked into the dining room for supper. "With that baby, I suppose. I'll never understand why you care more about that stray than you do your own sister."

"Not now," Violet whispered. She took the empty seat on Lily's right and bowed her head just as Sister Immaculata started the blessing.

Lily waited, open-eyed, for the moment when the Catholics would start crossing themselves, her signal that the prayer was almost over.

*"In the name of the Father . . ."*

All of the women except for the Morgan girls lifted their right hands to their foreheads.

"Do you even know what today is?" Lily couldn't contain herself.

Violet tipped her bowed head in her sister's direction, opened one eye, and glared. "Amen."

Sister Immaculata gave a nod, and napkins snapped open, some spread across laps and bellies, others tucked under chins. Ladles clanked against pressed-glass tureens as a hearty stew made its way around four long tables. Lily wrinkled up her nose as Violet filled their bowls.

"This doesn't look anything like Mother's." Lily poked at chunks of gray meat swimming among the potatoes and carrots in the thick brown broth.

"That's because it's mutton," Violet said, "not beef. Now be grateful. Plenty of mouths are going unfed tonight." She took two pieces of hard-crusted bread and handed the plate past Lily to the woman seated on her left. "Here," she said to her sister, tearing one of the slices into small chunks and scattering them in her bowl.

"Mother always makes dumplings," Lily said, stirring the bread pieces to soak up the gravy.

Violet lifted her spoon to her mouth and held it there. "Mother rarely makes anything," she mumbled, "and certainly not dumplings." She licked the spoon clean and set it alongside her bowl. "And if it's dumplings you like, you have me to thank." She picked up her slice of bread and pointed it at her sister. "And while you're at it," her was tone slightly elevated, but controlled, "you can thank me for ironing your dresses, plaiting your hair, teaching you how to skate . . ." She paused, the bread still aloft, thumbing through her mind's catalog. Getting Lily's breakfast. Reading her stories. Tucking her into bed. "And checking your sums every night," she blurted out, as if she hadn't thought about that one for a long time, "the year you had Miss Philips in grammar school!" Violet closed her eyes for a moment and inhaled deeply. She took her spoon and pushed it around in the bowl. "Onions are cooked down," she finally said, "the way you like."

Without looking up, Lily leaned toward the stew and started eating. "First Muriel leaves me." She reached for the saltcellar near the tip of her knife, threw a few pinches into her bowl, and stirred. "And then you forget what day it is," she said, pulling another slice of bread from the plate.

Violet's head snapped up. "Is there any word on Muriel?"

Lily pointed to a girl across the table, thin strands of blond hair skirting her eyes. "Carol says Sadie's still in with her."

Carol nodded and pushed back her bangs. "According to Ann, anyways."

They all turned to Ann Lehman at the next table, her stomach so swollen that she balanced her stew on top of it. "Saw Sadie my own self this afternoon," she said wearily. "Says I'm not ready yet. Says I must be carrying an eleven-month baby since my dear husband passed ten months ago."

Carol howled. "Your nose is growing, Annie."

"Hand to God." Ann's fingers flew to her heart, spilling the contents of her bowl. "Now look what you done."

Sister Immaculata lumbered over with a handful of napkins. "Enough," she said to both girls. "I don't want to hear another word out of either of you." She sopped up the mess on Ann's stomach and led her out of the room.

"An eleven-month baby," Carol laughed as soon as Ann and the nun disappeared single file through the doorway. "Ain't that the funniest thing you ever heard?"

When supper was finished, the Reverend Mother stepped into the dining room and rang a small bell. "We'll be saying the Rosary in fifteen minutes," she said and walked back out the door.

Violet stood to leave.

"Where are you off to now?" Lily pushed herself away from the table. "You're always going somewhere."

"Not everything is about you, Lily Morgan." When girls at the table stopped their conversations to listen, Violet lowered her voice. "There's others with troubles. It's high time you learned that."

"And what's so special about that baby, anyway?"

"Keep it up and you won't get your gift."

Lily clapped her hands. "I knew you wouldn't forget!"

"I have half a mind to go back downtown and return it."

"You wouldn't dare." When Violet didn't answer, Lily offered up her sweetest smile. "You're so good to me."

"I can't imagine why."

"Where is it?"

"Don't get excited," Violet said, too late. "It's not much. Meet me in the nursery after chapel."

Lily stood up and kissed her sister's cheek. "Sorry for being cross with you." She clapped her hands again. "I should have known I could count on you. You always do right by me."

*No matter how dear the price*, Violet thought as she pictured Stanley, framed inside that streetcar, looking straight at her.

An unusually fussy Michael squirmed in Violet's arms when she rocked him. "It must be catching," she said of her mood, and offered the child her finger to suck. His tiny fist flailed, landed, and pulled the finger greedily into his dented mouth. "Maybe Stanley didn't see me," she said to the baby. Violet looked at Michael as if he might concur. "At worst, he'll think his eyes were playing tricks on him. The gray day. The swiftness of the trolley. The automobile exhaust." She punctuated each reason with a nod, trying to convince her mind that her body knew the truth.

The first note of a cry sounded from one of the cribs. Violet held her breath and peered across the dimly lit room. The Dennick baby stirred for a moment, then settled back to sleep. "We have to be quiet," she whispered to Michael. His eyes held onto hers.

The door flew open, and light from the hallway poured into the nursery ahead of Lily. "I'm here," she announced.

Across the room, Michael's head popped up and Violet's finger flew to her lips. *The babies*, she mouthed, motioning for Lily to shut the door and lower her voice.

Once inside, Lily snaked her way through the rows of cribs, sweeping her fingers along the bars like a child with a stick on a picket fence. She counted twelve babies in all, including the one in Violet's arms. "How many are girls?" she whispered.

Violet lifted Michael to her shoulder and patted his back. "Seven, and they'll be here a good bit. The boys go quicker, according to Sadie."

"Why's that?" Lily pulled a second rocker over to Violet and sat down next to her.

"Fathers want sons." Violet nodded toward the baby. "Is he sleeping?"

Lily leaned over, observed the infant's half-shut eyes, and shook her head. "Almost." She moved closer and inspected his marred face for the first time. She knew about the harelip, but seeing it up close made Lily shudder. *A woman oughtn't look at a crone or a cripple when she's in the family way*. Lily hugged her stomach briefly before remembering something. "The baby started kicking this morning."

Violet flattened her free palm against her sister's belly, but when nothing happened, she pulled her hand back.

"I'll let you know if she does it again."

"So she's a she," Violet said.

"More than likely."

"Why's that?" Violet switched Michael to her other shoulder.

"Mother only had girls, and her mother before that. Just seems natural." Lily glanced back at the cribs.

"What about the father's people?" Violet tossed the question out, hoping to unearth some detail that would reveal who was responsible for Lily's condition—George Sherman most likely, though Violet couldn't be sure. "Do they have many girls?"

Lily refused the bait. "So where's my present?" She glanced around the room.

"In a minute." Violet carried a sleeping Michael over to the empty crib.

Lily's eyes settled on her sister. "You look good with a baby." She checked to see if Michael's face was turned away, and when she saw it was, she stood up and walked over to the pair. "It suits you somehow."

"You think so?" Violet cooed in the infant's ear. "We'll have trouble adopting him out with his disfigurement."

"We? We who?" Lily searched her sister's eyes. "He's not yours, you know."

"I know," Violet said, but without conviction.

"He can't be. I mean it." Lily watched as her sister placed the child in his crib. "Look at me. You can't even think about it. You'll ruin everything if you bring him home."

Violet walked the rows, tucking cast-off blankets around her sleeping charges. "I'm not taking anybody home but you," she replied.

Lily continued pleading as if Violet hadn't said a word. "And what about Stanley? How could you ever explain a baby to him?

"Stanley's a good man. He'd understand."

"No man is that good. Not even Stanley Adamski. Besides, you swore you'd never tell him about this. You told me yourself: no good would come of his knowing. You even made the widow promise."

"I know I did," Violet said. "And I don't need you reminding me. The Reverend Mother is working hard to find him a good family. It's just going to take some time."

"Do you mean it?" Lily made her way back to the rocker and sat down.

"Of course I mean it."

"I just don't want you ruining my reputation. Sometimes that's all a girl has."

"Now I've heard it all. You're worried that I'm going to ruin . . ." Violet paused, giving weight to her next word, "your reputation?"

"You don't understand. You never do." The back of Lily's hand flew to her forehead. "I can't talk about this anymore. Not on my birthday."

A full minute of silence passed before Violet spoke again. "Worry about your own reputation, and stop looking for trouble where there's none to be had." When tears sprang to Lily's eyes, Violet softened, "Especially on your birthday."

Lily dabbed her face and looked up expectantly. "Do I still get my present?"

Instead of answering, Violet crossed the room and pulled the red hatbox out from behind two milk crates filled with empty bottles.

"Well, we know it's a hat." Lily said, reaching for the box, balancing it sideways on her lap, and spinning it like a wheel. Her left hand landed on the crumpled section of cardboard. "What happened?"

"Never you mind." Violet leaned down and righted the package. "Now open it before I change my mind." Pointing her nose toward the babies, she went to the cribs to determine which child had a soiled diaper. "And remember to keep your voice down," she cast over her shoulder in a whisper.

Lily untied the string, pried off the lid, peeled back the layers of tissue paper, and squealed in spite of Violet's admonition. "It's beautiful!"

"You really like it?" Violet found the baby who needed changing, picked her up, and turned back to Lily. "I was so afraid you'd be . . ." Her tongue landed on the roof of her mouth, ready to push the first syllable of *disappointed* through her teeth, but the word dissolved when Lily lifted the present out of the box.

Stunned, Violet watched as Lily ran the side of her hand over the knife-like crease on the crown of the hat—not the straw hat that Violet had purchased, but the modern felt one she'd so admired. *But how*? "I tied that string good and tight," she'd heard Mr. Widenor say before she'd left the store. He'd wanted her to be surprised.

Lily tipped the brim toward the dim lamplight and fingered the silk forget-me-nots and matching ribbon. "Periwinkle," she said. "Why, Violet, that's your favorite color, not mine." She placed the hat on her head and admired herself in the faint reflection of the closest window. "I love it, though."

"I'm not sure it suits you." Violet regretted the words as soon as they slipped out. Jealously—a fine way to repay Mr. Widenor for his kindness, she thought, heading to the changing table.

"Thank you."

Violet cleaned, powdered, and diapered the little girl before addressing Lily. "I'm happy if you're happy." She thought about her words as she returned the baby to her crib and decided that she mostly meant them.

Lily pulled off the hat and placed it back in its tissue-paper nest. She set the hatbox alongside the windowsill and stretched her arms out so Violet could help her up. "I need to get to bed before Attila the Hun comes in with her clipboard."

The image of Attila the Hun in a wimple struck Violet as so funny, she was rendered useless for the better part of a minute. When she finally composed herself, she grabbed Lily's hands and started to tug. Given Lily's awkward body, the rocker's natural movement, and the giggle fit that overcame them both, it took half a dozen tries to get her on her feet.

Once the laughing subsided, Lily steadied herself and grabbed the hatbox. "I can't wait to show Muriel!"

The mention of Muriel's name sobered both of them instantly.

Violet watched the color drain from Lily's face and immediately regretted her words. "I'm sure she's fine," she said, trying for a convincing tone.

Lily burst into tears. "I'm so scared."

"Sadie's taking good care of her." Violet pulled out a handkerchief, dabbed her sister's eyes, and walked her out to the hallway. "What you need is a good night's sleep."

Lily dropped the hatbox on the floor and threw her arms around Violet's neck. "I'm not brave like Muriel. I'm not brave at all."

A gust of cold air blew past the pair as the front door swung open at the end of the hallway. Both sisters looked up as Dr. Peters crossed the threshold and stood still for a moment, eyeing them in the distance. The pocket doors on his left split open, and Sadie Hope stepped out.

"No time to waste," she said, waving him into the maternity hospital.

# C HAPTER NINE

DR. PETERS FOLLOWED SADIE HOPE through to the hospital. Freshly painted wainscoting, the green of a summer pear, covered the bottom half of a long hallway. A copy of Leonardo da Vinci's *Madonna and Child* hung high up on one of the white walls. An inexpertly stitched Mary Magdalene tapestry adorned the other. In the first room on the right, Judith Dennick, still recovering from her difficult labor a week earlier, snored loudly.

"It's Muriel Hartwell." Hands trembling, Sadie pushed back the door on their left and held it open. "Bled some in the last hour." She hurried her words as if hoping to carry the doctor along with them. "Poor dear's been laboring since three this morning." She nodded toward a curtained area behind her. "And her temperature keeps spiking."

The doctor walked in with his medical case in hand, though he hardly needed it in such a well-stocked operating room. After ten years of service, the good sisters never questioned his requests. "Whatever it takes," the Reverend Mother would say, "to deliver our girls safely." Gauze, tape, Kelly pads, and cotton sponges lined the upper shelves of a gray-enameled steel cabinet, the first of two, next to the doorway. Vials of sutures, mostly silk and catgut, were arranged in rows across the back of the cabinet's worktable. Batches of bleached white towels and sheets were folded into the drawers below. The adjacent cabinet held the usual supply of drugs—chloroform, ether, diluted Lysol among them, and an unmarked bottle of whiskey, should a patient need a bit of courage.

A low moan crossed the divide from the curtained side of the operating room. The doctor tucked his medical case in the corner, bloused his sleeves over his armbands, and waited next to a small sink. "How far along?"

"Seven months." Sadie lifted her pale eyebrows. She slipped a rubber apron over the doctor's head, and then a muslin one, tying it snug around his broad waistline. "Her water broke a good ten hours ago," she said, turning on the faucet. She grabbed a nailbrush and a cake of green soap, and offered them to the doctor. "Can't coax more than a finger in after all this time."

Dr. Peters clasped Sadie's wrist and snatched the items out of her stilled hand. "And the contractions?"

Sadie draped a cloth across the top of a wheeled table and pushed it to the far side of the sink, next to two more cabinets filled with surgical instruments and appliances. "Four minutes." Lowering her voice, she added, "I'm worried something awful. The child's exhausted and talking out of her head."

"I'm not surprised," he said, soaping and rinsing his hands before wiping them on his apron. "These girls have no idea what's coming." Another moan rose up from Muriel's side of the room and the doctor bristled at the sound. "Clean her good," he said, handing the bottle of Lysol solution to Sadie. "I'll be in momentarily."

Dr. Peters pulled the wheeled table over and smoothed its cover with his palm. He rooted through the medicines; glass bottles clanked up against one another, making way for his meaty hands. He lined the drugs up on the table in order of height. Next, he stepped over to the instrument cabinet and began unraveling the cotton wrappers from the surgical tools—scalpel; metal catheters; artery clamps; ether mask; scissors; forceps, mouse-toothed and thumb; needles, curved and straight—and arranged them on the table.

Muriel's moaning escalated into screams, causing the doctor to swing around and face the curtain. "That's of no help to anyone," he said with the matter-of-fact tone of a schoolmaster. He turned back to the last cabinet, grabbed the brass base of a well-used ether inhaler, and placed several sponges inside. Finally, he set the glass-domed lid on top of the contraption and washed his hands again.

Muriel's eyes squeezed shut tight as fists at the start of her next contraction. "Get him away from me!"

"Who?" Sadie dipped a rag into a bowl of cool water and wrung it hard. "Dr. Peters? He's a good man," she whispered, laying the cloth on Muriel's hot forehead. "He studied for the priesthood before he got the call to medicine." She brushed damp strands of hair away from the girl's face and eyed a mahogany dresser pushed up against the opposite wall. Its low, broad design made it a practical place to tend to a newly born baby. That morning, Sadie had stocked the top with clean towels, a flannel blanket, dressing for the cord, and mineral oil for the newborn's skin. But something was missing. She looked again and spotted the bottle peeking out from behind the blanket. Boric acid. She'd need it to wash out the infant's eyes and mouth.

A moment later Muriel opened her eyes and started to breathe more easily. "Where is he?"

"Who, child?"

"Papa. I seen him standing in the doorway."

"Nonsense. That's the fever talking." With the back of her hand, Sadie felt the girl's cheeks. "Dr. Peters," she called out, before returning her attention to the patient. "He'll do right by you."

"He best do right by me." Muriel aimed her words toward the doctor's side of the curtain, but they landed far short of their goal. "I can't do this no more," she said, her voice clouded with tears and exhaustion.

Sadie looked past the iron headboard to the crucifix hanging on the wall. This brass Jesus had finished with His suffering. Eyes closed, head lolled. He just needed someone to take Him off that cross so He could get back among the living. She glanced at Muriel. The worst of her suffering still lay ahead. "Not too much longer now," Sadie said, scooting down to the foot of the bed where the smell of Lysol lingered. She tented the untucked blanket up on the metal bedposts, steadied her trembling hands on Muriel's pale knees, and split them open.

Goose bumps rose up on the girl's calves and she started to shiver. "It's too soon," she cried.

"Seven-month babies can survive. I've seen it with my own eyes," Sadie said. "All things are possible with the good Lord." She glanced at the crucifix again as if to make sure the good Lord had heard her.

"Not for me." Muriel shook her head. "Not after what Papa done to . . ." Her voice trailed off.

Metal rings scraped across a wooden rod as Dr. Peters pulled back the curtain. He wheeled his table to the foot of the bed.

Sadie looked up. *No change,* she mouthed and stepped back.

Without warning, the doctor reached between the girl's open legs and shoved two chapped fingers inside her.

Muriel yelped like an injured dog.

"The cervix is firm," he said. "Unyielding." He drew back his fingers and wiped them across his apron. "Disinfect the abdomen."

Sadie folded Muriel's nightgown up to her breastbone

before rubbing an alcohol-soaked cloth across her belly. "No need to worry," she told the girl. "Dr. Peters will see to everything."

"Rest assured." The corners of the doctor's mustache lifted around his tight-lipped smile as he poured ether onto the sponges in the inhaler's brass base. He quickly set the glass-domed lid back in place and attached a length of rubber tubing and a cone-shaped mask to a protruding knob. He smiled again, hanging onto the expression a little longer. "You'll hold her down?" Although the last word lifted into a question, the tone did not allow for refusal.

Sadie kissed Muriel's brow. "It'll all be over soon." She pressed her weight against the girl's arms as Dr. Peters lowered the mask over her mouth and nose. Muriel bucked up several times before succumbing to the anesthesia.

"She's a fighter," the doctor said. "I'll give you that." He eyed Muriel's bare abdomen and picked up a scalpel. The tip of the blade caught the light before disappearing into the taut flesh just above the navel.

All through the evening service, Mother Mary Joseph ruminated on the infant incubator that Jack and Mamie Barrett had donated. *Could a machine really keep a premature baby alive?* she wondered. *Would tonight be the night they'd finally put it to the test?*

"I'm going to see about Muriel," the Reverend Mother said, walking past Sister Immaculata and exiting the chapel. "Will you check on the nurseries," she called back, "after you get the girls settled?"

Mother Mary Joseph headed straight through the pocket doors and into the hospital.

She paused for a moment when she reached the operating room, but continued down the hallway to the second door on the left. In the dim light, the incubator on the far

wall resembled a narrow stove with its pipe running up behind it. The Reverend Mother switched on a lamp and examined the machine, an iron-and-glass oxygenated box on
slender white legs. The stovepipe look-alike connected to a
central boiler and thermostat. As the nun stepped forward,
a mesh metal hammock, intended to cradle a premature
infant inside the box, swayed to the floor's vibrations.

In this age of science, Mother Mary Joseph always felt
conflicted about these modern inventions. How could she
be sure of God's will? If a baby came into this world unable to survive on his own, should man intervene? Dr. Peters
didn't think so, and she certainly valued his opinion.

Though she continued to ponder this matter, the Reverend Mother reached behind the incubator, making sure
Sadie had already opened the valve that allowed the oxygen
to fill the glass chamber. "If it saves one child . . ." she said
aloud and walked back into the hallway toward the operating
room.

After cutting through the abdomen, Dr. Peters applied two
hemostats to control the bleeding. With the anterior uterine
wall exposed, he traded his scalpel for a pair of angular
scissors. Using his finger as a guide, he made an eight-inch
incision, sufficient for the baby's head. He nodded toward
the patient, so Sadie could see that the placenta lay on top
of the infant—unusual, but not harmful.

Sadie stood close by, clenching a large white towel,
ready to receive the baby. "I understand," she said, aware
that he would have to cut through the afterbirth to get to
the child, creating a frightening amount of blood.

Dr. Peters plunged through the membrane, slicing away
the placenta with one hand and pulling the baby out with
the other. When he lifted the lifeless boy into view, he and
Sadie both gasped.

"God have mercy on our souls," Mother Mary Joseph said, as she walked into the operating room and eyed the creature in Dr. Peters's arms.

A neckless head jutted faceup from the infant's shoulders, as if he'd purposely thrown it back in laughter or despair. The mouth hung open, unable to contain such a broad and swollen tongue. Two centered holes hinted at a nose, and froglike eyeballs bulged through thick folds of skin. A shock of red hair started at the place where a forehead should have been, and trickled past a flattened skull. Below the crownless head, blue-tinged flesh stretched across what appeared to be a perfectly formed body.

In addition to her hands, Sadie's whole body shook as she reached for the stillborn baby. "I'll see to him." Staring ahead at the bottles, the mineral oil, the diapers, the towels, anything other than the hideous creature in her arms, she carried the newborn and laid him out on the table.

"God have mercy," the nun said a second time, joining Sadie.

"An anencephalic monster." The doctor steadied himself and looked down at Muriel. "A brainless abomination," he said. "The devil's work." He glanced around, making sure the Reverend Mother and Sadie had their backs to him before slipping a curved needle up into the left corner of Muriel's exposed cavity. His knots were small, tight, practiced. Knotting the tubes was the form of sterilization he used most often. He had hoped to try one of the newer methods discussed in *The American Journal of Obstetrics and Gynecology*, but with both women in the room, he decided not to take the risk. Given the Good Shepherd's habit of ministering to the morally depraved, he'd have other opportunities to experiment soon enough.

Dr. Peters cut the thread close to the ligature, and repeated the tying process on the right side. He had to work quickly. The sisters at the Good Shepherd would certainly never approve of his actions. They were women of God, sheltered from the realities of modern life. He'd been ignorant himself while he'd been studying for the priesthood, but then he'd attended a lecture on eugenics. He'd immediately put his faith in science and his efforts into improving the human race, as God intended. Sacrifices had to be made, he thought, as he sutured the abdomen before him, but what good would ever come from allowing this girl or others like her to bear more children?

"She's lost a good deal of blood," the doctor finally said, finishing the last stitch. "Only time will tell." He rinsed his hands in the bowl of water next to the bed and picked up his stethoscope.

Both women shook their heads while they tended to the baby. Sadie washed its heavy-lidded eyes and awestruck mouth with the boric acid solution and cleaned his bluish flesh with mineral oil. For no other reason than dignity's sake, the Reverend Mother trimmed the baby's cord closer to his body, the way a careful hand would have after a favorable delivery, and dressed the wound in fresh cotton.

With the body prepared, the nun covered the tiny form with the flannel blanket and pressed her palms together. Sadie and Mother Mary Joseph dipped their heads.

At the conclusion of the prayer, Sadie asked, "Shall I send for the priest?"

Before the nun had a chance to answer, the infant began to cry.

# CHAPTER TEN

DR. PETERS YANKED THE STETHOSCOPE out and looked upon Muriel in her etherized state. "If she makes it through the night," he said, "she'll have a fighting chance."

"Hush." Sadie cocked an ear toward the dresser.

"I beg your pardon." His cheeks flushed with indignation.

The Reverend Mother waved a hand at the doctor but kept her eyes locked on the newborn.

A small foot, just starting to pink up, kicked out from under the cover, as the infant cried a second time.

"It's not possible." Dr. Peters started over toward the women but stopped halfway.

This time a tiny fist pushed past the cover as the baby whimpered thinly. Mother Mary Joseph peeled back the blanket, and the women parted to make room.

With his stethoscope still in hand, the doctor walked to the dresser and shook his head. "Fetal asphyxia," he said. "I'd swear my reputation on it." He put the stethoscope back in his ears, while never taking his eyes off the infant. When he pressed the metal chest piece against the breastbone, the baby appeared to flinch. Dr. Peters listened for a full minute, his mouth hanging open as if imitating his patient. "It's not possible," he said again.

"Thought so myself, and I handled him," Sadie said, standing near the baby's oddly shaped head and studying its awkward position.

The Reverend Mother glanced toward the inner door that opened into the incubator room but said nothing.

"Heartbeat is slow and irregular." The doctor draped the blanket back over the infant's face. "He'll not survive."

"That may be so," the Reverend Mother said, pulling the cover back and tucking it around the well-formed shoulders, "but until then, it's our duty as Christians to provide comfort."

"Of course, Sister." Dr. Peters returned to Muriel, lifted her eyelids, and started to untie his apron.

"Do we try to feed him?" Sadie asked.

The Reverend Mother nodded at the question.

"Pointless." The doctor dropped his surgical clothes to the floor and unrolled his shirtsleeves. "Let nature finish what God started."

Mother Mary Joseph's eyes traveled to the incubator room, then she looked back at the infant. "No time for the priest," she said. "I better baptize him myself."

"Baptize!" Dr. Peters spit the word out as if it were spoiled cream. The women turned and stared at him, but remained silent. "Sister," he said, starting back toward the infant, "I understand the importance of the sacrament, but look." He pushed the baby's hair aside to show a dark red tangle of vascular tissue where the crown of the head should have been. "He's more brainless than an imbecile." He let the strands of hair drop back into place.

"It's your duty to take care of their medical needs." Mother Mary Joseph dipped an empty bottle into a basin of water. "It's my duty to see to their spiritual ones."

"Baptize? How?" He ran his hand over the baby's odd features. "There's no brow. Where will you make the sign of the cross?"

The nun wiped up a few drops of spilled water and tossed the damp cloth in a nearby hamper. "If you'll excuse me, doctor."

"I won't," he said. "Father Finetti will not approve of this."

"Father Finetti is not here, so the decision rests with me."

"You've read the decrees from the Sacred Office regarding the *abnormal fruits of conception.* You know what they suggest."

"I'm quite familiar with the Church's teachings." She tightened her lips but the words pushed through. "I finished my religious training, as I'm sure you know." She swaddled the infant and cradled him in her arms. "*Ego te baptize in nomine Patris, et Filii, et Spiritus Sancti,*" she said, pouring water over the misshapen head.

Dr. Peters stormed out of the room.

An hour later, the baby perished in the Reverend Mother's arms.

Thanks in large part to Sadie Hope, Muriel's story made its way through the convent. At breakfast, the girls spoke in hushed tones. *She had a rough time of it. Almost didn't pull through. She gave birth to a monster, may he rest in peace.* To Sadie's credit, there was no mention of words between Mother Mary Joseph and Dr. Peters, though Sadie did make it clear that the baby could be buried in consecrated ground, giving those who were Catholic a bit of relief.

After the morning Mass, Lily headed straight for the infant nursery. "Did you hear about Muriel?" she said a little too loudly, and one of babies cried out.

"I know." Violet put the last pin in the Dennick boy's diaper and set him in a nearby crib. "It's so sad," she said, opening her arms. "The Reverend Mother says Muriel will make it though."

Lily's eyes brightened. She stepped back and held both of Violet's hands. "You have to go see her. That ridiculous

Sister Immaculata won't let me. She says I'm too delicate. But you can go."

"I'm not sure I—"

"For me." Lily put Violet's hands together, pleadingly.

"I'll think about it."

"She has a husband, you know."

Violet's brow lifted.

"Well, she *could* have one. She said she did." Lily sighed. "What difference does it make? I can't stand to think of her all alone in there. She needs someone to talk to. Someone who's not a nun."

"If Mother Mary Joseph gives her permission, I'll go to see Muriel this afternoon."

"I knew I could count on you." Lily smiled tremulously and turned toward the doorway. "Find out exactly where they cut her open."

Violet's face dropped. "I'll ask nothing of the kind."

"You must." Lily's eyes teared up. "I need to know." When Violet stood in silence, Lily continued: "I can't be cut open. I can't!" She started to cry. "No man will ever want me. How would I explain the scar?"

Violet turned to the changing table and started folding freshly washed diapers. "You're a selfish girl," she said to Lily. "Poor Muriel. What she went through, and all you can think about is yourself."

"You don't understand. You'll never understand. You have Stanley. I have no one. I'll end up a spinster."

"You made your bed." The anger hardened Violet's tone. "It's Muriel you should be thinking about now."

"I thought you loved me. I thought you wanted more for me." Tears poured down Lily's face as she left the room.

Violet refused to run after her. Not this time. She had her hands full with the babies who depended on her, and she liked it that way. Since arriving at the Good Shepherd, she'd grown accustomed to this temporary world, and looked forward to her duties in the nursery. She enjoyed routine. It had long been her companion, a bit of predictability in an unpredictable world. Ever since Daisy's death, Violet liked to know what was coming. She counted on it, like she counted on Stanley. He came to her mind again, as he had all night. She stood in front of the changing table, wondering once more if he had seen her from the streetcar, cursing herself for having taken such a chance.

*You're a selfish girl.* Violet's words to her sister came back on her. *You're no better than Lily*, she thought. *It's Muriel you should be thinking of now.*

That afternoon, Mother Mary Joseph sent one of the postulants to relieve Violet in the nursery so she could go visit Muriel. "Perhaps you can lift her spirits a bit," the nun had concluded.

Since the first door on the right was ajar, Violet caught a glimpse of Judith Dennick propped up in bed, paging through her Bible, the only reading material allowed in the maternity ward. Violet had heard that the Dennick baby was going to be adopted out the following week to a couple from Altoona, and she wondered if Judith knew. At the next door, Violet knocked twice and waited. When no invitation came, she turned the knob and poked her head inside. "Would you like some company?"

Muriel lay in her bed, staring at the ceiling, and did not respond.

"I can come back later if you're not up to it now." Not knowing whether to stay or go, Violet stood at the threshold for a moment. "You get your rest," she finally said, and started to pull the door.

"I never even got to see him." Each word crackled along Muriel's parched tongue.

Violet made her way over to a pitcher of water on the nightstand and filled a glass. "Drink," she said, lifting Muriel's head and holding the glass to her lips.

Muriel took a halfhearted sip, but most of the water dribbled down her chin. She pushed the glass away, dropped back on the pillow, and winced. "They took him away before I woke up. They should have waited."

Violet looked around for a cloth to wipe Muriel's face. When she found none, she used the hem of her skirt. "They probably wanted to spare you the pain."

"They should have waited."

Not knowing what to say, Violet pulled a chair alongside the bed, sat down, and held Muriel's hand.

"He told me I'd be punished."

"Who?"

"*Wicked girls get what they deserve,* he'd say. And he was right."

"Stop dwelling on such nonsense. Anyone who would say such awful things doesn't deserve a sweet girl like you." Violet wondered to whom she was referring, but settled on a different tack. "It won't be long now." She tried for a lighter tone. "The Reverend Mother says you'll be back home before you know it. She's already sent word to your father."

Muriel squeezed her eyes shut. "How long?"

"Three weeks. Plenty of time to recover first." As Violet studied Muriel's pained expression, a question jumped to her own lips. "Who is it that calls you wicked?"

"They should have waited," Muriel said and turned her head away.

# EXCESSIVE LIBIDO IN WOMEN

*When the libido in woman is so excessive that she cannot control her passion, and forgetting religion, morality, modesty, custom, and possible social consequences, she offers herself to every man she meets, we use the term nymphomania . . . Nymphomaniac women should not be permitted to marry or to run around loose, but should be confined to institutions in which they can be subjected to proper treatment.*
—*Woman: Her Sex and Love Life,*
William J. Robinson, MD, 1929

Starting the work is two-thirds of it, as we Welsh like to say. And with Easter only six weeks away, there's plenty of work to be done. Clean the church, wash the choir robes, sew new scarves for the Communion table—purple for Lent and white for Easter. We always have a good crowd that day. Even the most reluctant Christians heed the resurrection.

We have to wonder if the Morgan girls will be home from Buffalo by then. Violet will almost certainly lose her position at Walsh's if she's away much longer, and Lily could get held back if she misses too much school. More importantly, George Sherman seems to have taken a shine to Lily and has been asking all over town for her. If Lily wants to improve her lot, she needs to be in Scranton where she can catch his eye.

If they're not back by Easter, surely they'll be home in time for Mother's Day. We count on them to help pass out the flowers. It's a beautiful service. The mothers are invited down front for a carnation. Red if her own mother is living. White if she's passed on. That first white flower is always the hardest. Heartbreaking, really, but you can't change tradition. The preacher has us order enough carnations for all the women in the church. After the mothers have made their way back to their pews, he calls the spinsters and the barren forward so they don't feel left out. It's a magnanimous gesture, and one we're sure is appreciated by the childless women who show up to church that day.

# CHAPTER ELEVEN

JUDITH DENNICK KNEW BETTER than to go into the infant nursery that morning, but she went just the same. She'd been etherized during the delivery and never got a chance to see her baby boy. Keeping the child was out of the question, but Judith sorely wanted to hold him before his adoption, which would take place later that day. Sadie had warned against it. "Lay eyes on him and it'll break your heart." But at nineteen, Judith had already had more than her fair share of pain. What difference could one more broken heart make?

She slipped out of her room, hesitating a moment at the sound of Muriel's muffled cries next door. *I'll check on her later,* Judith thought as she slipped through the hospital doors, into the foyer, and down the hallway. *First, I have to see my baby.* She paused briefly, leaned against the wall outside the infant nursery, and cradled her stitched abdomen. It still bulged somewhat under her binder. Judith stood for a few seconds, steadying herself. Sixteen days of bed rest had taken their toll, but the Reverend Mother insisted on extra recovery time for the girls who'd had cesarean operations. Judith hadn't even been allowed to go over to the church for ashes the previous Wednesday. Father Finetti had come to her hospital room after services to prepare her for Lent. Judith's legs quivered beneath her flannel nightgown.

A moment later, she drew in a breath and turned the doorknob. Inside, three rows of cribs stretched out in front of her, each ending at a long sunlit window. Were those forsythia branches tapping against the glass, and was it possible they were already starting to green amid the lingering snow? How long had she been at the Good Shepherd? Four months? Yes, she thought. March 10. What else had happened outside those windows while she'd been hidden away?

"You're not supposed to be on your feet yet." Violet shifted a baby to the crook of her left arm and dragged a rocker over to Judith with her free hand.

Looking around, Judith realized with some relief that Violet was the only adult in the room. "Which one is he?" Judith's pale cheeks flushed at the question. Shouldn't a mother know her own child without having to ask? She walked up and down the rows, grabbing onto the cribs for support.

"Hasn't been three weeks," Violet said, motioning her toward the seat. "Mother Mary Joseph says—"

"I need to see him." Judith's legs started to buckle, and she dropped into the rocker. "Just once," she said, "that's all."

"Wait." Violet went over to the cribs, trading the baby in her arms for another. "He's beautiful," she said, handing the child to Judith.

The infant squirmed inside a loosely swaddled blanket before settling into his mother's embrace. "Mama's here," was all Judith could think to say. "Mama's here. Mama. Mama." Her lips opened and closed around each syllable. "Mama," she said again, nodding at such a simple word. She traced the arch of her son's eyebrows, the angle of his nose, the curve of his mouth, the slope of his chin and cheeks. "So perfect."

When the baby started to fuss again, Violet handed over a bottle that had been warming in a pot of hot water. "I think he'll take some, if you want to try."

"I was never meant to be a mother." Judith brushed the bottle's nipple back and forth along the baby's lips. "My milk never even came in." At first, the infant refused to be coaxed, but he finally started sucking. Judith shook her head and asked, "What kind of woman can't nurse her own child?"

"That happens sometimes." Violet pulled another rocker over and sat down. "It doesn't mean anything."

Judith shrugged as she stared spellbound at the baby. In the next moment, her eyebrows shot up in dismay. She handed the bottle to Violet, laid the infant across her own lap, opened the blanket, and started counting.

"They're all there," Violet said. "Ten fingers. Ten toes."

Relief supplanted panic as Judith pulled the ends of the blanket back over the child, drew him to her breast, and inhaled his scent. "What kind of woman gives up her own baby?"

After a long moment, Violet said, "Maybe you can keep him."

"And what should I do?" Judith stood and carried the child over to his crib. "Take him with me? Show up at home with a baby? Just say, *I'd like you to meet my son?* as if that sort of thing happens every day?" She laughed at the absurdity of it, and tears started rolling down her face. "Do you have any idea what those people would do to me?"

Violet shook her head but kept her eyes focused on the girl.

"They'd run me out of town. Or worse. They'd ignore me. I wouldn't be welcome. No one in the neighborhood would talk to me. I wouldn't be invited to sit at their kitchen tables for a little gossip. *I'd* be the gossip. And worse still, my boy would be the gossip." Judith kissed the baby's forehead and lowered him into the crib. "What chance would he ever have?"

"I'm sorry I . . ." Violet walked over to Judith and took her hand. "You're giving him the best life possible. That's what good mothers do."

"That's what desperate *women* do." Judith wiped the tears from her face and smoothed her nightgown.

"I'm so sorry," Violet said again.

"Thank you," Judith walked toward the door, "for letting me hold him." She folded her arms in front of her chest, closed her eyes, and felt the weight of her baby once more. Her lids flew open wide when Sister Immaculata squeezed into the room.

"The Reverend Mother is asking for the Dennick infant." The nun followed Violet's eyes to Judith. "Bring him out when he's ready." Sister Immaculata blushed slightly. "The couple from Altoona is waiting in the front parlor."

"He's ready." Judith stepped around the nun and into the hallway. As she passed the parlor, she turned her head in the opposite direction and continued toward her hospital room.

Hours later, Violet was still pondering the question Judith Dennick had brought up—how could a mother give up her own child? Violet wasn't judging. In fact, she understood. It was exactly what Lily was there to do. And Lily did not have a choice either. She'd be ruined if she returned to Scranton with a baby. No one would give her a chance. She'd be forced out of school, out of the church. What kind of life would that be? Lily couldn't stand up in the face of such shame; she didn't have the constitution for it. She'd had everything handed to her. It was their fault, of course. The whole family. They'd spoiled her, their miracle baby, coming on the heels of Daisy's death. They hadn't prepared

Lily for life's difficulties. Violet accepted her part in this. She knew the dark side of life; she'd lived it every day since Daisy's death. She had no intention of exposing her sister to such pain. Maybe if Lily had someone like Stanley by her side, someone she could depend on in her darkest hours, then she'd be able to do right by her child. *Stanley,* Violet thought. *A man who could forgive almost anything.*

When Michael started to stir, Violet lifted him out of his crib and smiled.

More than a week had passed since Stanley thought he'd seen Violet from the streetcar window. The streetcar was only the latest sighting. There'd also been Boathouse Row, Wanamaker's, and the concert hall. And here he was, strolling purposefully along Market Street, hoping to run into her again. The first time it had happened, he'd gone so far as to catch up with the woman whose black curls beat against the back of her bright red dress as she walked toward the pier. "Violet!" he'd shouted, tugging her red sleeve. The woman had screamed so loudly a nearby policeman rushed over. The officer eventually released Stanley, mumbling something about college boys and the girls they'd left back home. After that, Stanley's heart continued to play tricks on his eyes, but common sense told him to hold back. He'd watch from a safe distance, knowing that the look-alike would never turn out to be his beautiful Violet.

Stanley sat down on a bench and rubbed his eyes, trying to erase the memory of the raven-haired girl running away from the streetcar with a red hatbox in her hand. After all, Violet was in Buffalo, farther from him than ever. That's what the letter that Evan had delivered had said. The last letter Stanley could expect for some months, according to Violet, though he still couldn't understand why. He reached into his jacket and removed the pages, shiny from wear. He inhaled deeply, hoping to catch a trace of the lilac perfume that had worn off days ago.

*My Dearest Stanley.* How many times had he read her words? *I have such good news.* That's how she had put it—her sudden trip to Buffalo to help her mother's sister set up her new house. *Aunt Hattie's husband* and *lucky to find work at all.* Even if that were true . . . Even? Of course it was true. But why couldn't she write to him? *I can't send letters without raising Aunt Hattie's suspicions.* This made no sense to him. They'd managed to correspond through Babcia over the years. Why couldn't they do that now? He pored over the letter as if a different answer would appear, but her words remained unchanged. *Aunt Hattie knows all the tricks. If she sees the widow's return address, she'll be on to us.* And further on, *can't take the chance when we're so close to our dream.*

Something had changed, but for the life of him, he couldn't figure out what. And why hadn't he heard back from the widow yet? He'd written to her, hoping she'd have some answers. Stanley skipped ahead, craving the reassurance at the bottom of the second page. *My love for you is everlasting.* He closed his eyes and imagined Violet saying the words to him. *My love for you is everlasting.*

Everlasting. He held onto the word as though it were a prayer or an incantation. Just for a second, he caught the scent of lilacs, a trick of the nose, but lovely all the same. What if just this once he opened his eyes and found her standing before him?

He looked up and found an empty sidewalk, as he knew he would. When he stood to leave, he noticed the gilded sign across the street for the first time. *Widenor's Hats.* Just then, a paunchy woman in a fur stole walked out of the store and started down the steps, a red hatbox dangling from her hand.

* * *

Long after everyone else had fallen asleep, Violet continued to stare at the ceiling. Her heart still ached for Judith who'd given her baby up that morning, and for Muriel, and for all the other girls who'd been forced into motherhood too soon, only to lose their chance in the end. Violet glanced at Lily, still two and a half months short of her time, wondering what would become of her after giving up her own child, her flesh and blood. How would she ever recover from such a blow?

Knowing that sleep would not come this night, Violet threw off her covers, put on her robe and slippers, and headed down to the nursery. Just as she reached the top of the stairs, the convent's front door groaned shut. Had someone left another baby in a cradle? Violet continued down the steps, past Mother Mary Joseph's room, to the foyer. She found the cradle empty, and glanced to the right noticing that the pocket doors to the hospital were ajar. She headed down the long hallway, looking in first on Judith, who lay fast asleep, and then Muriel. Violet tapped lightly on the door, and entered. When she found an empty bed, and then an empty washroom, she rushed back to tell the Reverend Mother, who was now standing in her doorway.

"Muriel's run off!" Violet shouted, disregarding the late hour.

Still dressed in full garb, Mother Mary Joseph's brow furrowed. "Hush." She pressed an index finger against her lips and glanced toward the nursery. "Yes." The nun looked down the hallway, then back at Violet. "Well, there's nothing we can do about it now."

"Nothing we can do? We can send for the police," Violet said, wondering if she should wake Sister Immaculata, or Sadie, or one of the other nuns. "We can go out and find her ourselves." When the Reverend Mother didn't respond,

Violet added, "It's only been nine days since she had the baby." Her voice dropped. "Since she lost her baby. She's not strong enough."

The Reverend Mother reached for the rosary beads at her waist. "We'll pray on it."

Violet searched for what she could say to convince the woman something had to be done immediately. "Her father will be here soon," she remembered. "What'll we tell him?"

"We'll tell him nothing." Mother Mary Joseph's needle-sharp tone seemed to surprise even herself.

"He may not be the kindest man, but no one deserves . . ."

The nun took a breath and started again: "You don't know the whole story. This was Muriel's choice. All we can do now is pray for her safety."

A door creaked open on the second floor, and some-one poked her nose over the banister. The Reverend Mother looked up with her jaw set, and the girl retreated.

"She'll never survive," Violet said once she heard the upstairs door close. "She has no food, no money."

"We can't be sure of that."

Violet's eyes narrowed. "You knew." She said the words slowly, trying to make sense of them. "How could you . . ." Her voice trailed off. "She's all alone," she finally said. "We have to help her."

"We're never alone," the nun said, "when we have God in our hearts."

"Well, if you're not going after her," Violet started toward the steps to get her coat, "I will."

Mother Mary Joseph took Violet's arm. "If you go look-ing for her," she paused as if to consider her words, "you'll lead him right to her."

"Him?"

"She doesn't want to be found. I don't want her to be found. Not by that monster."

Violet thought about Muriel's pregnancy, the made-up husband. "Her *father*?" Bile rose up from her stomach and burned her throat.

"Her father," the nun repeated, and she patted Violet's damp brow with a fan of sleeve.

# CHAPTER TWELVE

STANLEY KNEADED THE SCARRED STUMP at the end of his left forearm. Pressure sometimes relieved the ache that accompanied a storm. Though no one could see the rain through the heavily curtained windows, the sound of it competed with the convivial atmosphere inside the Fin and Feather, a speakeasy at the back of a downtown taxidermy shop. It had been a month or so since he'd spoken to the proprietor of Widenor's Hats, six weeks since Violet's last letter. Stanley had started frequenting the speakeasy after a fellow Socialist Club member vouched for him. The first time Stanley stopped by, he was surprised to see both men and women inside. Decent women too. Mostly. Not decent by Scranton's standards, but what did that matter to him? Stanley had lived in Philadelphia long enough to broaden his thinking beyond the borders of his hometown.

"Another whiskey," Stanley said, pulling out a few coins, carefully avoiding Violet's medallion, which weighed like an anchor in his pocket.

Mounted above the bar, a large-mouthed bass and a good-sized walleye bookended a fish hawk frozen in flight. Stanley sat on his stool, eyeing the stuffed bird, its wings spanning at least five feet, its talons gripping a reinforced branch that jutted out from a beam. On the opposite wall, a brook trout taunted the impotent hawk, daring it to swoop in for the kill. Stanley closed his eyes to summon the bird's distinctive *chip, chip, chip* whistle. As a boy, he'd studied all the winged species indigenous to Pennsylvania, and his only real regret after his accident was that he was no longer able to do two-handed bird calls.

"A fresh whiskey," the barkeep said, setting a drink in front of Stanley and scooping the coins into his palm before moving on to the next customer.

Stanley picked up the glass, touched it to his lips, and set it back on the bar. He had no business being in a speakeasy, that night or any other, and it had little to do with Prohibition. He knew Violet's opinion on the matter of alcohol, and understood her reasons. She'd seen what drink had done to her father for the year or so following Daisy's death and had no intention of living that life with her own husband. Assuming she still wanted him for a husband. Stanley wasn't sure of anything anymore. He slipped his hand into his pocket and fished out the medallion.

> *Scranton Central High School*
> *Valedictorian*
> *Class of 1923*

"A present for her sister," the man had said. But why was Violet in Philadelphia buying something for Lily, and why had she run away? He took a sip of his whiskey. And what about Buffalo? Had that been a ruse all along? He tipped the drink back, draining it this time. There had to be a good explanation. He started to push the empty glass forward, but changed his mind. This was Violet, after all. His Violet. As true as the day was long. He stood to leave, resolving not to return to the Fin and Feather and not to pass judgment on Violet until he had a chance to hear her out. Or the widow. She knew something about all this, Stanley was sure of it. Her response to him had been uncharacteristically vague, easy to do in a letter, but he'd be home in a month and a half, and then he'd get his answers.

As Stanley fingered the medallion, a voice behind him said, "Well, it's official. These eyes have seen everything." Lorraine Day, a blond pixie of a girl, pulled out the stool next to Stanley but remained standing. "Stanley Adamski in a gin mill." Looking at the ground, she added, "Don't mind me. I'm just waiting for hell to freeze over." She laughed and sat down.

Stanley put the medallion back in his pocket and remained silent. No matter how worldly he'd become, the idea of a woman willingly sitting at a bar startled him.

"Cat got your tongue?" She squeezed his forearm and smiled.

"How long has it been?" Stanley finally managed, trying to remember what year he'd taken her to the St. Valentine's dance.

"Buy me a drink and I'll tell you," Lorraine teased.

As Stanley leaned in to flag down the barkeep, he caught a heady whiff of Lorraine's perfume.

"And get another for yourself," she said, patting his empty stool. "In Philadelphia, it's considered un-gent-le-man-ly," she stretched each syllable as if to emphasize the offense, "to allow a woman to drink alone."

After two hours and twice as many whiskeys, enough time and alcohol for Stanley to lay bare his troubles, he concluded, "I should have married Violet long before now." He shook his head and stood to leave, weaving as if on the prow of a ship.

"She's a lucky girl. I'll say that for her. Any other man would have flown the coop by now." Lorraine rose and took Stanley's arm. "A lucky girl," she said again as they staggered out to find the rain had stopped.

Stanley paused for a wave of dizziness to pass. "How is it I can say things to you I can't say to anyone else?"

"I understand, is all. I've been double-crossed myself." She tipped her head up at him. "I've had my heart broke a few times."

Stanley looked at Lorraine, really looked at her for the first time. Here she stood, not a foot away, the streetlight bouncing off her painted lips. He slid his hand behind her neck, pulled her in, and kissed her. She looked surprised at first, then pleased by this development. She answered him with kisses unlike any Violet had ever bestowed upon him. Lorraine's mouth was hot, moist, deliberate.

"Take it somewhere else, pal," a voice called out from the doorway. "We don't need nobody calling attention to the joint."

Stanley blushed, but Lorraine simply took his hand and led him down the street to a two-story house covered in green asbestos shingles. "Around back," she said, leading him to what appeared to be an added-on room with its own entrance. "What do you think?" she asked as she stepped inside. Stanley remained at the door. "Don't tell me you want to be carried over the threshold," she laughed.

"I'm not sure . . ." Stanley tried to think of what came next, but all his words melted to the floor. "I . . ."

"At least have a drink with me." Lorraine walked past the spindle bed and pulled a bottle out of an open dresser drawer.

Stanley pocketed his handless arm, and followed her to the other side of the room. He ran his tongue across his lower lip, tasting the last trace of her.

Lorraine passed the bottle and two sticky glasses over to Stanley. "It's ungentlemanly to let a woman pour."

Stanley's hand trembled, but he managed.

"Still want to talk about that girl of yours in Scranton?"

He threw back his drink, poured another, and downed that one as well. He licked his lips again, and tasted Lorraine still. And what about that girl of his? Where was she tonight? Whose lips had *she* kissed?

Lorraine smiled and fingered the bow at her neckline. She placed the two dangling ends in Stanley's hand. "Pull," she whispered into his ear. One loop disappeared and then the other. Stanley watched as the now-unfettered blouse slipped to the edges of her shoulders.

Without speaking, Stanley kissed her neck, the tops of her arms, the tip of her nose. He unfastened one button, and then another. He pushed the blouse gently and watched it drift to the floor.

A last drink for each of them, and then, somehow, he found himself on top of her, kissing her, liberating her corseted breasts, cupping them one at a time, taking turns with them, cursing his misfortune, his missing hand. He closed his eyes and kissed her again, her lips, her tongue, and uttered a single word: "Violet."

His eyes shot open, and he found Lorraine underneath him, half naked. He sprang up from the bed, picked up her blouse, and threw it over her. "I'm sorry," he said, and ran out the door.

The rain started up again, soaking Stanley, hunched in a vacant lot, vomiting the last of the whiskey. He was no stranger to alcohol; he had cut back, even stopped for long stretches, first to win Violet over, and then to please her, but he hadn't given it up entirely. Yet he was retching like a boy who'd just swilled his first few pints. Even with no one around to witness the scene, Stanley felt like a damn fool.

Guilt, that's what it was, he thought as he straightened up and started walking again. What had he been thinking? And when had Lorraine become that kind of girl? Like most fellows his age, he'd frequented "the Alleys" back home. He could spot a tart when he saw one. You never know, is all. But it wasn't his place to judge Lorraine, and he knew it.

Violet was his strength, his courage, his heart. His world. Nothing else mattered. He'd simply lost his mind for a moment, upset by his meeting with the milliner; upset that he could not put together the pieces of this strange puzzle. It was the drink. He would stop. No one needed to ever know about this.

Drenched, he slipped into the boarding house and up the stairs to his room. *Never again*, he thought, peeling off his clothes and dropping them where he stood. He choked back a wave of nausea, stumbled to his bed, and lay down. In an instant, the room seemed to have set sail on choppy seas, so he pulled himself up and sat back against the headboard, searching for a single point of focus to calm the waters. He followed a sliver of moonlight to a hook on the opposite wall where his mechanical hand dangled from a canvas harness. He'd slung it there when he'd moved in, and there it had hung, unused.

The widow, notoriously frugal when it came to her own needs, was generous to a fault with Stanley. He'd never had an interest in a prosthetic; he made do, even flourished, in spite of his missing hand, but that didn't stop the widow. "You want a jury listening to your words, not looking for your hand," she'd said, and she had a point. So she'd joined forces with Doc Rodham, who researched the matter and discovered that the Germans had made significant strides with artificial limbs after the Great War. Doc Rodham took the casts and measurements, and sent them to a company overseas. Two months later, the device arrived—an aluminum hand with jointed wooden fingers that could be closed and opened by means of a cable. The hand screwed into a metal sleeve that stopped halfway up Stanley's forearm.

Leather straps connected the sleeve to a cuff that buckled around the upper arm near the elbow. A canvas harness kept the apparatus in place. The maker recommended the use of gloves for a more "natural appearance." He also included a hook that could be screwed into the sleeve instead of the hand for times when manual labor was required.

Stanley had tried the hand for a month, but the pressure and friction against the stump never subsided and proved too painful. He hated to let the widow down, so he'd kept the thing, with the intention of trying again someday. Someday never came, and there it hung, reminding him that he was broken.

But so was Violet, after the death of her sister. They'd known each other whole, and they'd known each other broken. That's why it worked. That's why Stanley would never hold another woman in his arms. And when he'd see Violet next, she'd tell him all about what brought her to Philadelphia that day and why she couldn't tell him. And though he couldn't imagine what it could be, she'd have a good reason because she was a good woman. The kind of woman who makes you a better man. The kind of woman you love for life. The kind of woman who makes you whole.

# CHAPTER THIRTEEN

IN THE TWO MONTHS following Muriel's disappearance, daily life at the Good Shepherd took on a quieter tone for Lily. She'd become more serious about her situation, somehow indifferent to the frivolities of friendship. No longer interested in breaking the rules, Lily settled into the routine of Mass, meals, and classes in the domestic arts, and she'd slip into the nursery at least once a day to see her sister.

Violet continued her own routine—up every morning no later than five and into the nursery by five forty-five. She worked well into the night, breaking sometimes for lunch or supper in the dining room, though she often stayed put and ate in with the babies.

And while Violet could honestly say she loved all of the charges in her care, she took particular pride in Michael. In spite of his disfigurement, he grew stronger each day, and the Reverend Mother credited Violet with his progress. "You're doing something right," the nun would remark when she'd see Michael in Violet's arms.

For the first time since arriving at the Good Shepherd, Violet slept until six thirty when Sister Immaculata came into the ward to wake the girls.

"Why didn't you come for me?" Violet asked when she finally made it to the nursery.

Mother Mary Joseph sat in a rocker, trying to soothe a fussy Michael. "He's all yours," she said, handing him up to Violet. "You're the only one who can do for him." She watched as the baby settled quietly in Violet's arms.

"I'm so sorry." Violet carried Michael over to a basin that had been prepared for his bath. She ran a damp cloth along his gums, over his face, and around the triangular cleft under his nose before unpinning his diaper and placing him in the water.

"I rather enjoyed myself." Smiling, the Reverend Mother walked up and down the rows of cribs, touching each infant briefly on the forehead. "And you haven't had a wink of sleep since Muriel . . ." she waited for the right words to land on her tongue, "left us."

"Neither have you." Violet wrapped Michael in a towel and carried him over to the table. "I've seen the light under your door when I go to bed." Violet coaxed a lone tuft of hair on top of Michael's head into a curl. "What's to become of him?" she asked the nun who stood alongside her now, rubbing the baby's legs.

"If he's still here next spring, St. Patrick's Home for Boys." She nodded toward the window. "Just down the road. A cheerful enough place." She glanced around the cramped nursery. "Once they start walking, they need room to run."

Violet looked out the window but she couldn't see any farther than the asylum's side yard. By May, the yellow forsythia petals had long since fallen, and the peonies stood ready to bloom. The waiting seemed endless at the Good Shepherd, and yet, almost three months had passed since Violet and Lily had arrived, making Michael about four months old. If no one intervened, he was well on his way to spending his days in a boys' home, and though Violet should have expected it, the realization stunned her. "And his face?" she asked, trying to smooth the tremor out of her voice.

"God has a plan."

"How can you be so sure?"

"He brought you here, didn't He?" Mother Mary Joseph stroked the baby's plump cheek with her index finger. "Look at the change in him. That's your doing. God's hand is in that."

"Lily's indiscretion brought me here, and I'm certain God's hand was not in that." Violet finished dressing the boy and laid him in his crib. "So we just wait, and hope someone comes along to help him?" she finally said.

"This is on God's timetable." The Reverend Mother pushed open the window and inhaled the spring day. "We wait. We pray."

"That's it?"

"And see what Dr. Peters says about the matter."

"Dr. Peters?"

"I asked him to see if there was someone at the hospital experienced enough in matters like these." She ran a finger across her own fully formed upper lip. "Someone willing to perform an operation for free."

"What about God's timetable?"

"No harm in giving Him a little nudge." With her finger still resting lightly against her mouth, Mother Mary Joseph smiled and walked out of the room.

"You're always gone without so much as a *Good morning*," Lily said as she lumbered into the nursery after prayers.

"Good morning." Violet lowered a baby into a carriage, and lined that carriage up behind four others pointed at the door.

"Not even a *How are you this fine day*?" Lily glanced at the infant closest to her and wrinkled her nose.

"They're ready," Violet said to a novice standing nearby. The young nun pulled the first carriage into the hallway and headed toward the front door. Violet looked over at her sister. "And how are you this fine day?"

"I've been better." She lowered herself into a rocker. "My back aches something awful."

Alarm crossed Violet's face. "Did you tell Sadie? You're too close to your due date to ignore any symptoms."

"I'm telling you, Sadie's not family. You are." She adjusted her position, pushing her lower back up against the rocker.

"There you are." Carol stood in the hallway, peering into the nursery at Lily. "Elocution lessons start in five minutes." She looked at Violet, who was pushing the last carriage toward the door. "It's a wonderful class," Carol said, as if Violet had asked her opinion on the subject. "Sister Immaculata teaches us how to say no like real ladies." She threw her head back and laughed.

Lily scowled.

"Come on," Carol said. "I can always get a rise out of you with that one."

"She's out of sorts today," Violet said.

"I'm stuck." Lily stretched her arms straight out.

Violet grasped Lily's hands and pulled her to her feet. Violet stood stunned, noting the size of Lily's belly. Could the baby have grown that much in a day or two? "It's pretty quiet in here today," Violet said. "How 'bout you save me a seat at lunch?"

"I best not miss my lessons," Lily said, making her way slowly toward the doorway.

Violet took her sister's arm and the two walked down the hallway with Carol just ahead. "Ask Sadie to look in on you in the meantime," Violet said. She dropped her sister off at the door of the classroom at the end of the hall, then headed for the front porch to sit with the babies.

* * *

The late-morning sun burned through the clouds, carrying the promise of summer. A gentle breeze freed the remaining blossoms from the dogwood trees, and a flurry of white petals settled on the grass in the front yard. Violet sat on the porch, surrounded by eleven napping babies inside six wicker carriages, imagining a world where she could return to Scranton with Michael in her arms. Maybe the neighbors wouldn't judge her harshly. Just maybe they'd say, *That woman's a saint*, when they saw her with the child. *No one else would have taken on such a burden. What choice did she have?* And perhaps she could convince Doc Rodham to perform the operation. He was a good Christian man, and he'd always loved her family. Of course there was Stanley to consider, but how could he say no? He'd been adopted himself and would probably welcome the chance to do the same for some other poor soul. She'd have to come up with some explanation for the baby—found in a basket on a set of church steps; abandoned on the seat of a streetcar—but surely God would forgive such a small lie. Maybe taking Michael home was part of God's plan as well.

Two pairs of booted feet scraped up the stone steps. Violet's eyes flew open and she wondered in that moment how long they'd been closed. "May I help you?" she called out as the pair reached the top.

The woman spoke first. "We're here about a baby," she said, glancing from one carriage to the next. "Any boys?"

"Four." Violet stood up to shake off her drowsiness. She studied the couple before her, their clothes patched, their faces as worn as their boots. They looked barely able to feed themselves, let alone a child.

"I don't have all day," the man said to the woman, who stepped a few feet closer to the carriages and started to peer inside.

"Perhaps you'd better to speak to the Reverend Mother." Violet placed her hand on the woman's back and pointed her away from the babies and toward the door. "Through the foyer, then the first room on the right. She's giving lessons, but they should be over any time now."

The man stayed planted on the top step. "I'm not so sure about this." He shoved the toe of his boot into the railing.

"I'm not leaving empty-handed," the woman said with a resolve that seemed to surprise them both. She took a breath and steadied herself. "Not again." She turned and walked through the door.

Mumbling to himself, the man gave the railing one good kick, pushed past Violet, and headed inside.

Half an hour later, with the help of the novice, Violet got the babies back to the nursery. As she walked past the parlor, she noticed the man and woman were standing up as if to leave. Not surprising, she thought, as she pushed the last carriage down the hallway. No matter how much a couple wanted a child, Mother Mary Joseph had to be selective about the families.

Once the babies were settled, Violet headed across the hall to have lunch with Lily. Sadie met Violet just outside the dining room door. "She's starting to drop. Could be any day now."

Violet's breath caught. She had been aware that Lily's time was coming, but knowing the truth didn't make the hearing of it any easier. "What did she say when you told her?"

"She's in a bit of denial. It happens at this stage."

"What do we do?" Violet peeked into the room and spotted Lily at the end of a table.

"Keep an eye out. I've alerted Dr. Peters." Sadie started down the hall.

"Aren't *you* going to deliver her?" Violet called out.

Sadie swung around. "I'll assist," she said, "but Dr. Peters made a good point the last time he saw her. She's narrow-hipped. Best to have him on hand. Better safe than sorry."

After lunch, Violet brought Lily back to the nursery. "You should rest in the afternoon from now on. No need to go to classes if you're not up to it." She held onto her sister's arm as Lily dropped into the rocker. "Can I get you anything?"

"A footstool." Lily leaned down toward her feet. "My ankles swell so." She made an attempt to lift her legs into the air but quickly abandoned the idea.

Violet pulled an empty milk crate over and lifted Lily's feet onto it.

The Reverend Mother walked into the room clapping her hands. "Wonderful news!" She headed over to Michael's crib and lifted him into the air. "Our prayers are answered." Mother Mary Joseph raised the baby into the air one final time before handing him to Violet. "Sister Immaculata is on her way to relieve you. As soon as she gets here, meet me in the front parlor with Michael. There's someone I very much want you to meet," she said as she rushed back out of the room.

"What's all the fuss about?" Lily asked as soon as the nun disappeared.

"Sounds like Dr. Peters found someone to do Michael's operation." Violet tried to look cheerful, but the worry in her eyes belied the smile on her lips.

"Well, that's good news." Lily started to fan her face with both hands. "He'll be able to live a normal life now."

"Yes," Violet said, lifting him out of his crib, "I suppose."

"You better get going," Sister Immaculata said as she walked into the room. "Mother Mary Joseph is expecting you two." She looked at the baby in Violet's arms and shooed both of them to the door. "Go on now, they're waiting for him."

Michael cooed as Violet carried him down the hall. She thought about Dr. Peters and wondered if she'd judged him too harshly. If he found someone to do the operation, perhaps he wasn't a scoundrel after all. At the very least, she thought as she stepped into the parlor, she needed to thank him for going out of his way in this instance.

"There you are," the Reverend Mother said. "I'd like to you meet Michael's parents."

Violet stopped cold at the sight of the impoverished couple from the front porch. "You can't have him." She turned to Mother Mary Joseph. "They can't adopt him. It wouldn't be fair."

"This is not your decision." The nun's tone left no room for discussion.

"I'm sorry. I'm sorry. I'm so sorry," the woman cried as she stared at the baby in Violet's arms. "I never should have left you here."

The man looked around the room and settled his eyes on a portrait of Pope Pius. "Let's hurry this along," he said. "I've already missed half a day's work."

"It's you?" Violet said, trying to recognize something about the woman—her shape, her voice.

"I'm so sorry," the woman said again and broke into choking sobs.

Mother Mary Joseph directed the woman to a chair and turned to Violet. "I told them they have you to thank for their son's good care."

"Yes," the woman managed, and she extended her hand to Violet. "Thank you."

"You're his mother?" Violet said, ignoring the proffered hand. "You left him in that cradle?"

"It was too much," the woman said. "We have three other mouths to feed, and my husband didn't think . . ." She stopped. "It's different now. We've come to take him home."

"As long as they can fix his face," the man looked up from the painting, but averted his eyes from the child, "we'll keep him."

"I found work," the woman explained. "In a hospital. One of the doctors says he knows how to do the operation. Says he'll do it for free if they let him."

"Answered prayer," Mother Mary Joseph said, nodding for Violet to pass the baby to his mother.

But Violet could not let go.

"It's always better to be raised by your own," the nun said. "The way that God intended." She lifted the baby out of Violet's arms and handed him to his mother. "And will he be named for his father?" she asked, avoiding Violet's tear-filled eyes.

"God no!" The man's face reddened as he turned to his wife and said, "If he's coming with us, he's coming now."

"Henry," the woman answered as her husband pulled her up from the chair. "My father's name, God rest his soul. You'd be hard pressed to find a better man." She walked toward the door and turned back. "Thank you, again," she said. "And God bless both of you for watching over my boy."

Violet burst into tears, pushed past the couple, and ran into the hallway.

"Hurry!" Sadie yelled from the foyer. "Lily's baby is coming, and she's asking for you!"

# CHAPTER FOURTEEN

LILY CRIED OUT FROM HER HOSPITAL BED, but Dr. Peters remained unruffled on his side of the curtain. He pulled a long, thin, fine-tipped cautery electrode from his medical bag and placed it next to several pairs of forceps on the wheeled instrument table. "I'll be in momentarily," he said in Lily's direction. A well-thumbed copy of *Eugenical Sterilization in the United States* lay open in front of him.

"She's crowning!" Sadie hollered. "You better hurry!"

"Don't let her push!" the doctor snapped as he filled a syringe with a novocaine-adrenalin solution. According to the book, a physician who'd been testing cauterization of the tubes as a method of sterilization suggested numbing the vaginal walls before burying the electrode to keep the patient from screaming out. Although tubal ligations resulted in the highest success rates, they could only be performed undetected when patients delivered a baby by means of a cesarean operation, making that technique impractical for a significant number of Good Shepherd girls who gave birth vaginally. If effective, Dr. Peters felt, cauterization at the horns of the uterus held great promise for the science of eugenics and the betterment of the human race. It would allow physicians on the front lines of the movement to sterilize women who were deemed morally, intellectually, or racially unfit, and no one would be the wiser. Dr. Peters studied the diagram provided in the textbook and reviewed the experimental procedure.

From the other side of the curtain, Lily kicked as Sadie gently tried to press the girl's knees together. "Not too much longer," Sadie said, but Lily would have none of it. Her body could no longer allow her mind to deny the baby inside her. Something bigger than Lily, something beyond reason and pride, coursed through her.

"I can't wait," she said to Violet, who bent over her, rubbing her head and holding her hand. *Don't let her push!* Was he insane? Lily wondered. Try telling a swollen river to keep within its banks, for in that moment she was a river whose natural path had been choked off from its rightful destination with fallen leaves, twisted branches, and shattered notions of how life was supposed to have been. But suddenly, she knew that if she pushed hard enough, down and over and through, she'd finally rid herself of this one complication and find her way back to the life she'd deserved all along.

She pushed.

Dr. Peters be damned. And George Sherman, and Little Frankie, and everyone in Scranton who ever looked down their noses at her for being the daughter of a miner.

She pushed again, knowing that soon this baby business would be behind her, and the old Lily could return home to make something of her life.

She pushed once more with all her might, and when she opened her eyes, Sadie stood at her feet, cradling the baby in her arms, clearing its mouth with her fingers.

"A girl." Violet's voice cracked as she spoke. "A healthy girl."

Boy or girl—it made no difference. Lily watched as Dr. Peters wheeled his instrument table over to her bedside. She focused on his liver-spotted hands as he cut the umbilical cord, severing the last connection she'd ever have to this child. Her contractions started again, milder this time, but insistent.

"I'll deliver the afterbirth," the doctor said to Sadie. "She needs a few stitches. You two run along and tend to the baby."

Violet hesitated. "Can't she hold her? Just for a minute?"

"No reason to," Lily said, turning her face to the wall. "She's not mine." As the pain rose again, she winced.

"Let's get you cleaned up." Sadie said to the bundle in her arms, and carried her across the room to the changing table. "Dr. Peters will take good care of your mother."

Violet started to walk away, but stopped in the center of the room, her head turning from Lily to the baby and back again.

Dr. Peters marched over and pulled the curtain shut, cutting Violet out of the scene.

"You can't be in two places at once," Sadie said, nodding toward a bottle of boric acid beyond her reach. "It's either Lily or this baby."

Violet stood for a moment, staring at the curtain. "I'll clean her up," she finally said, grabbing the boric acid on her way to the changing table. She saturated a square of cotton batting and patted it around the baby's eyes. "Blue." The word tethered itself to her breath and floated out in a whisper.

"She has her mother's eyes," Sadie said, as the baby flailed her limbs like a ladybug that had somehow landed on its back.

"And Daisy's." Violet wiped mineral oil across the baby's brow and over her cheeks. Tears fell from her eyes onto the infant's slicked skin.

Sadie didn't say anything. She simply watched as Violet cleansed and swaddled the child, all the while whispering that name.

Violet picked up the infant and breathed her in.

"Nothing like the smell of a baby," Sadie said, straightening all the bottles then straightening them again. "Let's get her over to the nursery and see if she won't take a bottle." She walked to the door and held it open.

"There's no denying it." Violet stood a moment longer, running her fingers through the shock of dark hair at the top of her niece's head. "You're a Morgan all right. So much like Daisy." The thought of her older sister pierced Violet's scarred heart, and she pulled the newborn into her chest, a salve on a chronic wound. She glanced at the closed curtain before carrying the infant through the door and down the hallway.

On the other side of the room, Dr. Peters palmed the syringe and said, "You may feel a slight pinch."

Lily stared at the wall without saying a word.

After Lily's ten-day hospital confinement, she returned to the girls' ward for observation and waited for permission to travel—another week or so at most, according to Dr. Peters. This was good news for Violet, who was anxious to get back to Scranton, where she hoped Stanley would be waiting for her with open arms. Violet was almost able to convince herself he hadn't seen her from the trolley. The Stanley she knew would have jumped off that car, no matter how fast it was moving or how crowded it was, to get to her. Most days, though, she knew she had fences to mend when she returned, and she prayed that Stanley would accept whatever story she chose to tell him, though she had absolutely no idea what that would be.

She'd always believed in the value of truth—for the sake of virtue, yes, but also as a matter of practicality. Hard truths were easy to remember. Lily had a baby. There'd be no forgetting that. But would Violet remember all the lies she'd have to tell in order to make that first one about going to Buffalo ring true? "A lie begets a lie," their Sunday school teacher used to say. And what about Lily? Would she remember to tell the exact same lies, the exact same way? Truth had a way of making itself known.

Yet Violet couldn't tell Stanley about the Good Shepherd. She'd given her word to Lily—foolishly, reluctantly, but she'd given it. No going back now, she thought. Besides, she loved Lily and wanted the best for her. A clean slate for the price of a lie. A bargain made.

Maybe it was best that Dr. Peters advised them to wait another week before traveling. Violet needed the time to figure out what she'd say to Stanley when she saw him. And she also enjoyed the idea of spending time with her niece. She knew enough to guard her heart from the child. Michael's return to his parents had taught her that much. Still, this baby was family, and unlike Lily, Violet couldn't just ignore that fact.

Mother Mary Joseph had named the child Bernadette, until the adoptive parents came along, but secretly, Violet called her Daisy. She always knew that someday she'd name her own daughter after her deceased sister, so what harm could come from using the name now?

At the end of the week, when Dr. Peters had finally released Lily from his care, Violet pulled the cowhide suitcases out from under her bed and opened them on the bare mattress.

"I'm so relieved to be done with all this," Lily said, stepping away from her dresser to make room for Violet. "When do you think I'll get my figure back?" She patted the barely perceptible bulge of her belly.

Violet shot a look over her shoulder as she emptied the drawers. "I could use some help here."

"I'm afraid people will notice." Lily clenched her stomach muscles and straightened her back.

"Don't forget your hat." Violet glanced at the red box. The thought of Stanley entered her head, and she shook it away. *I can't think about that now.* "It's under your bed." As she turned back to the suitcases, something in the top drawer caught her eye. "What's that?"

Lily reached in and pulled out one of Muriel's movie magazines. Clara Bow smiled up from the front cover. Tears sprang to Lily's eyes, but she quickly wiped them away while Violet's back was to her. "It's an old one," she said, tossing the magazine back inside and shutting the drawer.

"You'll be sorely missed," the Reverend Mother said as she embraced Violet. "The children have certainly taken to you." As if on cue, the DeLeo baby, born two days earlier, cooed from across the nursery. Violet started to cry, and Mother Mary Joseph held her at arm's length. "What is it, child?"

"I've grown so attached to all of them. To all of you."

"You'll always be welcome here." The nun gave her one last hug. "But it's time for you to go and be with your family. They need you now."

"May I?" Violet glanced toward her niece.

"Of course." The Reverend Mother walked with Violet to the infant's crib.

Violet took the baby into her arms, nuzzled her neck, and whispered, "I love you, Daisy."

"I'll find her a good Christian home," the nun said, taking the child. "You have my word."

"And I'm sorry about your mother," Violet murmured to the baby. "I'm sure she loves you in her own way."

Violet picked up the suitcases in the corner of the room. The weight of them seemed enormous somehow. How had she carried both of them from the train station to the Good

Shepherd? She turned and looked at the Reverend Mother who was still holding Daisy. "Take good care of her." A wave of emotion—love, or regret—welled up inside her. Violet dropped the suitcases, went back to the baby, and kissed her one last time. "Be a good girl." Then she picked up the suitcases and walked out the door.

Lily sat at the kitchen table, drumming her fingers impatiently. "The train leaves the station in two hours," she said.

Violet took one long look around the kitchen, picked up the suitcases, and led her sister to the back door. Just as the pair was about to leave, a new girl, considerably further along than Lily had been when she arrived, pushed the door open. The Morgan sisters stepped around her, and Lily called back, "The latch slips shut. Wouldn't want to lock all your gentlemen callers out." She followed Violet down the sidewalk and onto the road, laughing lightly, though her heart wasn't in it.

Twenty minutes later, the sisters arrived at the train station and found an empty bench. Violet glanced at a large clock built into the marble wall. "One hour," she said. "We arrived in plenty of time." She started searching through her bag for their tickets.

"I'm hungry," Lily said. "What are we going to do about eating?"

Violet reached into her pocket, handed Lily an apple, and continued rummaging through her bag.

Lily took a bite and stared straight on at her reflection in the glass. "I look positively frightful," she said, tugging at her hair. "What will people think when they see me?"

"That you've been on a train from Buffalo for eight hours." Violet found the tickets and pulled them out. "And you best remember that or all our efforts will have been in vain."

"Who's coming to meet us?"

"No one knows we're coming home today." Violet exhaled loudly. "I didn't want anyone to see us getting off a train from Philadelphia."

Lily continued to adjust her curls. "Where's that hat you bought me for my birthday?" She wound her long hair as if to secure it in a bun, but let the locks drop loosely. "The one with the flowers," she said, twisting her hair again.

Violet's head sank into her hands. "It's the only thing I asked you to remember."

"So what do we do now?"

"We?" Violet shot up from her seat. "*We?*" She closed her eyes and inhaled hard. "Stay here," she finally said, and headed back to the infant asylum.

# C HAPTER FIFTEEN

ON THE WAY BACK TO THE GOOD SHEPHERD, Violet seethed over Lily's thoughtlessness. *I'm going to keep the hat myself,* she thought. *Spoiled brat. What do we do now? We!* "I'll tell you what *we* do," she said aloud, and the elderly couple with whom she'd been sharing a sidewalk crossed the street. She put her hand to her mouth and cleared her throat, as if to suggest the comment had been a bit of phlegm, but anger quickly usurped her embarrassment. "We're going to make some changes," she called across the street. And then more quietly, "Starting today." The woman steered her husband toward a set of steps and pulled him up into a shop. The sign out front read, *Widenor's Hats,* in gold letters. Violet's legs almost buckled at the memory, and she dropped onto the bench facing the store. She'd given up her valedictorian medal, and for what? *A thankless child,* if she remembered her Shakespeare. But what of a thankless sister? What would he say about that? Violet closed her eyes and saw the streetcar in her mind, Stanley standing next to the window, gripping the leather handhold. And the split second when he faced her. What had he seen?

The one o'clock whistle blew, and Violet jumped up with a start. Their train was pulling out at two o'clock sharp, and they'd need to board early if Lily was to get an aisle seat. Lily liked knowing she could get up and move about the car freely, though she rarely did. *Maybe* I'll *take the aisle seat,* Violet decided, and quickened her pace.

As Violet approached the infant asylum, she noticed Jack Barrett's maroon Model T sitting empty in the driveway. Apparently Mamie Barrett had tired of being carted along on days when benefactors met. Maybe she'd finally set her husband straight. Maybe she'd told him these visits to the Good Shepherd were too painful. If so, it would have been her first sane act since the death of her baby girl.

Sister Immaculata stood alone on the porch, shading her eyes to see who was approaching. Violet waved to the woman and started climbing the stairs, but before she reached the top, the nun disappeared inside.

Violet pulled the front door open and nearly slammed into the Reverend Mother, who stood on the other side of the threshold with the red hatbox in her hand. "Something told me you'd be back."

"I have half a mind to keep it for myself." Violet took the box and threaded her fingers through the taut string. "It would serve her right."

"God be with you," Mother Mary Joseph said evenly, and she turned toward the hallway.

"Thank you," Violet called out, wondering at the nun's curt manner. When Mother Mary Joseph disappeared into the parlor, something anchored Violet to the porch, though she knew she must leave soon. She peered past the foyer into the now-empty hallway. She couldn't help herself and slipped inside. As Violet neared the parlor, she heard voices and stopped to listen. Jack Barrett was saying, "How good this will be for Mamie. Something to clear her mind."

Violet peeked in to see the Reverend Mother sitting across from him, nodding sympathetically. "It may just be the answer," she said. "Of course, you'll have to give her time to get used to the idea."

"Yes, of course," he replied, "but she'll come around. I once put a litter of setters on the teats of a hound when their own mother died birthing them. Hand a baby to a woman and she'll start mothering."

"Shall we go see how they're doing?" The nun rose from her chair.

Mr. Barrett fingered a chain that dangled from his vest pocket and pulled out a watch. "Let's give them a few more minutes," he said. "About how old did you say she was?"

"Three weeks tomorrow," Mother Mary Joseph answered, taking her seat again.

A wave of nausea choked Violet as she tiptoed past the parlor door and headed toward the nursery. *She? Almost three weeks old?* Mother Mary Joseph would never hand Daisy over to a woman so crazed with grief. Violet must have misunderstood, or at the very least, it must be someone else's child being adopted out.

Violet rested her hand on the doorknob for a second before stepping inside. On the far side of the room, Mamie Barrett sat in a rocker, her eyes unfocused, a dark-haired baby lay crying in her arms. Mrs. Barrett remained unfazed. Smiling tightly, Violet set down the hatbox, walked over to the pair, and lifted the infant. "Time to sleep," Violet said quietly, and carried Daisy to an empty crib. Mrs. Barrett continued to rock, her face expressionless. With no time to waste, Violet picked up the hatbox, tugged off the string, and shoved a few clean diapers and a half-empty bottle under the brim of the hat. She quickly replaced the string, then searched the room for pen and paper and wrote: *It is always better to be raised by your own. You taught me that,* and then she added, *God help me,* before dropping the note on the changing table. Violet scooped Daisy up with one hand and grabbed the hatbox with the other. The pair passed through the kitchen, out the door, and into the street.

* * *

She half-ran back to the station, though carrying Daisy and the hatbox slowed her down considerably.

"All aboard!" the conductor shouted from the front of a nearby platform.

"What on earth?" Lily gasped. "What do you think you're doing?"

"Grab those suitcases," Violet said shortly, hurrying toward the train, sweat moistening the back of her neck and underarms.

Lily stood firm. "Return that baby at once!" she cried, and several heads turned toward them.

"I'll do no such thing," Violet said and stepped up into the train.

A moment later, Lily caught up with her, a suitcase dangling from each hand. "I don't understand," she said. A porter passed by and she handed him the suitcases. He slung them on a rack overhead and tipped his hat, but Lily ignored the gesture. "I don't want to be a mother."

"But I do," Violet said, surprised by the truth of her words. "*I* do." She took a step back so Lily could slide across to the window seat.

"You're ruining my life! I'll never forgive you for this," Lily said as she stormed off to the next car.

Violet's feet twitched as if to follow, but the urge subsided, and she settled peacefully into her seat on the aisle. She swayed back and forth, feeling the weight of the baby in her arms. "Let's get you home," she said to Daisy, "where we both belong."

"Next stop, Scranton," the conductor announced as he passed through the car. Lily trailed behind him and settled in the empty seat across from Violet and the baby. "If you're trying to humiliate me," Lily said, "you're doing a fine job."

Violet handed her sister the empty bottle and a cup of milk she'd gotten from the porter. "Make yourself useful," she said. "We'll be getting off in about ten minutes."

"What are people going to say?" Lily angrily poured the milk into the bottle and snapped the nipple over its mouth.

"They're going to say . . ." Violet paused. What *would* they say exactly? "They're going to say, *Did you hear the Morgan girl got herself in trouble?*" Before going to the Good Shepherd, a revelation like that would have severely shaken Violet. Instead, she simply accepted the truth of it.

"They'll say more than that," Lily snapped. Blood rushed to her cheeks, then drained away just as quickly. "Which Morgan girl?"

"Let's get something straight," Violet said. "If you are ever going to lay claim to Daisy, do it now."

"You've named her?"

"Otherwise," Violet considered her words, "I'm raising her as my own. No one will ever know your part in it."

"And I'm just supposed to sit by and watch? She's mine, not yours!" Lily scanned the car to see if anyone could hear her. Most of the passengers within earshot were either sleeping or lost in their own conversations.

"Not from where I'm sitting," Violet said. The train's wheels screeched to a stop. "So what's it going to be?"

"You're being impossible. I'll not stand for this."

"Which is it going to be?"

The porter hurried up the aisle and pulled down their suitcases.

"I'll never forgive you for this," Lily said. "I'll always be known as the girl with a floozy for a sister."

Startled, the porter dropped one of their suitcases in the aisle. "So sorry," he said, tipping his hat without looking at the pair.

Violet reached into her purse and brought out a few

coins, which she settled in the porter's hand. She glanced at the hatbox on the floor, gathered up the baby, and started for the exit. Lily grabbed their luggage and followed at a distance.

*I might be making the biggest mistake of my life*, Violet thought as she balanced the baby on one arm and took hold of the handrail with the other, *but if I don't do this, I will die*. She kept her eyes lowered as she navigated the three steps down from the train. As soon as both feet landed on the platform, she looked up and saw Stanley staring right at her.

# PART II

## ADVICE TO THE MARRIED
## AND THOSE ABOUT TO BE

*. . . Whether you are newly married or have been married a quarter of a century, be sure that your underwear is the very best that your means will allow you, and that it is always sweet, fresh, and dainty. It will help you to retain the affection of your husband.*

—*Woman: Her Sex and Love Life,*
William J. Robinson, MD, 1929

Never thought we'd see the day. Protestants, Catholics, Jews, even the Episcopalians (just a fancier way of saying Catholic if you ask us) working together to feed and clothe those hit hardest by what the papers are calling "The Great Depression." Last month alone we distributed 1,729 quarts of soup and 513 pairs of children's shoes to Scranton's neediest. We say *neediest*, but truth is, we're all hurting these days. Some worse than others, is all. The Archbald Mine's only been worked eight weeks in the last year. That kind of hand-to-mouth living steals a man's dignity.

With so much misery in the world, it's a wonder more people aren't coming out to church on Sundays. If hard times don't fill pews, what will? Reverend Sheets is determined to add to his flock. Says new blood will do us some good. He might be right. Then again, nothing ruins a congregation faster than an overeager preacher.

Take Violet Morgan. She certainly deserves a second

chance, and we're all happy to give it to her if she's truly repentant. She'll be a married woman soon, and if that's reason enough for the elders to reinstate her, so be it. But does that mean we have to allow her to exchange wedding vows at Providence Christian? Reverend Sheets seems to think so, especially since she's promised to raise that little girl of hers in the church. The preacher's heart is pure, and yes, there's the child to consider, but in order to be a beacon of light in these dark days, it seems to us we should be cleaving to our morals, not abandoning them.

Of course, the die is cast. Reverend Sheets made his decision, so no sense chewing over it again. Time to focus on other matters—the coal drive, for example, set up at St. Stanislaus's. The Polish church on Oak Street. Nice enough people if you like that kind. Poverty sure makes strange bedfellows, but we don't mind. Tending to other people's troubles helps us to forget our own.

# CHAPTER SIXTEEN

"It's wedding day!" Five-year-old Daisy ran into the bedroom, waving a calendar over her head like a kite. She pointed to the date, *Saturday, October 12*, circled in red, and climbed up next to her mother on the bench seat at the dressing table.

"There's my doll baby." Violet pulled the child into the curve of her hip and kissed the tip of her nose.

"And Indian summertime day." Daisy put down the calendar and pointed out the window to an autumn morning already wrapped in sun. "Look at me!" She made a long O sound in the back of her throat while vigorously patting her mouth. "I'm a summertime Indian."

Violet didn't have to ask where her daughter had learned such common behavior. The Wilson twins next door were holy terrors. Only six years old and those boys had already gotten into trouble more times than Violet could count. That mother of theirs never seemed to notice. Violet caught them trying to shoot Mrs. Harris's chickens with a bow and arrow set they'd found down by the creek. Violet made them hand it over.

"Nice little girls don't play *Indians*," she said sharply to Daisy.

One last low-pitched O leaked through Daisy's flattened fingers.

"Do you want Grandma and Grandpa to see you acting that way?" Violet wagged her finger and glanced at the open bedroom door.

Shrugging, Daisy dropped her hand in her lap.

Violet immediately regretted her impatience. "I'm sorry," she said. "My nerves are getting the best of me today."

Daisy loosened a hairpin from a tangle of them on the dresser and yanked both ends apart. "But it's a happy day."

"A very happy day." Violet looked in the vanity's oval mirror and practiced her smile. Thirty years old. At this age, she thought, she should be embracing spinsterhood, not marriage. "Just nerves," she said again.

"Make me pretty." Daisy held up the hairpin, now bent out of shape like wire legs from a pigeon-toed insect.

"You're already the prettiest girl in town," Violet said, taking a brush to Daisy's long curls. "You have your mother's . . ." She set the brush in her lap and cupped Daisy's plump cheeks in her hands. "You have Morgan features. Morgan eyes." Violet turned and faced the mirror. Same dark hair, same nose, same smile. They looked enough alike to keep gossip to a minimum.

"Blue, like Aunt Lily's." Daisy tossed the hairpin back into the pile and stared at her own reflection. "Grandma says so."

"Yes, doll baby." Violet pressed her lips into thin lines and gripped the handle of the brush. "And like your Aunt Daisy before her. Does Grandma tell you that?"

"God rest her soul," the child said, reminding her mother of the words that were always recited at the mention of Aunt Daisy's name.

"God rest her soul," Violet repeated, her lips loosening into a smile. "You're Mama's good girl."

Daisy scooted off the bench, stretched out her arms, and spun around the room in her bare feet. The hem of her nightgown caught the air, opening like a bell.

"Be careful," Violet said as she watched the reflection of her daughter's dance. Daisy whirled past the open closet door where a mauve A-line dress hung from a bar. Violet had originally intended to borrow Lily's white crepe silk, the very dress she'd worn that past November to marry George Sherman Jr., but Violet's mother had thought mauve would be a better choice, "given the circumstances."

Violet hated that saying. Circumstances had a way of entering a room before her. *Unwed mother. No husband. A disgrace to her family.* People shunned her because of her circumstances.

"I'll never forgive you," Stanley had said the afternoon she'd stepped off the train with a baby in her arms. She'd wanted to tell him the truth. Maybe she would have if he had stopped yelling long enough to give her the chance. And maybe not.

Of course, some folks treated her with kindness, but Violet suspected her "circumstances" prompted what they thought of as good Christian behavior. Tommy Davies seemed to be the only friend she could depend on besides the widow Lankowski.

Dizzy and winded, Daisy staggered to the bench and draped her upper body over the tapestry-covered seat next to her mother. "It's wedding day!"

"And when Reverend Sheets says, *I now pronounce you man and wife*," Violet prodded, hoping Daisy would remember what they'd practiced, "what do you say?"

Daisy peeled herself off the seat and stood for a moment in thought. Finally, she blurted, "I love you, Daddy Tommy!" and threw her arms straight up in the air.

"Just *Daddy*," Violet corrected as she pulled the little girl in for a hug.

"I love you *Just Daddy*," Daisy said solemnly.

* * *

Covered in coal dust, Tommy Davies headed up Spring Street toward the only home he'd ever lived in. Like all the other company houses in the Providence neighborhood of Scranton, it had originally belonged to George Sherman Sr., owner of the Sherman Mine. Seven years earlier, Sherman had started selling off his properties, a trend among fellow coal barons. While Tommy had a mother to support, he'd been single longer than most, and without a wife and children to feed, he'd been able to scrimp, even on a miner's wage. His family home had gone up for sale a year before the crash. The banks were still in the business of lending, and he'd been able to put enough money down to get a mortgage. He wished Violet's father could have done the same when, a few years later, Sherman put the Morgans' house up for sale, but banks weren't making loans by then. No one was buying either, thank goodness, so Sherman allowed the Morgans to stay on as renters, even after miner's asthma forced Owen to give up his job inside the mine. "Once a man, twice a boy," Owen used to say, along with all the men before him who'd been sent back to work in the breaker, where they'd started out as small boys, sorting coal from slate by hand. Sherman uncharacteristically continued to give Owen a miner's salary because George Jr. had insisted they help his father-in-law. When he married Lily, he told her Owen would get his full pay whether he put in his time or not. That had been a godsend, especially in the last few months when her father couldn't work at all. Owen had strong opinions about charity, so the idea never set well with him, but what choice did he have? As hard as things were six years after the crash, the man was lucky to be collecting a paycheck.

In the past few months, twenty men had been laid off at the Taylor Mine, and sixty workers from the Von Storch had been fired outright, though it could be said that they'd brought it on themselves. Earlier that year they'd joined the United Anthracite Miners, a group of hotheads who'd broken away from the United Mine Workers of America after accusing them of siding with the owners on wages, hours, and safety issues one too many times. In September the insurgent union had staged a spate of strikes throughout the region. Picketers and miners exchanged their fair share of punches before state troopers stepped in to restore the peace with billy clubs.

And now there was talk of a UAM strike at the Sherman Mine first thing Monday morning. Stirring up that kind of trouble made no sense to Tommy. While Sherman Sr. was no saint, he always paid a fair wage for an honest day's work. The same could not be said for many of the mine owners up the line.

Since only a handful of the men in Providence had been fool enough to join up with the UAM, Tommy felt no obligation to picket. The Sherman Mine still had enough work for a full crew, and in such dire economic times, fighting for better working conditions seemed indulgent. A family man needed to have a dependable income, and by day's end, Tommy would have a wife and daughter to support.

Tommy smiled at his good fortune, setting flecks of loosened coal dust adrift in the warm breeze. He'd provide for Violet and her daughter. His daughter, soon. And if he could just keep working, in another eight years he'd own his house outright, giving them a permanent place to call their own.

He walked up his front steps, crossed the porch, and ran his palm up and down the seat of his porch swing. The varnish still shone like a new penny. *A good effort*, he thought. He'd started building that swing the same morning he'd decided to try his hand at courting Violet. Being inexpert on both fronts, he soon discovered the virtue of forbearance.

Five weeks to build a swing, five years to win the heart of the girl next door.

Glancing up, Tommy hoped to catch sight of his bride-to-be. All the shades were drawn against him. She knew he'd be looking and wouldn't want him to see her before the wedding.

*Two more hours*, Tommy thought, checking his pocket watch. He'd been glad to only work half a shift, unusual for a Saturday, but lucky for him. He'd have plenty of time to clean up before heading to the church. Violet had wanted to get married at Providence Christian. She held no malice toward the congregation in spite of the fact they'd excommunicated her when she'd returned to Scranton with Daisy. "They did what they saw fit," she'd said. Tommy had not been as forgiving, but he knew enough to keep quiet, especially since the elders had recently voted to bring Violet back into the fold "for the sake of the child." *And for the sake of the collection plate*, Tommy thought. Lily had convinced George Jr. to use his financial influence to get his sister-in-law reinstated on the rolls. Lily and Violet didn't seem to agree on much most days, but they were both desperate to have Daisy raised in the church.

He'd even held his tongue when nosey Mrs. Evans, whose backyard butted up against the Morgans', remarked to Violet about Tommy making an honest woman of her. Such talk infuriated him, and had she spoken to him that way, he would have told her so. Violet was the most honest woman he'd ever known. And who was Myrtle Evans to sit in judgment? If he could forgive Violet's indiscretion, why couldn't Myrtle? Why couldn't the whole town, for that matter? Wasn't that the Lord's way? Frankly, it was Stanley's behavior that infuriated him. How could he not do right by Violet? It was obvious to Tommy that Stanley had seduced her with promises of marriage and financial security, and then discarded her as damaged goods. This was Stanley's fault, and why the people in the Providence area couldn't see that was beyond him. It did take some getting used to—no question—when Violet came home with Daisy, but he'd grown to love the child, and the woman who so bravely shouldered the town's scorn. Violet was a good woman who sacrificed her needs for those of others. Especially when it came to her daughter. This made her virtuous in his book. Violet once told Tommy that Stanley refused to hear her out when she first returned to town. Well, Tommy didn't need to hear her out. He knew her true nature. She was sorry for her sins. Christians were supposed to forgive. Hypocrites, the whole lot of them.

Tommy took one last peek at Violet's house, knowing that a glimpse of her would soothe him. Just as he was about to go inside, the curtains on the parlor's side window split open, and Daisy stood at the glass, blowing a kiss. He touched his hand to his heart before returning her kiss again and again.

Violet arrived at the church on foot, with her mother and daughter in tow. Unable to catch a decent breath, her father had stayed home in his chair in the parlor. Lily, who after her own wedding had gone to live with her moneyed in-laws in the Green Ridge neighborhood, drove up to the church in an automobile. "Of all the silliness," Grace said of her youngest daughter. "A woman at the wheel."

Louise Davies, Tommy's mother, was the only other guest. Violet had invited the widow, but in the end she'd decided not to come. "You know I couldn't love you more if you were my own," she'd said when she'd stopped over that morning to give Violet a handmade lace tablecloth. "But Stanley needs me today." She stared down at her gnarled fingers and rubbed the swollen joints. "No question, this is all his doing. Still, he's tore up inside, and . . ." Her words trailed off. Relief swiftly displaced Violet's disappointment. Even though Tommy had never said a word on the matter, the widow was the closest thing Stanley had to a mother, and there was no question that her presence at Violet's wedding would have discomfited him.

After the "I dos," Grace invited everyone back to the house so Owen could be part of the festivities. Her pot roast was just starting to catch on one side when they walked through the door. "Something wrong with your nose?" she yelled to Owen as she passed into the kitchen. Water hissed while she poured it into the cast-iron pot.

Owen flared his nostrils as if taking in a lungful of air. "Smells fine to me," he said and stretched out his arms for Daisy to climb into his lap. "Just the way I like it."

"*Just the way I like it*," Daisy mimicked from her perch.

Violet bent down and kissed the top of her father's balding head. With Daisy settled on his lap, Owen took Violet's hand and kissed it. "Where's that son of mine?" Tommy stepped forward. Owen took Tommy's hand, placed it on top of Violet's, and laid his own hands on theirs. "A Welsh blessing," he said. "Wishing you a house full of sunshine, hearts full of cheer, and love that grows deeper each day of the year." He kissed their hands. "Love," he glanced into the kitchen at Grace, "so much love."

Lily stood in the archway between the parlor and the hallway to the bedrooms, taking in the scene.

Grace worked in the kitchen, grumbling about the pot roast out of habit, not anger, while Louise helped her with last-minute preparations. In the parlor, Tommy set up a table they'd borrowed from the church. The words *Providence Christian* were scrawled on its underside. Violet spread a cloth on top, opened the nearby folding chairs, and set seven places. She added a couple of Montgomery Ward catalogs on the seat next to hers, so Daisy would be able to reach her plate.

"Get to the table!" Louise yelled, placing a butter-topped bowl of mashed potatoes next to a steamy dish of rutabaga. Even with Violet's assistance, Owen moved slowly across the room, giving the others enough time to stand and admire the meal before them.

"You outdid yourself, Mrs. Morgan," Tommy said, pulling out her chair.

"Mother," Grace said. "You're family now."

Lily cleared her throat at this and took her seat.

Tommy blushed. "Thank you, Mother Morgan." He swung Daisy up and set her on her chair. "Best food in Providence."

Louise glanced sidelong at her son, snapped her linen napkin open, and draped it over her lap. "Had I known you felt that way, I would have sent you over here for supper all these years." She turned to Grace. "Looks lovely."

"Almost as grand as my wedding supper." Lily pinched her lips into a smile. She reached over and laid Daisy's napkin on her lap. "I still can't believe how generous George's people were."

Violet took Daisy's napkin and tucked it into the neckline of her dress.

Since no one seemed to be listening, Lily turned to Daisy, as if the conversation had been intended for her all along. "The Mayfair Hotel, of all places." She pushed Daisy's long hair behind her ears. "The most special day of my life."

In the eleven months since her wedding, Lily had shown no signs of expecting—a surprise to everyone—and, to Violet's great concern, she was suddenly giving a lot of attention to little Daisy.

"The Mayfair Hotel," Daisy repeated.

"I know," Lily said, patting the child's hand. "I'll take you there for lunch one day."

"Don't put ideas into her head," Violet said.

"You'll come with us, of course," Lily replied, reaching for the platter of meat.

"We haven't said the blessing." As hoarse as Owen's voice had become, it retained its head-of-the-household authority. Lily pulled her arm back and folded her hands on her lap.

"And where is that husband of yours?" Owen asked.

"Your *other* son-in-law?" Lily said. "He's helping his daddy. A mine doesn't run itself. You of all people know that."

"Don't tell me what I know." Owen's sharp tone set off a coughing spell.

Grace hopped up from the table and rubbed his back while he spit into his napkin. "I'm right here," she said. Everyone waited for the moment to pass, inhaling carefully and deeply as if trying to breathe for him.

"Stop your fussing," he finally said when his breath came back to him. "Son," he turned to Tommy, "will you ask the blessing?"

Lily left as soon as the meal was over. "Don't want my husband thinking I got lost." She laughed a little and hugged her sister lightly. "I'm happy for you." Her words sounded like those verses of scripture they'd been forced to recite as children. They came out in the right order, but lacked conviction.

An hour or so later, with a little nudging from Louise, Daisy asked to see her new bedroom. Tommy offered to take her next door and his mother followed, anxious to show off the brightly patterned quilt she'd made for the child. Violet remained behind to help her mother with the dishes and ended up staying long enough to get her father settled for the night.

"It's your turn now," Owen said from the edge of his bed where he sat to catch his breath.

"My turn for what?" Violet fluffed three pillows and stacked them against the headboard.

Owen swung one leg up and then the other and angled the pillows so his head would remain upright, allowing him to breathe easier through the night. "I love Lily. I love both my daughters." He ran his thumb across Violet's brow. "But Lily's not as strong as you are. She could never do what you did."

"What I did?"

"I may not be book smart, but I'm not a stupid man." He glanced at a framed picture of Daisy on the night table. "She's your daughter now. And it's for the better."

"You knew?" Tears filled Violet's eyes.

He nodded.

"Why didn't you say anything?"

"No reason to. And mark my words, I'll not speak of it again. But I want you to know something." He took Violet's hand. "You can be good in this world *and* you can be happy. You don't have to choose. Now . . . go and be happy."

Violet kissed her father and wiped the tears from both their faces before returning to the kitchen.

"I have a little something for you," Grace said when Violet approached her at the sink.

"I'm worried about him." Violet cast a look toward her parents' bedroom.

"He'll be fine." Grace dried her hands on a dish towel, then handed Violet a present wrapped in blue tissue paper. "In fact," she said, coating her words in a lighter tone, "I think his color was better today. Now take a quick peek," she nodded toward the gift, "and then get yourself home to that husband of yours. We've kept him waiting long enough." She let out a light laugh.

Violet peeled back the paper. Inside was a lace-trimmed dressing gown the color of pearls. "It's beautiful," she said, too modest to examine the garment fully in front of her mother.

"It's supposed to look like this princess slip." Grace handed her a page torn from a catalog. "Yours is ivory, not white," she said, "but still, a good likeness, I think."

"A perfect likeness." Violet sat for a long minute, running her fingers across the silky fabric. Finally she said, "I'm scared."

"Every woman is. But Tommy is a good man. A kind man. He'll take the lead and nature will do the rest."

Nodding, Violet stood and folded the paper back over the gown. "Thank you, it's beautiful."

Grace hesitated. "Wait." She went to the sink and came back with an unopened bar of Fels-Naptha soap and tucked it inside the tissue paper. "It's good for stains. After he's asleep," she said, "wash out the blood in cold water before it sets. He'll never know."

Violet hugged her mother, harder than she remembered ever hugging her, picked up her gifts, and headed next door.

# CHAPTER SEVENTEEN

"SHE WENT DOWN WITHOUT A FIGHT," Tommy said of Daisy. "I think all the wedding excitement tired her out."

Violet looked around the parlor—the Davies's parlor—her parlor now too. She spied the two cowhide suitcases Tommy had carried over the night before last, when she had finished packing her belongings. They'd now seen her through two journeys—to Philadelphia and to the house next door. Violet would unpack them in the morning and put the suitcases away for Daisy to use someday.

Tommy patted the spot next to him on the couch. "Although I did have to promise you'd wake her to say good night." His mouth lifted into a half-smile. "Ma's asleep as well."

"I'm sorry," Violet said, setting the package from her mother on a sideboard and glancing around the room again. "It took some time to get Father settled."

Everything around her was at once familiar and strange. Since her mother and Louise Davies were best friends, Violet had spent a good portion of her childhood in this house. She knew it well: The gray, almost lavender wallpaper. The dresser-sized Heatrola in the corner. The scars on the wood floor from the casket stand where Tommy's father Graham had been laid out. Violet had been only four, but it was the first time she'd seen a dead body, so she still remembered.

The day after the funeral, eight-year-old Tommy donned his father's denim trousers, cut down and cinched with a rope belt, and went to work in the breaker. That's how it was. When a man died in the mine, his eldest son took his father's place or the family lost their house. Tommy hadn't had a choice in the matter, but all these years later, Violet had never once heard him complain about his lot. *That's a good man*, she reminded herself, and sat down beside him. "I should have been here sooner," she said, nervously tugging on the scalloped edge of an afghan draped over the back of the couch.

"My mother's handiwork." Tommy traced a length of the blanket's zigzag pattern before moving his hand to Violet's cheek. He turned her face to him. His fingers traveled along the curve of her chin, the length of her neck, before finding refuge in the soft flesh of her throat. "You're here now. That's all that matters." He allowed his hand to journey back up, toward her lips, so soft, so tempting. Violet shivered. Without a word, he outlined each feature—her lips, nose, each eye, the worry spot between her brows—memorizing her face, its contours. And in that moment, looking at such beauty, he wished his cracked and calloused hands were those of an artist instead of a miner, if just for one hour, so he could sculpt this vision for all to admire.

Violet closed her eyes and lifted her chin, allowing her lips to part. Tommy leaned in and felt the heat of her breath on his face. He shut his eyes, inhaling the scent of lilac on her skin and rose water in her hair.

The kiss landed softly, his lips brushing up against hers like feathers. He pulled back and saw that her eyes were still closed. "I promised Daisy you'd be in to say good night."

Violet opened her eyes slowly. "Daisy," she whispered but remained seated.

Tommy stood up, took Violet's trembling hands in his,

and lifted her to her feet. "I'll be waiting." Feeling a little embarrassed, he simply nodded toward the bedroom before disappearing down the hall.

"Sweet dreams, doll baby." Violet kissed Daisy's forehead, and the little girl looked up at her with blue eyes so reminiscent of the first Daisy's that Violet had to hold in a moan.

"Is Daddy Tommy my real daddy?" the little girl asked. "He's your real daddy now and that's all that matters in the world. Remember that, my doll baby."

"I will . . ." Daisy's lids closed as she drifted off to sleep.

Violet kissed the child's forehead again and tiptoed toward the bathroom. Tommy and a buddy of his who worked for Sears Roebuck had put indoor plumbing in after Tommy's first year of failed attempts to court Violet. Tommy later told Violet that if he ever married, his mother would insist the couple make the family home their own. A fair deal, since it was Tommy's pay that had kept a roof over their heads all these years. And it was Tommy's sweat that had allowed his younger brothers to stay in school. Now, two out of three Davies boys had high school diplomas, families, and homes of their own. Not the perfect record his mother had hoped for, but a respectable one for a family from Spring Street.

Violet hid the Fels-Naptha underneath the skirted sink, unfolded the negligee, and shook it out. *A true work of art*, she thought to herself. She undressed, then slipped it over her head and looked at her reflection in the mirror. She pinched a little color into her cheeks.

"He's a good man," she murmured to herself, before crossing the hallway to the bedroom.

Tommy sat on top of the yellow chenille bedspread in the flicker of a single candle. After serious deliberation, he'd removed his suit coat, tie, suspenders, and shoes, but remained dressed in his shirt and trousers, out of respect for his bride. This would not be his first time, of course. At thirty-four, Tommy had drunk his share of whiskey, tried his hand at cards, and indulged in carnal delights when urged on by alcohol, his friends, and the "ladies" they met in "the Alleys" downtown. Those encounters had thrilled him in the moment, but they always disgusted him in the morning, so he'd given all that up before his thirtieth birthday.

Violet stepped into the room, and for a moment Tommy couldn't breathe. She stood in the doorway, unable or unwilling to move. Tommy knew he should get up, take her by the hand, and lead her to their marriage bed, but he sat a moment longer, taking in her beauty. The dressing gown dipped just below the neckline, revealing the tops of her breasts. It flowed down the length of her body, slowing at each bend like a country stream.

She waited another moment, then took one tentative step, and another, until she stood at the edge of the bed. Rather clumsily, Tommy tugged the spread and sheet out from under him and draped them over his lap to hide his excitement. He slid across the mattress, making room for Violet, and lifted the bedding, inviting her to sit next to him. She slipped in, immediately covering herself with the bedspread, and stared straight ahead.

That close, Tommy shut his eyes and breathed her in again, inhaled her delicious fragrance.

"Thank you," she whispered, "for loving me. For loving Daisy."

He opened his eyes and looked into hers. "I'll always love you," he whispered back, and kissed her gently. After Violet returned the kiss, he fumbled under the covers, and soon his shirt, trousers, socks, and summer union suit tumbled to the floor. He sidled up next to her, their bare arms pressing together, his naked thigh against her silk-covered one. He reached for her hand and turned his face toward her cheek. "I love you."

Violet tilted her ear toward his voice, and he inhaled the perfume in her curls. She lifted her head and met his face with her shivering mouth. She kissed him hard this time, as if to still those lips. Emboldened, Tommy wrapped his arms around her and pulled her down on top of him, making sure to keep the covers over her. He ran his hands hungrily across her silky back, occasionally daring to cup the bounty of flesh at her bottom. Both shivering against each other, Tommy rolled over with Violet in his arms. That luscious hair fanned out behind her, redolent of rose water, wild and untamed. On top now, he needed to be a part of her, inside of her. He reached for the gown and yanked it up to her hips. He grabbed her hands and pushed against them as he tried to enter her. She continued to tremble, and her body resisted his efforts. "I love you," he whispered into her ear, and thrust again, this time more forcefully. With every muscle tensed, he squeezed inside of her just in time to explode, then collapsed on top of her, rolled onto his back, and shut his eyes. "You've made me a happy man, Violet Davies. A very happy man."

In order to keep Tommy from discovering her secret, Violet knew she had to tend to her stained gown, but she couldn't slip out until she was sure he'd fallen asleep. There she lay in what was now and would forever be their marriage bed, making no movement, trying to quiet her breathing. She hardly knew what to make of what had just happened. She was no fool. At thirty, she had some sense of what should be expected on the wedding night, the mechanics of things, at least. Given that Lily had been married for the better part of a year, she'd proved helpful with information. But somehow Violet felt let down. When she'd overheard some of the women at the Good Shepherd talking about "the deed," they'd spoken of it as a pleasure. Violet had no way of knowing if she'd take delight in such amorous pursuits, but she had hoped intimacy would spark the kind of love she'd only ever felt toward Stanley. That breathless, stirring, starry-eyed love.

What foolishness. One of the most decent men in the world lay next to her, and instead of being grateful, she was brooding. And thinking of another man. A man who'd shunned her. A man who had taken one look at her at the train station with a baby in her arms and without a moment's hesitation accused her of the most wicked behavior, and worse. Accused her of never loving him at all. Yes, she had lied to him, but for good reason. She had tried to speak her truth to Stanley, and for that split second he'd actually stopped yelling. There had been no time for hesitation, and she should have seized the moment to answer him. But what had she done with that briefest of windows? She'd looked over at Lily, dissolved in shame, tears streaming down her face. So lost, begging silently with those blue eyes. The baby's eyes. And Daisy's before her. And the moment passed. Stanley stormed off, but not before vowing to never speak to Violet again.

Next to her, a light wheezing sound worked its way into a full-blown snore. With Tommy finally asleep, Violet slipped out of bed and into the bathroom. She stood naked in front of the mirror, scrubbing at the stain with the bar of soap, soaking the gown in cold water, and scrubbing it again. Patience, she thought. That's all it would take. Wait awhile and the love will come. She hung the gown on the back of the door to dry and put on a cotton one she'd retrieved from her suitcase. If Tommy asked about the change of clothes in the morning, she'd tell him she'd wanted to sleep comfortably. *A lie begets a lie.* The last one, she thought. No more.

Violet tiptoed back down the hall, taking great pains not to wake Mother Davies or Daisy along the way. When she arrived at her door, she gingerly opened it and found Tommy sitting up in bed, holding the still-lit candle, staring at the bloodstained sheet.

# C HAPTER EIGHTEEN

THE WAXING MOON CURLED AGAINST THE SKY like a shaving of pinewood. For as much light as it threw, there may as well have been no moon at all, but it made no difference to Lily. Her eyes had adjusted to the dark night a minute or two after she'd gone out on the balcony. Violet's wedding that afternoon had been especially taxing, and the day unseasonably warm. Lily welcomed the bite in the evening air. This immediate discomfort demanded her attention, forcing all her cares to fall in line behind it. On the other side of the French doors, George's half of the turned-down bed remained empty.

*Concentrate on the cold.*

A beam of light pierced the night like a shot. Lily leaned over the railing to discover its source: the study. Mother Sherman always read by that lamp near the window. Poor woman, an insomniac. Lily assumed the lack of sleep had something to do with her mother-in-law's sour temperament. The woman lacked for nothing, living in this relatively large house with a husband, two sons still at home, and servants to tend to her every need.

As Lily straightened, she noticed how the lamplight bounced off the front fender of her LaSalle Coupe. A "split chrome fender" the sales specialist had called it, pointing out what separated the '34 from earlier models. He'd also mentioned the long, V'd radiator grill, the bullet-shaped headlights, and the torpedo hood ornament, as if Lily knew enough about automobiles to appreciate such improvements. Up until she and George met, Lily had spent very little time riding in cars, let alone driving, but according to her husband, she'd turned out to be a quick study, considering her gender. The LaSalle had been a wedding present from George. "Lily blue," he'd called the customized paint color, in reference to her eyes. She actually wanted the yellow convertible they'd seen in the motor company's showroom, but George didn't approve. He found yellow too showy for such hard economic times and advised her on the pitfalls of flaunting their wealth. Instead, he'd ordered the coupe in what she thought of as sapphire, and a nearly identical-looking sedan, save for the greater length and two extra doors, in that very same color. "We'll need the extra room," he'd said of the five-seater he'd bought for himself, "when the babies start coming."

Lily turned, stealing a glance inside at the stately bed with its hand-carved headboards, and was annoyed at her husband's absence. If he'd wanted her to give him children, he should be here.

*Concentrate.*

The cool breeze stung her eyes and chilled her forearms. Where did he go when he left the house, sometimes before they'd even had supper? Oh, she'd believed him at first, the stories about board meetings and Masonic business. At least in the initial months of their marriage, he'd always returned home by midnight, smothering her with kisses when she'd cry over being left alone. And in those early days, he'd always make it up to her with some little present, a bag of sweets from Cali's Confections; a pair of stockings from the Globe Store; and once, after a particularly unbridled episode of tears, a silver brooch from Levy's Jewelers.

To hear other people tell it, they should still be in the honeymoon stage after only eleven months, but George seemed to tire of Lily not long after their wedding, especially when she didn't immediately conceive. Ironic, of course, since she'd gotten pregnant the first time she'd ever had relations—with Frankie Colangelo, no less. What a scandal that would have been, if it hadn't all worked out. George would never have married her. As he had explained the night he proposed, he wanted to marry a virtuous woman. *The joke's on you, George.* She looked back at the empty bed. *And me.*

Now Violet was married to Tommy, a man who loved not only her, but her illegitimate daughter as well. How could someone as decent as Tommy love a woman with a past? Not that Lily wanted Tommy Davies or any man of his sort. Lily deserved better than a life of want and sacrifice. She'd seen her mother go off to church in the very same dress every Sunday morning for the better part of a year. A miner's wife would not be Lily's lot in life. Yet Tommy's devotion to Violet and Daisy rankled her. If anyone deserved to have the kind of man who loved her beyond reason, it was Lily.

A block away from home, George pulled up alongside a streetlamp and fished in his pocket for a few Sen-Sens, something to take care of the vodka on his breath. If only it were that easy to mask the smell of Janetta's cheap perfume. Perhaps he'd buy her a bottle of Shalimar so Lily would think it was her own scent clinging to his clothes. He unrolled his shirtsleeves, folded back the cuffs, and threaded a pair of cuff links through the openings. At each of his wrists, a fourteen-carat gold sea nymph reclined against a gilded wave. Lily hated them. George ran his thumb across a naked torso, remembering the day his father had taken him to the jeweler downtown.

"This is between us," his father had said with a wink. An awestruck George accepted the cuff links, sure that his thirteenth birthday would be the best one by far. His father had trusted him with a secret, and a bawdy one at that.

"He's all boy," the jeweler had said, watching as George gingerly touched the golden breasts.

"We're about to find out," his father had laughed, leading George Jr. out of the store and three blocks over to Lawrence's, one of the better whorehouses on Penn Avenue. His father sat in a velvet chair as George Jr. followed a woman in a burgundy silk robe up to the second floor. A woman to a thirteen-year-old, but when George thought about it now, she was probably only sixteen, eighteen at the most. As soon as they entered the room, she slipped off her robe and sat down on the edge of the bed. "Call me Baby." George had never seen a naked woman, and he stood in front of her, awed and terrified. "You look just like your daddy," Baby said sweetly, in an almost motherly tone. "Don't worry," she laughed, "this won't take no time at all."

Later, when it was George's turn to wait in the velvet chair, he heard Baby say, "A chip off the old block," as she led his father upstairs.

George popped another Sen-Sen in his mouth, put on his sport coat, and peeked around to see if anyone might be looking out at this late hour. He could appease Lily if he had to, but if his mother got wind of his antics, he'd never hear the end of it. Janetta had been hounding him again about getting a divorce, so he'd left her apartment before he'd finished dressing.

George started the engine and glanced at his watch. Twenty minutes after two. A little late, even for him, but hopefully everyone would be sound asleep. He loved Lily, but the last thing he needed tonight was another go around with her, especially after his fight with Janetta.

The blue coupe sat in the driveway just ahead of him, so George pulled up and parked next to it. Just before he cut the engine, he noticed how the headlights lit up the front of the house, illuminating Lily on the balcony.

Stanley pushed his glass toward the barkeep, who picked up the whiskey and poured. Hunold's Beer Garden had become Stanley's regular haunt when he'd moved into one of their upstairs rooms four years earlier. His accommodations lacked the warmth of the widow's house, but at least he didn't run the risk of seeing Violet every time he stepped out his front door. Downtown may have only been a few miles away from Providence, but people in Scranton stayed close to their own neighborhoods, a fact that gave Stanley a modicum of comfort, tonight of all nights. No chance of running into the just married Mrs. Davies.

Violet Davies.

That would take some getting used to.

"Another dead soldier," Stanley said, hearing the clank of an empty bottle as it landed in the garbage tin near the cash register. He gulped his drink and rapped his glass down on the bar. "Again."

The owner, a German fellow named Gus, eyed Stanley all around as if measuring him for a suit. "Are you certain, Mr. Adamski?"

"Never been more certain in my life."

Gus nodded as if he understood but hesitated a moment longer. "How's about a bowl of Mrs. Hunold's stew? Been cooking it all day."

Stanley nudged his glass a little ways down the bar. "Whiskey. Neat." He added that second word in case Gus got it into his head to start watering his drinks.

"And a beer." A lanky man in a three-piece glen plaid suit held out his hand. "Name's Woodberry," he said to

Stanley, his arm still extended. "Judson Woodberry. Judd to my friends." He waited a moment before running his unacknowledged hand through a few longs hairs on his mostly bald head. "Mind if I take a load off?"

"It's a free country," Stanley answered, watching Gus take a little longer than necessary to wipe up a spill behind the bar.

"I know it's been a tough day for you," Gus finally said, his tone sharp, "but don't nobody question how I serve my whiskey." He pulled a bottle out of a crate stamped *Jack Daniel's No. 7* and refilled Stanley's glass.

"Won't happen again," Stanley said, raising his right hand, staring straight ahead.

"Don't expect it will." The edges of Gus's words were sanded down some. He set the bottle on a shelf behind him before walking to the other end of the bar toward the tap.

"Broads are the worst," Judd said, as if participating in the give-and-take of an ongoing conversation.

Stanley cocked his head toward the stranger but didn't say a word. The man stretched his thin lips into a smile too big for his face.

Stanley turned back to his drink. At the other end of the bar, Gus used his index finger to slice the foam off the top of a beer and pushed it down the length of the wooden surface.

"Assuming that's what's troubling you tonight." Judd caught the glass, tipped it to his mouth, and took a timid sip. "More trouble than they're worth."

Gus made his way back to the two men and pointed a thumb at Stanley. "You're preaching to the choir."

"I knew it," Judd said. "Can always tell a man brought down by a woman. Looks as if he's had all the air sucked outta him."

Gus glanced at Stanley and nodded. "Ain't that the God honest truth."

"Must be a real looker considering his state." Judd

twisted his head back and forth between Gus and Stanley as if both men were engaged in the conversation.

Stanley swirled his whiskey and followed its path around the glass. The oaky aroma reassured him. Another drink or two, and he'd forget his troubles, if only for a few hours.

"Good looking?" Judd asked.

Gus cocked his head and shrugged. "I ain't never seen her myself, but when a woman's been around the block as many times as Violet Morgan . . ."

Stanley reached across the bar and grabbed Gus by the front of his shirt. "Say her name again," he pulled Gus closer, "and I'll kill you!"

Gus threw his arms into the air. "I didn't mean no harm," he said.

Stanley held his grip a moment before letting go and dropping down on his stool. "As long as we're clear."

Both men leaned back, taking in the silence. After about a minute, Judd finally said to Stanley, "I hear tell you're defending the miners from the Von Storch. About sixty workers fired in total."

"So that's it." Stanley turned and eyed the man for the first time. "Policeman or reporter?"

"I'm with the *Scranton Times*. Trying to put together a story on those firebrands from the UAM. So what's your strategy?"

Stanley stood up, dug in his pocket, and found three one-dollar bills. "Keep the change," he said to Gus. "You want a story? Come by the Sherman Mine the day after tomorrow. Men striking for a fair wage and decent working conditions. There's your story."

"I need a new story," Judd said, pulling out a notepad. "Something readers will care about."

"Make them care." Stanley drained his glass. "That's your job," he said, and he headed upstairs.

Stanley's room above Hunold's was larger than the one he'd rented in Philadelphia—four windows instead of two, and a small alcove for a table and chairs. He even had a closet where he kept the artificial hand so people wouldn't have to look at it if they came by. Not that he'd ever invited anyone up. In spite of its size, this room, like all the others he'd lived in, had the same feel. Rumpled. Cluttered. Detached. A few law books and a copy of John Reed's *Ten Days That Shook the World* lay scattered across his desk. A notebook peeked out from under the pile with the words *Von Storch Defense* scrawled across it. The miners had been arrested as much for striking as for joining the United Anthracite Miners, a rogue union, against the wishes of the United Mine Workers of America, a useful enough group in its day, but more and more they kowtowed to the pressures of politics. Thanks to a clause in the National Recovery Act giving miners the right "to organize and bargain collectively," Stanley felt sure he'd win the case, but not before the men lost a couple months of wages languishing in jail awaiting their trial. Which had been the point all along, of course. To threaten legal action in order to deliver a financial blow to the upstarts. Make sure the men paid a real price for joining the wrong union.

Stanley thought about the dangers of the coal industry. As a young boy, he'd worked bent over in the breaker, twelve hours a day, sorting coal from slate. A grueling job for anyone, but especially for a child. After a few punishing months, he thought he'd improved his lot when they'd brought him down into the mine as a nipper, where he had to open the shaft doors as mine cars came through, but he soon lost his hand—and almost his life—trying to stop an out-of-control car. Fortunately, the widow had nursed him back to health and taken him in, because the mine owners never bothered about their newly crippled workers. Unwilling to abide such callousness, Stanley vowed to fight for the rights of miners till his dying day.

He sat down at his desk and pulled out the notebook, but he didn't have it in him. It would take another drink or two to get Stanley to where he needed to be tonight. With no whiskey in his room and no interest in returning to Hunold's, he glanced out the window and hit on an idea. He'd go to Catherine Blair's, the yellow whorehouse with the red front door across the alley at the end of the block.

Catherine ran a respectable place, if such a thing was possible. Clean house, and clean girls thanks to yearly visits from the doctor. Reasonable rates, a dollar a throw, though she did charge extra for peculiarities. A few years back she covered all the windows in chicken wire to prevent men from sneaking in and out of the bedrooms without paying. Catherine said it was her way of keeping honest men honest. For her part, she paid the constable to keep away from her customers and her girls when he was in uniform. Off-duty, he was extended the same courtesies as every other man. Catherine liked Stanley. He was good to her girls and had defended them in court on a few occasions. She'd be glad to sell him a little whiskey. And if he was lucky, Stanley thought as he headed down the stairs, Ruby might make a little time for her favorite customer.

# C HAPTER NINETEEN

SITTING AT THE KITCHEN TABLE, Tommy waited for the coffee to percolate. He'd known Violet all her life, and in that time, he'd only ever seen her drink tea, but now, as he looked forward to their first breakfast together as man and wife, he doubted himself. Did she like coffee? He couldn't say for sure. Just in case, he'd made a full pot, knowing his mother would have something to say if a drop of it went to waste. "Times are tight," she'd scold. Well, he'd drink the whole damn pot before he'd let her say her piece, this morning of all mornings. And in front of his new bride, no less. Just let his mother try.

Tommy went to the stove with one of the cups and saucers that had been laid out. His mother always set the breakfast table the night before, and glancing back, he noticed the four place settings for the first time. Guilt replaced the annoyance he'd managed to conjure. She'd wanted Violet and Daisy to feel at home.

*What's got into me?* He poured his coffee, shuffled across the room, and propped open the back door. The earthy smell of night lingered in the predawn air, refreshing his stale lungs. Sunday. His body couldn't tell the difference between a day of rest and one of labor. Although he couldn't see the Morgans' kitchen from where he stood, he knew that Owen, as sick as he was, would also be awake. Like the constant trickle of water on stone, routine eventually cut a groove into a man.

Fortunately, Tommy had come to appreciate the solitude before the day broke on Sunday mornings. It gave him time to sort his own thoughts before folks tried to fill his head with theirs. Church in a few hours—that was the most immediate worry. It would be Violet's first time back at regular service since she'd come home with Daisy. *Please, Lord. Let her get through this day without a fuss. She never lets on, but just the same, I know it would mean the world to her.*

He closed his eyes, remembering how right she felt in his arms when she'd finally fallen asleep. After he'd unraveled the secret of Daisy, they'd talked for a considerable part of the night. He understood why she'd claimed the child, though he felt her actions had far exceeded the limits of sacrifice. And while he admired her decision, he also despised it, but he couldn't explain why; not fully. Perhaps he hated to see her paying for someone else's sin.

The matter had been resolved, so why did he still feel out of sorts? Tommy stood shivering at the door. Last night's chilled air had carried into morning. The day would warm up, but with October almost half over, he knew to appreciate the last of the temperate weather. Soon enough, the cold would have its way.

"You'll catch your death." Violet cinched the corded belt on her gray wool robe, covering the cotton gown underneath.

Startled, Tommy shut the door a little harder than necessary, spilling his coffee. "Damnit!"

"Sorry." She grabbed a towel from the sink and handed it over.

"No, no. It's my fault." He blotted his shirt. "I didn't hear you come in." His eyes settled on the whisper of cleavage at the top of her robe. Red-faced, he dropped his gaze.

"How'd you sleep?" He brushed past her, lingering a moment to take in the scent of her hair before pouring a fresh cup of coffee.

Violet clutched the fabric at her neckline, using her hand like a brooch to pin both sides together. "Fine," she said, filling the kettle. A moment of silence passed before she looked over at Tommy, now seated at the table. "And you?"

"The same." Then brighter, he said, "Slept like a log." Though he'd tossed for some time, and he knew she knew it.

"Give me your shirt," she said, and reached toward him. "I'll soak it."

"After breakfast." Tommy thought to kiss her hand but hesitated just long enough for her to turn away.

"It's a comfort to know my way around this kitchen," Violet said, reaching behind the cast-iron stove for the coal pail.

"Let me." Tommy jumped up, shoveled coal into the stove, opened the drafts, and stoked the flame. "I'm afraid we're not very modern around here."

"I wouldn't know what to do with a gas stove," Violet said, scooting around him to put the kettle on to boil. "This one will do me just fine."

The sun broke outside and pressed its nose against the kitchen window. They'd both grown shy in the morning light. The possibility of touching her now, stroking that hair, kissing those lips, like he'd done so freely last night, seemed as unthinkable as it had when they'd started courting. He recalled their first real date, the first time she'd said yes to him after her return to Scranton. He'd taken her to the pictures to see *All Quiet on the Western Front*, and afterward they'd gone back to pick up Daisy for ice cream. Daisy had been the key to winning Violet's heart.

Tommy watched as Violet steeped her tea at the sink. He felt unsettled, but was uncertain why. Perhaps because, until last night, he'd never thought to ask her for her story. Instead, he'd readily accepted the town gossip and prided himself for being the kind of man who could love a sinner in spite of her sin. What arrogance! He was no better than Stanley Adamski, who'd refused to hear her out.

"Should I start breakfast?" Violet opened the cupboard, then turned back to Tommy. "What is it you like to eat?"

"I'm sorry," he said, standing up and taking Violet's hands in his. "I should have asked you about Daisy when you first came home."

"That's water over the dam," Violet said, touching her lips to his cheek.

"But if I had asked," Tommy lifted her chin, "I mean, before last night, if I had asked, you would have told me, right? It's because I didn't ask."

Tears filled Violet's eyes. "No," she whispered. "I made a promise . . . to Lily."

That single, barely audible *No* resounded in Tommy's ears.

"Swing me again!" Daisy's arms shot into the air. Violet and Tommy each took a hand, lifted Daisy off the ground, and propelled her a few feet forward. A high-pitched "Weeeee" erupted from the trio. "Again!"

Violet mindlessly repeated the game as they headed up North Main Avenue, toward Providence Christian Church on the square. Occasionally, she'd sneak a glance at Tommy, trying to read his expression. When she finally caught his eye, she managed an uneasy, close-lipped smile. "What are you thinking?"

He tipped his head in Daisy's direction. "Not now."

Tommy's tone lacked reproach. His instinct was to protect her child. Both good signs, Violet decided.

Up ahead, old Myrtle Evans and her sister Mildred

played their own game. First they'd take turns looking back at Violet and her little family, and then they'd whisper in each other's ears. Violet was used to such behavior. She hoped they'd accidentally bang their hatted heads together as they gossiped.

"Here comes your sister." Tommy scowled. Behind them, an automobile ground its gears as it climbed the hill.

"It's your Aunt Lily," Violet said to Daisy.

Tommy shook his head as if to throw off his displeasure. He lifted the child onto his shoulders to give her a better view of the LaSalle.

"How can you tell without looking?" Daisy asked as she flung her arms around Tommy's neck.

"A lucky guess." He looked at the little girl and his countenance brightened.

Lily beeped the horn as she approached and veered in their direction.

"Keep your eyes on the road!" Violet shouted.

When Lily waved, Owen leaned across from the passenger side and took her splayed fingers and moved them back to the steering wheel. In the backseat, Louise and Grace dropped their heads into their hands. With one more toot of the horn, the car continued up the hill.

A few minutes later, Violet followed Tommy and Daisy single file past the LaSalle, which Lily had parked on the sidewalk in front of the church. Tommy turned around, annoyed.

"She's my sister," Violet murmured, hoping to pacify him.

"Don't I know it," was all Tommy said.

Once all three made it up the steps, Tommy lowered Daisy from his shoulders, smoothed her dress, and took her hand. When he looked up and saw Myrtle and Mildred lingering outside the heavy wooden doors, he grabbed Violet's hand as well.

Reverend Sheets pushed past the sisters and extended

his arm. "Glad to see you, Tommy." He nodded toward Violet. "Mrs. Davies. On behalf of your church family, I'd just like to say, welcome back."

Violet took in the scene—the warmth of the redbrick building, a perfect circle of stained glass over the entrance. "It's good to be home," she said. No matter what happened in life, she'd always been able to find consolation inside the church. Her church. Now, more than ever, she needed to feel that sense of peace again.

Myrtle and Mildred harrumphed in tandem and stormed into the sanctuary.

"Well, I suppose we're obligated to join them." The minister chuckled as he opened the door and waved the trio inside. Daisy pulled Tommy forward, so Violet was the last one through. As she passed, Reverend Sheets stopped her and said, "You're one of God's children. Enter His house with your head held high."

Violet smiled, both grateful and relieved, but only a few steps in, she heard a muffled "Jezebel" slip past Mr. Jenkins's hand-covered mouth. Mrs. Jenkins, her expression unchanging, thumped her husband's chest with her pleated fan. Violet faltered, but Reverend Sheets came up behind and whispered, "Head high," and nudged her forward.

She continued down the aisle while the preacher lagged back, reminding Mr. Jenkins about the perils of casting stones. Once Violet reached her parents, she stopped to kiss them, then walked up one more row to the Davies's pew where Tommy stood waiting to let her in.

"Is everything all right?" he asked.

She nodded. "It will be."

Tommy gripped her hand. "I love you," he whispered. Violet gave his hand a squeeze and smiled.

Louise slid across the seat to make room. "I'm so proud I could burst," she said.

Violet sat down next to her mother-in-law, followed by Daisy and Tommy. Once they were all settled, she turned around to her father. "Mother's right." Her worried expression belied her enthusiastic tone. "Your color's good."

"I feel good," he said, but they both knew it was a lie.

"Wild horses couldn't keep him down." Grace draped a flannel blanket over Owen's legs and tucked in the sides.

"Stop your fussing." He feebly swatted her hand away. "One person makes a remark to my daughter . . ." His cough started up, but he seemed determined to will it away. A moment later, and to everyone's surprise, he said with more strength than he'd mustered in some time, ". . . and they'll have me to deal with."

Violet glanced at her family, old and new, suddenly filled with gratitude for such bounty.

"This is the day that the Lord hath made!" Reverend Sheets shouted from the pulpit, immediately putting Violet in mind of the long-forgotten morning routine at the Good Shepherd. She didn't dare look across at Lily in the Sherman pew, but Violet knew they were both recalling Sister Immaculata's booming voice. So much had changed in the five years since, and all of it because of a single choice. Violet glanced at Daisy on Tommy's lap. *A very good choice*, she thought.

Violet held onto this thought through the hymns, prayers, and Communion. When it finally came time for the sermon, she tensed, worried Reverend Sheets would offer a veiled message about forgiving her trespasses, but when he started in on Noah's Ark, she knew the worst was behind her.

At the end of the service, several of the women came over to Violet to offer their good wishes on her marriage and to welcome her back into the church, and for the most part they seemed sincere.

"You'll never guess what just happened to me." Lily pushed through the little group, speaking to Violet and Grace directly.

Tommy cut in. "Don't you think you should ask your sister how she made out first?"

"Just look at her," Lily said. "She made out fine—as I expected. We're talking about Violet, after all."

"She's just excited." Violet hugged Tommy's arm lightly. "Do me a favor, will you? Help Father to the car."

"I don't need help," Owen said, pushing the blanket off his lap as he attempted to stand.

"Well, I could sure use some fresh air," Tommy said. "How about we start out and let the girls have their talk." He pulled Owen gently up from the seat and offered him his arm for support.

"Me too?" Daisy pulled at Tommy's sleeve.

"Especially you."

"Thank you." Violet was relieved to see Tommy's anger mollified.

"I'm just outside if you need me," Tommy said as he walked Owen up the aisle with Daisy on his heels.

"What was that all about?" Lily finally asked when Tommy was out of earshot.

"Tell us your news." Violet faced her sister, but watched her husband until he vanished out the door.

"Abigail Silkman herself invited me as she was walking out of church."

"Invited you where?" Grace lit up. Every move the Silkman girls made was reported in the society pages of the *Scranton Times* and, if Myrtle Evans could be trusted, even the *New York Times* on occasion.

"To a luncheon next week at the Omar Room in the Jermyn Hotel. According to Abigail, if all goes well, I should expect an invitation to join the Christian Ladies' Society!"

She leaned into the pew and hugged her mother. "Can you imagine?" Turning to Violet, she said, "Aren't you thrilled?"

"I'm very happy for you," Violet responded, though her mind was elsewhere. *What if Tommy never lets go of his resentment toward Lily?*

"That's wonderful news." Louise leaned forward and took Lily's hand into both of hers. "It's what you've always wanted."

"Isn't that the truth," Lily said. "Violet, you have to go to town with me tomorrow. I don't have a thing to wear and I need your honest opinion."

"What about George?" Louise said when Violet didn't answer. "Won't he want to take you?"

"He's too busy with the mine. He's down there now, dealing with some sort of rumor about a strike tomorrow. Anyway, I want my sister with me for something so important."

"Of course she'll go," Grace said. "I'll mind Daisy. The house is already too quiet without that child." She laughed and hugged Lily again.

"Not before noon," Violet finally answered. "There's wash to be done.

"Nonsense," Louise said. "I can tend to that."

Violet persisted: "And I still have to finish unpacking."

"I knew I could count on you," Lily said. "I can always count on you."

# C HAPTER TWENTY

"WHY'D YOU LET ME FALL ASLEEP?" Stanley stood along-side the bed, pulling on his undershorts, eyeing the floor for his pants.

"You don't pay me to be your keeper." Ruby Hart, na-ked as a robin, sat up, rummaged through the twist of sheets, and produced a pair of brown tweed trousers. "My finder's fee." She laughed and grabbed a few Lucky Strikes from a pack in Stanley's front pocket. "For later," she said, placing two cigarettes on the dresser while she held onto the third.

Stanley paused to take her in—the generous bosom, that fire-red hair, her emerald eyes. Almost beautiful, he thought, but for how long? Catherine Blair treated her girls right, but "right" for Ruby's line of work was still hard living and bound to catch up. He leaned forward, kissed the top of her head, and snatched his pants.

With the cigarette in her mouth, she pointed her chin up to Stanley.

"I'm late," he said, striking a match and holding it against the tip of the cigarette till it caught. Shafts of morn-ing light pressed through the chicken-wired window, painting crosses on the opposite wall.

"How late can it be?" Ruby closed her eyes, took a long drag, and exhaled slowly. "We only slept an hour or two." She picked Stanley's shirt off the iron bedpost and handed it to him. "I still can't believe Catherine let you in here after hours."

"I'm a good customer." He smiled.

"Don't I know it." Ruby watched as Stanley poked his handless arm into the left sleeve before slipping his good one into the right. "I'm a lucky girl. Got to spend time with my favorite gentleman caller twice in as many days." She leaned back, cupped one of her breasts, and slapped it up a few times. "Of course, three's my lucky number." When Stanley didn't respond, Ruby pinched out her cigarette and raised her arms in a V. "See anything you like?" She reached behind, grabbed hold of the headboard, and banged it against the wall.

"For crying out loud," a voice yelled from the next room, "it's six o'clock in the morning!"

"Sorry, Susie." Ruby laughed into a pillow then quietly asked Stanley, "So what do you say?" She flung her bare legs straight into the air. "Ruby needs a new pair of shoes," she said, swinging a foot toward him and tracing his lips.

He stared at the patch of red hair between her legs and sucked on her big toe. "You're trouble." He let go of her foot with a pained sigh. "Not now," he said, more to himself than Ruby. "Not today."

"Where you off to in such a hurry, anyways? You have a sweetheart here in town? A fella like you must have a sweetheart." She let both legs drop over the side of the bed as she sat up.

"The Sherman Mine." He finished buttoning his shirt one-handed, tucked it into his pants, and buckled his belt. "The UAM called for a strike. If it goes off, they'll probably be charged with contempt of court, since a judge ordered them to rescind the strike order. That's where I come in."

"The strike'll still be there in half an hour." She held him in place with her eyes while she unhooked his belt, undid the top button of his trousers, and slid her hand inside.

"I have a duty." His murmured words lost their conviction as soon as they hit the air. Stanley closed his eyes and shuddered.

Ruby unzipped his pants and let them fall to the floor. "That's not all you have." She laughed as she pulled him back into bed.

Tommy felt the slap of frosty air as soon as he stepped off the porch. So much for Indian summer. It couldn't last forever, but this was unseasonably chilly, even for October. Granted, the black bristles on the caterpillars outnumbered the brown ones this year. A harsh winter was in store. He just wished it wouldn't come too soon. Then again, maybe this cold snap would keep the strikers at home. That would be something, at least.

There were no lights on inside the Morgan house as Tommy walked by. That meant Owen was too weak to get out of bed. It was only a matter of time, but Tommy didn't like to think about it. Owen had been a father to him after his own father died in the mining accident, and he couldn't imagine having to say goodbye all over again. At least the Shermans had been good to the Morgans. Say what you will about George Jr., at least he took care of his own.

At the bottom of Spring Street, Tommy met up with a half-dozen of the more sensible men on his shift. "Strength in numbers," one of them had said the previous week when they'd heard the scuttlebutt about a wildcat strike. Tommy agreed. He had no intention of joining the strike, yet crossing a picket line didn't sit well with him either. He'd been a union man as far back as he could remember, and that meant something, but now was not the time to demand a five-day workweek and ten-hour days. There were plenty of men on the dole who'd jump at the chance to work twelve-hour shifts, six days a week. How those fools from the UAM couldn't see this was beyond him. And why split off from the United Mine Workers in the first place? It just didn't make sense to pit one union against another. Scabs and owners would be the only ones to benefit.

When the men reached Providence Square, they turned down Market Street and crossed the bridge. Twenty feet below, the Lackawanna River rushed angrily by as if to spite the coal sludge intent on choking it. "Looks like a lot of fuss for nothing," Tommy said, pointing through a patch of needleless evergreens, their branches covered in soot.

He squinted toward the colliery. "I can make out three, maybe four strikers near the road."

Relieved at such a poor showing, Tommy continued down the hill and over to the main entrance. In the distance, a couple of mule boys loitered near the above-ground stable, and nine or ten men stood near the cage, ready to be lowered into the mine when the hoistman gave the signal. As close to an ordinary workday as they had a right to expect, Tommy thought.

"They're yella," one of the miners from Tommy's group said as soon as they stepped onto Sherman property without incident.

Tommy hoped to God he was right.


"Hel-lo?" Lily sang out as she knocked on the front door and walked into the parlor carrying a small box tied with string. "Anybody home?"

"You're half an hour early," Violet called from the second floor. "I'm in Daisy's room."

"Perfect," Lily said, taking off her coat and looking around the Davies's parlor. "Feels strange calling on you here." She climbed the stairs and found Violet in a small room with a slanted ceiling at the end of the hall. "Where's Daisy?"

"Next door," Violet said, mating the child's clean anklets and folding them into balls. "I thought I told you noon."

"How come she's there so early?"

"Slept over last night. I think she misses her old bed."

"I bought her something," Lily said, holding out the package.

"Not again." Violet took the gift and set it on the dresser. "I don't like you spoiling her."

"What's an aunt for?" She paused in thought, then waved her hand. "Besides, it's nothing. A little pearl-toned mirror from Woolworth's with a matching comb and brush." Lily sat down on the bed. "Where's Mrs. Davies?" She smiled. "Or should I say, the *other* Mrs. Davies?"

"Over with Mother and Daisy."

"Then you have no excuse." Lily hopped up and took her sister's arm. "Off we go."

"Settle yourself," Violet said as she pulled free and put the socks in a drawer. "I still have a sink full of dishes to do."

"Can't that wait?" Lily followed Violet out of the room and back downstairs. "They'll be out of dresses by the time we get to town. The pretty ones, anyway."

"Where's the fire?" Violet asked as she walked into the kitchen.

"George telephoned. He left some papers at home and asked me to drop them off. He was very adamant."

"So do it now and come back," Violet said.

Lily shrugged. "Not without you."

"Is something going on between you and George?" Violet looked at her sister. "Is he treating you right?"

"You know I hate doing anything alone." Lily leaned forward. "Speaking of husbands, how's married life? Do you love him madly?"

"How could I not?" Violet started filling the sink and

turned around. "But you'd tell me if something was wrong, wouldn't you?"

"My life is perfect," Lily said. "Or it will be as soon as I give George a baby."

"These things take time."

"Not when you don't want them to." Lily sighed and waved her hand. "Don't mind me. I'm not sleeping well lately." She stood up and walked into the parlor. "It's just . . ." she stared out the window facing her parents' house, "when I look at you and Daisy together, I want that too."

Violet stood motionless. "You're a healthy girl," she finally said. "You'll have your own babies soon enough."

"You're right, of course." Lily's face brightened. She walked back into the kitchen and put on her coat. "In the meantime, I think I'll go next door and spend some time with Daisy. Come get me when you're ready."

"No." Violet pulled her hands out of the half-full dish-pan and dried them on a towel. "I'm ready now," she said, grabbing her coat. "Let's go find you the prettiest dress in Scranton."


By eleven thirty, there were close to a hundred men picket-ing outside the colliery, according to Buddy Parker, Eddie Parker's youngest. The boy had spotted the mob on his way to the mine to drop off his father's dinner pail.

"I never thought that many men would show up," Tommy said, lifting Buddy out of the wooden cage that had deliv-ered him to the shaft four stories below ground. "A hun-dred," Tommy marveled, still holding onto the boy till his eyes adjusted to the little bit of light thrown by the miners' headlamps.

"Thereabouts," Buddy speculated as Tommy handed him over to his father. No one doubted the boy's figure. Eddie always said the kid had a gift for sums.

"How'd you get past them?" Eddie asked, taking the pail and setting it on the dank ground near one of the timbers bracing the narrow tunnel.

"Slid down the bank on my bum." Buddy turned around and showed the smears of dirt across the seat of his pants. Twenty headlamps pointed toward him, throwing long shadows on the jagged walls.

"Your mother will tan your hide when she sees those britches," Eddie said.

"Couldn't help it. The road's blocked. Men at the entrance have picket signs. Them that don't is throwing rocks, like to warn people." He pressed his hand behind his ear. "I think one of 'em got me." He inspected the blood on his fingers and nodded.

"Is he hurt bad?" Tommy asked.

"He's eight years old, for chrissakes!" Eddie yelled, taking out a handkerchief and holding it to his son's head. "The bastards!"

"It ain't much." Buddy lifted his father's hand away.

"I don't give a tinker's damn how much," Eddie said. "You hurt my son, you answer to *me*."

Several "sons-a-bitches" and "bloody hells" rose up from the men.

"I've had it with those troublemakers. Tearing apart our union. Spitting on our jobs. And worst of all," Eddie picked up his son, "attacking my boy." Stepping into the cage, Eddie looked out at the twenty or so men in front of him. "They're going to answer for this one!" he yelled. "Who's with me?"

One by one, the miners climbed inside with their shovels and pick axes in tow. Tommy stood for a moment, considering the situation. "Hold on," he said. "I don't like this any more than you do, but there's a world of difference between a rock and a pick."

"They have it coming to them," Eddie argued. "Did you see what they did to my boy?"

"I did," Tommy said, "and they'll answer for it. But not this way." He stood motionless for a moment, wondering what in God's name he was supposed to do next. Wait them out? Walk away? Join the madness? Finally, someone in back said, "Davies is right," and tossed a shovel out onto the ground. "Let's make it a fair fight." After a bit of grumbling, the others pitched their tools as well.

Tommy nodded as he stepped into the cage, relieved and dumbfounded by the group's sudden change of heart. He signaled the hoistman with two sharp whistles, and as the cage began to ascend, he prayed that he was right.

Anxiety seemed to have lodged itself in Violet's stomach. *When I look at you and Daisy together, I want that too.* Of all the silliness, Violet thought as she headed down the front steps. Lily meant no harm. She'd simply said she wanted what Violet had, but with her own child.

Borrowing trouble. That's what her father would say, and he'd be right. It's something she'd always done, and it never served her. Not once. Violet slid into the passenger seat of Lily's coupe just as the noon whistle sounded down at the Lace Works.

"I'm telling George it's your fault," Lily said as she got behind the wheel.

"What's my fault?"

Lily looked into the rearview mirror and smoothed her hair. "He's going to think I took too long getting down there with his papers, and I'm going to blame you." Lily pressed the clutch, closed the throttle, inserted the key into the ignition, turning it to the *on* position, and pushed the starter button on the dash. "Are you listening? This is important."

"Yes," Violet nodded, finally catching up with Lily's

conversation. "I still don't understand why you didn't go before you picked me up."

"George won't yell at you." Lily turned the steering wheel and shifted into first gear. "And he won't yell at me in front of you." She pressed the gas pedal and let up on the clutch. Violet's mouth dropped open. "Lily Morgan," she finally said, "what's going on over at that house?"

"Sherman," Lily corrected. "I know you don't like George, and he knows it too." She pulled onto Spring Street and headed downhill. "It's written on your face whenever you see him."

"I just think he needs to pay more attention to you," Violet said. "Spend more time with you."

"George's moods run hot and cold, but he's a good man," Lily said. "Never laid a hand on me, and that's the truth."

That last bit of news did little to ease Violet's anxiety. "I thought I wouldn't have to worry about you once you had that ring on your finger."

"Always worry about me. I wouldn't want it any other way," Lily said as she started her turn onto North Main Avenue. "But trust me. You don't have to worry about George."

"I hope not." Violet worried about Lily, though it was Daisy she was most concerned about. If George had known he fathered her, he was a cad for abandoning Lily in her time of need. If he didn't know, he might try to claim the little girl if he found out now.

"Look!" Lily pointed to the Silkman house up on the left. "Is that Abigail on the porch?" She squinted. "Should I wave?"

"Pay attention to your driving," Violet said.

"If it's Abigail, I should wave." Lily leaned up over the steering wheel, veering into the middle of the road.

"Watch out!" Violet pulled on the wheel just as a

milkman's horse crested the hill in the opposite direction.

Lily slammed on her brake and skidded to a stop in time to hear an abundance of obscenities streaming from the milkman as he continued down the road.

"Thank goodness," Lily said, once she got the car going again. "It was only one of the housemaids."

Violet stared open-mouthed at her sister.

"Don't be like that," Lily said. "I just mean it would have been worse if it had been Abigail on the porch."

"Do you know how serious that almost was?"

"No harm done." Lily's relief quickly dissolved into worry. "Not a word of this to George, do you hear me?"

Violet just shook her head.

When they reached the corner of Main and Market, Lily carefully waited until all traffic had passed before making the left-hand turn. "No sense tempting fate," she said. Halfway down the hill, both sisters saw the picket squad, but it was too late to turn around.

The noon whistle blew at the Lace Works, momentarily drowning out Eddie Parker's rant. When the note ran out of steam, he started up again. "I'll give you one last chance!" Eddie lifted his son with one arm and pointed out the blood-matted hair with the other. The child squirmed under his father's unyielding grip. "Which one of you cowards done this to my boy?" When no one answered, he turned on Stanley. "Don't you go protecting that son of a bitch. Hand him over or I'll kill the whole lot of them!"

"And I'll help!" someone shouted from behind. Several of the men near Eddie echoed the sentiment.

Stanley scanned the picket line, as if considering the request. "We've made our point, fellows. Let's call it a day." He motioned for the strikers to clear out, but they refused to budge.

"This is your doing." Tommy stepped forward and thumped Stanley on the chest.

Stanley's eyes narrowed. "How do you figure that?"

"You're a lawyer, not a miner. This isn't your fight."

"You don't say." Stanley raised his handless arm and pointed the stump at Tommy. "From where I'm standing, looks like I have more of a right than most."

Both men glared at each other and held their ground.

"I still want to know who done this to my boy!" Eddie yelled.

"Take Buddy home," Tommy said, "before the troopers get here and start breaking bones."

Eddie paused. "This ain't over," he finally said, but he started up Market Street with his son in his arms. "Not by a long shot."

Eddie's departure seemed to take the fight out of the other men who'd been working in the mine. "We have a shift to finish," Tommy said, still scowling. "Keep this up," he looked at Stanley, "and someone's bound to get killed." He started walking back to toward the cage, but shouted, "And that'll be on your head!"

"We're all on the same side here," Stanley called out as the miners walked away. "Solidarity forever!"

"Solidarity forever!" the strikers repeated with fists raised.

Stanley turned toward them. "An injury to one . . ." he said, his face bright red, and waited for the response.

"Is an injury to all!" the men returned.

Stanley looked over and saw Judson Woodberry, the reporter from the *Scranton Times*, pull out his pad. "It's time to stand up to the mine owners," Stanley shouted, "who profit from your sweat but refuse to pay you fairly for it!" Stanley made sure his voice carried as far as Tommy and the other men still walking toward the cage. "They take your limbs, your breath, your life, but it's not enough for them! Twelve hours a day, six days a week! And if they could talk the Almighty out of that day of rest, they'd make it seven! It's time to say, *Enough!*"

"Enough!" the crowd echoed.

"There he is!" someone in the crowd hollered, and pointed to a blue LaSalle coming down Market Street.

"It's Sherman, that son of a bitch!" a second man shouted as he lobbed a rock at the car. It skipped past the torpedo hood ornament and disappeared somewhere near the right tire fender.

A more accurate arm launched the next rock directly through the windshield. The automobile shot forward, and the crowd scattered like buckshot.

The driver jerked the wheel, slammed the brake, and skidded off the road toward the embankment and the river below. Screams filled the air—women's screams—as the car rammed a dying evergreen. The trunk crumpled, and the upper two-thirds of the tree fell backward into the water. The fractured stump alone held the coupe in place, its front tires resting inches from the twenty-foot drop.

"It's the wife's car!" shouted Eddie, who was closest to the scene. He put his son down and looked through the opening where the windshield belonged. "Mrs. Sherman and her sister!"

"Violet!" Stanley yelled, already sprinting toward the mangled vehicle. A few men followed at his heels, though most of them either stayed put or slipped away.

With some effort, Eddie managed to wrench the driver's door free from its buckled frame. Lily sat dazed, but alive. "You hurt anywheres?" Eddie looked her over top to bottom.

"Violet," she said, turning to her sister slumped against the door, unconscious.

The tree stump groaned as it shouldered the vehicle's weight.

"Let's get you away from here," Eddie said, lifting Lily out of the car and onto the sidewalk.

"Violet," she called again.

Stanley reached the passenger side and yanked the door open, catching Violet as she spilled halfway out. "Wake up," he cried. Part of the tree stump splintered under the pressure, and the car lurched forward another inch or two. Stanley eased Violet the rest of the way out and held her in his arms. "Don't you do this," he muttered. "Wake up." He used his sleeve to dab at a thin line of blood on Violet's forehead, where a knot was beginning to form. "This can't happen."

Violet stirred, her eyes still closed as if savoring the last few seconds of a pleasant sleep. "Stanley," she whispered, nuzzling his chest, breathing him in. "Don't cry, my love," she said, opening her eyes and holding his gaze briefly. "Stanley." She smiled and closed her lids again. Then her eyes shot open a second time, and she blinked to clear them. "Stanley," she repeated, her voice now thick with confusion.

"Don't try to talk," he said, stroking her hair. "I love you."

"Get . . . away . . . from . . . my . . . wife," Tommy said, giving each word plenty of emphasis.

Violet sat up slowly, painfully, and took in the scene. The crashed car. Lily, watching a few feet away. Tommy, towering over her.

"I just had to see . . ." Stanley's explanation trailed off. With Violet sitting on her own, he stood up and backed away.

Tommy crouched down alongside Violet and inspected the lump on her head. He swallowed hard, damming up the tears. "Are you all right?" he quietly managed.

"I'm not sure." Violet's half-smile turned into a wince. "It hurts to breathe."

"Don't move." Tommy looked up as a fire truck from the station at the top of the hill pulled up alongside them on the road. "Help is here."

"You're here," she said. "That's what matters."

Tommy pressed his lips against her cheek, and they both started to tremble. "I thought I lost you." His tears broke loose and dampened both of their faces.

"I'm right here," she soothed, and watched as Stanley turned and walked away.

# CHAPTER TWENTY-ONE

GEORGE FELT UNEASY as he inched his LaSalle across the rutted back road that would take him off mine property and onto Green Ridge Street. It was almost noon, and Stanley Adamski and his gang of rabble-rousers were picketing over at the main entrance on Market Street. It was only a matter of time before the situation boiled over, yet George knew he had to get downtown by twelve o'clock in order to make sure this would be the first and only strike on his watch at the Sherman Mine. Since some of the men had joined that rogue union, they'd started grumbling more loudly than usual, so George had worked out a plan to solve his labor problem once and for all.

Of course, solving the problem meant convincing Little Frankie to buy into the plan, if he could even call it a plan, and that wouldn't be easy. They hadn't spoken in almost six years, since the day of the hayride, back when George was a freshman in college. Everyone in the neighborhood had known that Frankie was sweet on Lily, so when George left her on the blanket that afternoon to run after Janetta, Frankie never forgave him. And in a begrudging kind of way, George admired him for his convictions, even if they were wasted on a girl.

Publicly, a man like George, a deacon in his church, a pillar of his community, had no business fraternizing with the

likes of Franco Colangelo. But in this case George couldn't
pull his usual political strings, which meant he had to take
an underhanded approach. Federal agents were still shining
a spotlight on Scranton's government five years after round-
ing up seventy-eight men on racketeering charges—a former
mayor, the Civil Service commissioner, and a chief of police
among them. They had been getting kickbacks from a slot
machine syndicate operating within city limits. A syndicate
that included Franco Colangelo, though so far the feds had
missed his part in it. Frankie had turned out to be quite the
businessman, with interests in prostitution, gambling, and
untaxed liquor.

It took George almost two weeks to set up the meeting
with Frankie. Not that he was hard to find. For someone
in charge of such questionable enterprises, he was a fairly
visible man. He drove to Mass at St. Peter's each morning
and ate his noon meal at the Electric City Lunch every day
but Sunday.

George's hesitation had to do with an aversion to getting
his hands dirty. He'd learned early on to rely on other people
for that. He also had a distaste for treating a Guinea like
Franco Colangelo as an equal—Little Frankie, the greasy
kid with the big ears who used to supply the Green Ridge
boys with his uncle's wine. The thought of it turned George's
stomach.

He pulled up in front of the Mayfair Hotel, directly
across the street from Frankie's usual haunt. The clock at
the courthouse two blocks away started to chime the twelve
o'clock hour. As George turned off the engine, he had another thought. He hoped he wouldn't run into his wife and
that sister of hers while they were downtown. When Lily
had mentioned the shopping trip that morning, George had
tried to talk her out of it, but to no avail. Nothing to be
done about it now. He reached into the glove compartment

for his pistol, then decided against taking it inside. A good faith gesture. He needed Frankie to trust him.

George made his way across the street, inhaling the aroma of hot dogs sizzling on the grill inside the Electric City Lunch. The green-and-white-tiled building anchored the corner of Penn and Linden, with entrances on both streets. A sandwich board usually stood out front with the message, *Scranton's Best Texas Wieners*, but someone must have swiped it again. *Probably one of the cooks from Coney Island*, George thought. Coney Island was a wiener joint down on Lackawanna Avenue that made the same claim.

Although George had only been in the restaurant a handful of times, he loved to watch Gino, the cook, at work. Gino stood behind the counter, slicing each hot dog lengthwise, careful to leave the halves hinged, so when he tossed them on the grill, they'd land facedown like half-read books. No one waited on you at the Electric City Lunch. You could sit in a booth, at a table, or on one of the stools along the counter, but if you wanted to be served, you had to stand in line. Fortunately for his customers, Gino moved with a speed that seemed inconceivable, given his girth. He tucked the finished dogs into their buns, smothered them in mustard and onions, and finished them off in a chili sauce so spicy that Gino would often hand a plate across the counter and say, "Now tell me that doesn't have a bite." Thanks to Gino, people from all walks of life frequented the place— businessmen, shopgirls, beat cops . . . and Frankie.

Franco Colangelo did more than spend time at the Electric City Lunch. He owned it, and the second-floor betting parlor too. The house always made a healthy profit, but unlike some of his competitors, Franco threw a few more wins in the direction of his customers. "Keep 'em happy," he'd say, whenever someone in the organization questioned his methods, "keep 'em coming back."

*The afternoon regulars*. Franco stood in the doorway of his office, surveying the dozen or so men scattered about on rows of wooden chairs that faced the racing board in front. Black Mike, nicknamed for his Sicilian heritage, adjusted his earpiece as he worked the board, calling a horse race out of Kentucky. Over to the left, two men stood behind glass, ready to take the next round of wagers.

Not bad for a kid from Bull's Head. A gambling parlor, the wiener joint, a couple of whorehouses down in the next alley over, a few dozen slot machines, and a stake in the liquor trade—all by the age of twenty-three. And if he played his cards right, a chance to expand his territory into Jersey by early spring. Money equaled power, and lucky for Frankie, he had both. Police departments, local politicians, and pillars of the church in his pocket. Everything a man could want.

Almost everything.

One of Gino's sons, the younger one with the knock-knees, came pounding up the steps and over to the office. "That fellow you're waiting for just walked in, Mr. Colangelo."

"Mr. Colangelo," George echoed from the top of stairwell. "Has a nice ring to it." He paused to inspect the scene, and nodded. "Not bad." He crossed the room and tousled the boy's hair.

Franco tipped his head, prompting Gino's son to leave the men alone.

"How are you, Frankie?" George's extended hand hung in the air.

"George Sherman." Franco's lips curled up as he finally took the proffered hand. "Look what the cat dragged in." The men locked eyes and laughed guardedly. "Come on in." Inside the office Frankie gestured for George to sit on the leather club chair. Frankie moved to a mahogany desk on the opposite wall, stopping briefly to shut a door to a small adjoining bedroom. "What brings you here, George?"

"No beating around the bush, Frankie. That's what I always liked about you."

"And here I thought it was my uncle's *vino*." He laced his fingers and cupped the back of his head. "What do you want?"

At that angle, George couldn't help but notice the perfect seams on Frankie's black serge suit. Expensive. Custom-made. Italian, most likely. And that lining peeking through—pure silk. George had to hand it to Frankie. He'd figured out how to dress the part. Had anyone else been sitting behind that desk, George would have asked for the name of his tailor.

"You know why you don't like me, Frankie?" He reached toward the edge of the desk and mindlessly picked up a gold-plated tabletop cigarette lighter. "Because I knew you when you were poor." He pressed a square button on the side of the lighter. The top automatically glided open and the flame ignited. George shook his head. "Nothing you can do about that."

Frankie pushed a matching cigarette case forward. "I wish I had time to reminisce," he said, opening the lid, "but my father doesn't own a mine. I have to work for a living."

George glanced back at the betting parlor. "Is that what they call it?" He laughed as he waved off the cigarettes. "I suppose pulling a trigger *is* work." He placed the lighter back on the desk. "Of course, it's not my place to judge."

"You flatter me."

"My mistake."

"You know why you don't like me, George?" Frankie tapped a cigarette out of the case and lit it. "Because I'm a self-made man." He took a drag before adding, "That's something you'll never be."

"Well, you have me there, Frankie. Then again, I'll never be an alligator wrangler, and I don't imagine I'll miss that either."

"Is it a loan you need, Georgie? I'm not used to giving handouts," Frankie stood up and pulled a money-clipped wad of bills out of his pants pocket, "but I can make an exception in your case."

"Here's the thing," George's tone deepened, suggesting a seriousness of sorts, "according to my sources, the feds are sniffing around your operations."

"And here I thought your sources were doing time for racketeering."

"Nice to see you haven't lost your sense of humor." George pressed his lips into a smile. "You need me, Frankie. You know you do. You can pay off the cops from here to kingdom come, but once the federal government moves in, you're on your own. Unless . . ."

"Unless?" Frankie slipped the bills back into his pocket and took his seat.

"Unless," George nodded to a black rotary telephone on Frankie's desk, "I call a buddy of mine in Washington who can put the feds on a completely different track. A Maryland track, for example. Or better yet, Florida. I'm sure that kind of sunshine makes them do all sorts of things that need investigating."

"And what's in it for you?"

"Can't a guy just do an old friend a favor?"

A hearty, smoke-filled laugh erupted from behind the desk. "Assuming that we are friends," Frankie took a final drag on his cigarette before tamping it out in a marble ashtray, "what's in it for you?"

"One hand washes the other. Isn't that how the saying goes?" When Frankie didn't respond, George continued: "I need a little help with a union problem."

"And your buddy in Washington?"

"He can't make people disappear, just federal investigations."

"I don't know what you heard, Georgie, but I'm not in that kind of business." Frankie pushed himself away from his desk and stood up.

"I think you misunderstood." He motioned for Frankie to take his seat again. "I'm not talking about a permanent solution. Just something that'll bring a man down a peg or two. Something that might put him away for ten-to-twenty."

"And what man needs to learn this lesson?" Frankie sat down.

"Stanley Adamski. That lousy excuse for a lawyer is stirring things up at the mine, and I want him stopped."

"Stopped how?"

"I thought he might get himself tangled up in something that would complicate his life. Get him out of the way for a while."

"You don't need me for that. Hire yourself an investigator. Dig up some dirt."

"I put a tail on him awhile back." It was George's turn to stand up. He walked the length of the office and circled behind the club chair. "The son of a bitch is clean as a whistle."

"Goes to the whorehouse pretty regular."

"Who doesn't?" George laughed. "Shit, I even ran into Babe Ruth in the Alleys. I would've asked for an autograph too, if I hadn't been so hell-bent on getting inside myself. No, I need something big."

"So where do I come in?"

George returned to his chair, leaned forward, and steepled his fingers, pointing them at Frankie. "Use your connections. Set him up. I don't care how. Take him down. Hard."

Frankie rose again, and this time there was no question that the meeting was over. "Afraid I can't help you out."

"Think about it. That's all I ask." George got to his feet and extended his hand.

Just at that moment, Gino came lumbering up the steps. "Mr. Sherman, your foreman's downstairs. Said he saw your car out front. He's been looking for you."

"Now what?" George pulled his hand back and walked past the folding chairs to the stairs.

"Trouble at the mine, sir. Something about picketers and a rock through Mrs. Sherman's windshield. There's been a wreck."

"Lily! Is she hurt?" The intimacy of her given name conspired with the urgency in Frankie's voice. His heart had been exposed. "Mrs. Sherman," he corrected too late.

"My wife." George gave each word equal weight. "How is she?"

"Bruised up a bit, but nothing too serious. He says the sister's worse off."

"What about the car?" George asked. "Had her painted Yale blue for my alma mater, just like my LaSalle." He nodded toward the window.

"He didn't mention the car. His concern seemed to be for Mrs. Sherman."

George thanked Gino for the message and waited for him to go back downstairs before turning to Frankie. "That son of a bitch Stanley did this. You and I both know it."

Frankie nodded but said nothing.

"Give it some thought." George started down the steps, pausing to call back, "I know it would mean a lot to Lily. Adamski never did pay for abandoning her sister and that little girl."

# THE HYGIENE OF MENSTRUATION

*Cold tub baths . . . as well as ocean and river bathing are best*
*avoided during the period; at least during the first two days. I*
*do not give this as an absolute rule; I know women who bathe*
*and swim in the ocean during their menstrual periods without*
*any injury to themselves, but they are exceptionally robust*
*women; advice in books is for the average person, and it is*
*always best to be on the safe side.*
　　　　　　　　　—*Woman: Her Sex and Love Life,*
　　　　　　　　　William J. Robinson, MD, 1929

Something like this was bound to happen. We're just glad it wasn't worse. Cracked ribs and a concussion are nothing to sneeze at, but Violet Davies should thank her lucky stars the good Lord had His eye on her. And that sister of hers.

Not that we're saying this was all Lily Sherman's fault, but when you gallivant around town in a brand-new car like you're Mrs. Gotrocks while everyone else is living hand-to-mouth, well, God is bound to notice.

Of course, we can't blame a girl like Lily for trying to live above her station. She must've thought she'd died and gone to heaven when she married one of the Sherman boys. And you can't fault George Jr., Lily always knew how to turn heads.

We do have to wonder what Abigail Silkman was thinking when she invited Lily to that luncheon, though. Abigail's had a fine upbringing and should know better than to hobnob with someone of Lily's low birth. Next thing, she'll be inviting colored women to join the Eastern Star.

Not that it's any of our business. Live and let live is what we always say. God will get around to judging us all in His own good time.

# CHAPTER TWENTY-TWO

AFTER GATHERING MOST OF THE INGREDIENTS for her potato leek soup, Violet sat at the kitchen table to rest. It had been four weeks since the accident and her ribs had not yet healed completely. She adjusted the compression binder under her dress. The pain had lessened somewhat, but deep breaths and sudden movement still brought on a stabbing, almost unbearable sensation, and she tired so easily. Another month, maybe more, Doc Rodham had said. The ribs would heal, but not soon enough for Violet, with a five-year-old to care for and a house to keep; still, they would mend. But what about the longing she'd felt since waking up in Stanley's arms? How many weeks or months or years would it take to cure that? She closed her eyes and shivered, remembering her body cradled in his, the embrace sparking old feelings she'd all but forgotten.

A knock at the back door roused Violet from her daydream.

"Are you up to a little company?" the widow Lankowski called out from the threshold, her arthritic fingers already turning the knob.

"Come in." Violet stood up and turned too quickly. She held her breath through the twinge. "I was just going to make some tea," she finally managed.

"You sit." The widow grabbed the kettle from the stove and filled it with water. Even at seventy, the six-foot-tall woman had a formidable presence. "I didn't come over to be waited on," she said. "Are you any better?"

"Some."

"Not from where I'm standing." With the kettle on the stove, the widow took a seat and looked around. "Anyone home?"

"It's Mother Davies's day to visit the shut-ins, and I insisted she go. I sent Daisy next door for leeks so I can start a pot of soup."

"Good. Then tell me what's really going on with you."

"I don't understand," Violet said, but tears sprang to her eyes.

"Stanley is brooding more than ever." The widow patted Violet's hand. "Every time I come over here, you look like you lost your best friend. And it's all since that accident."

"Something's wrong with Stanley?" Violet asked, her voice an octave higher, her body rigid.

"So that's it."

When Violet didn't answer, the widow continued, "I'm not sure what's in that head of yours, but for what it's worth, I think you made the right choice with Tommy."

"I don't believe you." Violet pointed at the widow. "You're the one who always said Stanley and I were meant to be together."

"And I was wrong." The widow took Violet's hand. "I love Stanley. I'd die for that boy if it would make a difference. But he has enough of his father in him to worry me. I see that now, and no amount of love will change it."

"He's nothing like his father." Violet shook her head. "Stanley doesn't have a mean bone in his body."

"But he does give himself over to the drink," the widow said. "And that makes for a very unhappy life."

"I can't bear to think of him unhappy." Violet dropped her head into her hands.

"He's not your problem to solve. Do you hear me?" The widow lifted Violet's chin and looked her in the eye. "You married a good man. You and Tommy are well-suited and that means everything in the long run."

*Plink. Plunk. Plink. Plunk.* Violet wiped her eyes at the sound of Daisy hopscotching up the steps, across the porch, and through the back door. "Grandma says if you need more, send me back over." The little girl handed her mother a bouquet of two large leeks, sniffed her now empty palm, and grimaced.

Violet smelled her daughter's hand and crinkled her nose. "Stinky."

Daisy laughed. "Aunt Lily told me to tell you to wash my hands."

"She did now." Violet paused, trying to decide if she should be annoyed or worried. "What was Aunt Lily doing at Grandma's?"

"Babcia!" the little girl yelled when she noticed the widow.

"Come over here and give me a hug." The widow leaned down, opened her arms, and pulled Daisy in. "And what do you have in there?" she asked, nodding to a lump under the child's coat.

Daisy undid the first two buttons and pulled out a stuffed elephant. "Ta-da!"

"Where did you . . ." Violet's heart skipped a beat, as if Stanley himself had suddenly appeared in the kitchen. *Of all the silliness*, she thought, as she took the animal and examined it—the shoe-button eyes, the floppy limbs. The chintz hide covered in tiny flowers. Stanley had thought them to be violets, but it was clear to her even then they were roses. She hadn't corrected him, and now she tried to remember why.

"What's his name?" Daisy finished taking off her coat. "I found him at Grandma's. She said I could have him if you don't want him. Aunt Lily said you're too old for him."

Violet put on a smile and handed the toy back to Daisy. "*Her* name. And it's Queenie."

"Who's Queenie?"

"An elephant at the Nay Aug Zoo," the widow said, handing Violet a cup of tea.

"Can we go and see her?" Daisy lifted the trunk and pointed it at the leeks. "Stinky." She laughed.

"No, doll baby." Violet leaned over and patted the elephant's head. "Queenie died a few months ago."

"Like Aunt Daisy, God rest her soul?"

Violet smiled. "Yes, my sweet girl, like Aunt Daisy."

"I think they play zoo together in heaven." Daisy climbed up on the widow's lap.

"I wouldn't be surprised," Violet said. "Your Aunt Daisy loved animals."

Daisy's face lit up with an idea. "I want to see a real elephant."

In spite of herself, Violet thought about that day. The peanuts. The crowds. The long line in which they'd waited.

"I'll bet your father would take you to the zoo if you asked him," the widow said, wiping Daisy's hand with a wet cloth.

"Yes," Violet said, "we'll ask Daddy."

"You're a lucky little girl to have such a nice father," the widow said.

"I love Daddy Tommy." Daisy swung Queenie by her front legs.

"So do I, doll baby." Violet's answer sounded hollow. She tried again: "So do I."

"But Queenie's in heaven," Daisy said.

"They have a new elephant," Violet explained, "named Tillie."

Daisy whispered into the elephant's ear. "Do you like

Tillie?" She held the trunk up and listened. "Queenie says yes."

"I'm glad to hear it." Violet got up slowly, walked over to the sink, and started cutting potatoes. "And Tillie has a friend."

"Who's that?" Daisy asked.

"Joshua the donkey." Violet handed Daisy a small, raw, peeled potato to eat. "They came to the zoo together."

"A donkey and an elephant? That's silly."

"It's sweet," the widow said. "They have each other."

"They're different." Daisy took a bite out of her potato. "They don't belong together."

"Why not?" And in that instant, Violet could hear her father say, *Unevenly yoked*. "I think it's good to have all kinds of friends. Remember that."

"I will," Daisy said, hugging Queenie.

The widow listened but said nothing.

Lily had gotten greedy. When her monthly time didn't arrive five days earlier as it should have, hope swelled inside her breasts and belly. Finally, someone to soothe the ache she felt every time she saw Daisy. A baby of her very own to love. When she'd visited her mother and father that morning and found Daisy at the house with that silly elephant, Lily was happy to see the child, but not as a secret daughter for once, rather as a niece who would grow up with the cousin that Lily was carrying. She'd indulged herself with that fantasy until just after dinner, but when she stood up to see George off to yet another meeting, she knew.

Bent over the bathroom sink, Lily added more ammonia to the salted water, then pressed her palms against her eyes to staunch the tears. All that was left now of the bright red blood was a rust-colored outline near the inside seam of her peach silk bloomers. Another soak, scrub, and rinse might eliminate the stain altogether. She'd stand at the basin all night if that was what it took to erase such a glaring reminder of another failure.

But how could this keep happening? She'd put honey in her tea, lay with her husband during every full moon, and ingested countless spoonfuls of Lydia Pinkham's Vegetable Compound because, as the saying went, *There's a baby at the bottom of every bottle*. God was punishing her. This was the price she was paying for abandoning Daisy.

Lily glanced at her reflection in the mirror and fingered the half-inch scar above her right eyebrow, the only lasting trace of the recent car accident. In spite of the gash and no new dress, Abigail Silkman had invited Lily to join the Christian Ladies' Society during their luncheon at the Hotel Jermyn the week after the crash. And since then, Abigail had asked her to attend a lecture they were sponsoring at the Century Club on November 19, eight days away. Lily had taken the invitations as a sign of good fortune. Maybe her penance was over. And then, when she was late, she dared to think her life was finally beginning. Her real life.

*So foolhardy*, she thought, leaning against the bathroom sink, her hands raw from the salt and ammonia, scrubbing away her rust-colored shame.

When Violet drew her bath, she added a cup of hot milk to the water, her mother's trick for soft skin. Tommy had insisted on putting Daisy to bed so Violet could take some time to "settle her nerves." He'd broached the matter as delicately as possible. The accident had probably taken a far greater toll on her than she'd realized. "How could it not?" his mother had asked, as if on cue. Under normal circumstances, Violet would have put an immediate stop to such nonsense, but after talking with the widow that afternoon and seeing the stuffed elephant again, she decided to heed her husband's advice.

Violet turned down the wick on an oil lamp she'd carried in with her. Electrical lighting had its place, but the low flame soothed her in so small a space. She dropped her robe and stepped into the warm tub, grateful Tommy had installed a Pail-a-Day in the cellar, making hot water available on a moment's notice. Such thoughtfulness. Violet's comfort was always at the forefront of Tommy's mind. She appreciated him for that and for so much more.

As Violet sat down, she lifted her long hair, leaned back into the cool porcelain, and dropped her curls over the tub's rolled rim. Stretching her legs forward, she pressed her feet against the opposite end, allowing her slightly bent knees to fall open. Ripples of milky water licked the edges of her body, until the motion dissolved into a quiet stillness. Violet closed her eyes, absorbing the heat, savoring the ache inside her. When the silence threatened to consume her, she splashed water up over her breasts, onto her belly, and between her legs. The runnels trickled back down along the same fleshy paths, stoking the passion that Stanley had ignited in her.

When Violet opened her eyes, she saw light spilling under the bathroom door. Tommy was awake, waiting for her across the hall. She stood up carefully, patted herself dry, slipped on the nightgown her mother had given her on her wedding night, and joined him in their marriage bed.

# C HAPTER TWENTY-THREE

"THAT WAS SOME PERFORMANCE LAST WEEK." Judson Woodberry applauded as Stanley entered Hunold's. The reporter turned and faced Gus behind the bar. "How's this for a headline?" He raised his hand and tapped each word as it hit the air. "*Lawyer Brings Vaudeville to Courthouse.*"

"What'll it be?" Gus asked Stanley as he sat down at the opposite end of the bar.

"A whiskey on me." Judd edged over to Stanley and pulled up a stool next to him.

"A beer," Stanley said. "Trial starts back up at nine o'clock tomorrow. Hoping to wrap it up in the next day or two."

"Well, if this week is as entertaining as the last one," Judd started chuckling, "we're in for a treat."

Stanley accepted his drink without a word and glanced around the dimly lit room at the Monday-night crowd, a dozen or so regulars, and George Sherman Jr. with that girlfriend of his. As he turned back, he saw Ruby emerge from the shadows and walk toward him at the bar.

"Another old-fashioned, Gus." She handed the glass across and sat down on a high stool.

"I was just on my way to see you," Stanley said.

Ruby shrugged. "Have me a night off."

"How's that?" Stanley said as he paid for her drink.

"Got a tip about a raid tonight. Catherine told us all to clear out. Anyways," she said, pointing her glass in Judd's direction, "I want to hear this fella's story."

"You and me both," Gus said.

"I'm surprised you haven't heard it yet." Judd smiled. "Best opening statement I ever witnessed. Do you want to tell it," he said to Stanley, "or should I?"

Stanley drained his beer, pushed it forward, and, in spite of his best effort, cracked half a smile and shook his head. "I don't know what got into me."

"I do," Judd said. "That damn judge started sleeping the moment you opened your mouth. Not much of a union man, I'm afraid." Judd hopped up on his stool. "Stanley begins by explaining how the rights of sixty men from the Von Storch are being trampled. Just then, the judge leans back like this," Judd demonstrated as he spoke, "crosses his arms, and closes his eyes. That doesn't stop Stanley." Judd's eyes widened. "He talks about the families and how they're suffering with their daddies in jail, breadwinners, all of them. He tells the jury these men deserve to be back home in time for the holiday."

"And I meant it. It's already the eighteenth," Stanley said, holding up his empty glass for a refill and nodding for Gus to get Judd a drink as well. "Thanksgiving is only . . ." He stopped to figure.

"Ten days away," Gus said, delivering the beers.

"That's right." Stanley took a sip and shook his head. "It's a disgrace what they're doing to the workingman."

"Get to the good part," Ruby said.

"A few minutes in, the judge, he's still not listening to a word." Judd stopped to take a sip. "So what does this fool do?" He points to Stanley. "He starts in on the chorus of some old labor song."

"Joe Hill's 'There Is Power in a Union,'" Stanley said.

"That's it." Judd started singing to the tune of the old hymn "There Is a Power in the Blood":

*There is pow'r, there is pow'r*
*In a band of workingmen.*
*When they stand hand in hand.*

Stanley joined in and harmonized with Judd:

*That's a pow'r, that's a pow'r*
*That must rule in every land—*
*One Industrial Union Grand . . .*

The two men slapped each other on the back, drained their drinks, and flagged Gus down for two more.

"What did the judge do?" Ruby reached under her skirt and started to roll down one of her stockings.

"Opened his eyes," Stanley said.

"And threatened to charge him with contempt of court." Judd laughed. "Said a night in jail might do his voice some good."

"Can you imagine?" Ruby straightened up. "You in the hoosegow instead of me? What is this world coming to?" She started rolling the other stocking. "How 'bout you unionize all us 'sporting girls'?" she said. "Fair wages for skilled workers."

"You're skilled all right," Stanley gave Ruby a pat on the behind.

"And I will be tomorrow," Ruby smiled, "when I go back to work." She stood up, pecked Stanley on the cheek, picked up her drink, and moved to an empty table a few feet away.

"I don't know what Violet ever saw in you," George said as walked up behind Stanley to get to the bar.

Stanley didn't bother to turn around. "I'm sure her sister would be interested in hearing all about your night out," Stanley said, sitting back down on his stool.

"And I'm sure Violet would like to know all about your little friend." George nodded toward Ruby. "Oh, that's right, she's married now." He peeled a dollar off the top of several bills and laid it down. "To someone else," he said, grabbing his drinks and heading back to Janetta.

"What the hell . . ." Judd started, but Stanley cut him off.

"Tomorrow's a big day. I'm going to finish this beer in peace, then head up to bed."

Judd nodded and moved a few stools down the bar.

Stanley closed his eyes and tried to quiet all the thoughts suddenly competing for his attention. The judge. George Sherman. Ruby. The craving for whiskey.

And Violet.

He'd thought of her nonstop in the five weeks since the accident. His Babcia had noticed. She'd told him to forget about Violet. She reminded him that she was married now. Everyone reminded him of this as if they thought he might forget. And yet, he did forget for a moment. He'd held her in his arms, thinking she was dead, and all of it slipped away. The marriage. Her infidelity. Wiped clean. He loved her and he always would.

Stanley opened his eyes, finished his drink, and motioned for another, just as a rather stout customer entered the bar, took off his coat, and sat down next to Judd.

"Name's Woodberry," the reporter said. "Judson Woodberry, but my friends call me Judd."

"Nice to meet you, Judd." The man extended his hand. "Scranton sure seems like a friendly town."

"Your first time here?" Judd pushed his seat back a bit, away from the man's girth.

"It is," the man said, stroking his beard and looking

around at the crowd. "I hear tell that it's an easy place for a man to find a little . . ." he paused for the right word, "companionship?"

"Over a hundred cathouses at last count." Judd smiled. "If it's companionship you want, you've come to the right town."

"Any recommendations? Someplace clean."

"I'd say Catherine Blair's place, but Ruby over there," Judd pointed toward her table, "said they're closed for the night. Something about a police raid."

"I certainly don't need to get caught up in that." The man turned around, looked Ruby up and down, and nodded. "What are you drinking?" he called over to her.

Ruby looked at the man and dropped her eyes. "I'm drinking alone," she said and turned her back to him.

"I'll make it worth your while," he coaxed. "I have a lovely room at the Mayfair. No chance of a raid there."

"Another time," Ruby said, propping her chin on her hand, as if to shield her face. "I'll hang my shingle out tomorrow night."

The man got down from his stool with his drink in one hand and his coat in the other, and walked over to Ruby's table. "I won't be here tomorrow." He sat down uninvited. "I'm passing through tonight and in need of some affection."

"Like I said," Ruby kept her back to him and eyed the door, "another time."

The man held Ruby's glass up so Gus could see. "We'll take one of these."

"That's very nice of you," Ruby said, "but I was just leaving."

"Stay," the man said. "If nothing else, I could use a little conversation." He pulled out a five-spot and tucked it into Ruby's curled palm.

"That's a lot of cabbage for a little chitchat," Ruby said,

tucking the bill between her breasts. "So what do you want to talk about?" She kept her chair turned so he could only catch her profile.

Gus delivered the old-fashioned to the table and stood uncertainly for a moment. "You let me know if you need anything," he said to Ruby and finally walked back behind the bar.

"How long have you been in this game?" the man asked.

Ruby counted on her fingers. "Almost five years."

"And what put you on this path?"

Ruby laughed. "I was born on this path. Like my mother before me, or so I'm told. It's in the blood."

"What are you, a cop or a Bible thumper?" Stanley called out from his seat at the bar.

"Neither one," Ruby said to Stanley as if she had some personal insight. "I can tell you that."

"Thank you," the man said. "I've always been an inquisitive sort. Helps with my vocation." When Ruby didn't ask the question, the man added, "I spend a good deal of my time on research." He wrapped his foot around the front leg of Ruby's chair, turned her toward him, and leered at her generous bosom. "You're certainly built for this profession."

Now face-to-face, Ruby stared into the man's eyes for several seconds before sliding sideways out of the chair. "I'm calling it a day, Gus." She waved to the barkeep. "And Stanley," she flashed a smile, "you're still my favorite."

The man from the table grabbed hold of Ruby's arm from behind. "Where do you think you're going?" He pulled her back. "I haven't gotten my money's worth."

"Let me go," Ruby replied calmly but firmly, "or I'll break that hand."

Stanley stood up and took a few steps, but he stopped short when Ruby said, "Don't worry. I know how to take care of bullies."

"I'm sorry," the man said, more to Stanley than to Ruby. "Where I come from it's the men who are particular, not the whores." He released his hold on Ruby by pushing her forward a step or two.

"Then maybe you should go back to where you come from," Ruby said, rubbing her arm.

"I've known my share of women," the man laughed as he bent to pick up his coat, "but I have to hand it to you. Scranton prostitutes are some of the most highfalutin I've ever encountered." He came up alongside Ruby and eyed the five-dollar bill in her cleavage.

Stanley stepped around Ruby and faced the outsider. "I wouldn't try it if I were you."

"Defectives and degenerates," the man said, glancing at Stanley's stump, then back at Ruby. "Abominations, the pair of you."

Stanley swung for the man's jaw, misjudged, and caught him in the eye instead. The man, whose bulk kept him on his feet despite the surprise slug, fingered his socket, smiled, and said, "We'll rid the world of your kind yet."

"Next time I'll kill you!" Stanley yelled as the man walked toward the door.

# C HAPTER TWENTY-FOUR

LILY PARKED IN FRONT OF THE CENTURY CLUB on Jefferson Avenue. The night before, she'd arranged to borrow George's LaSalle since hers was still at the garage for repairs. She had no intention of taking the streetcar, and for once, George had agreed with her. Being able to drive distinguished her from other women, and they both liked that. She scanned the invitation once more before slipping it into her purse.

*Christian Ladies' Society Lecture Series*
*Century Club of Scranton*
*Tuesday, November 19, 1935*
*Three O'clock*

According to Abigail, the talk was open to all married women whether or not they were associated with the Christian Ladies' Society. Abigail had promised the speaker a full house, so she'd asked Lily to invite her mother-in-law to come along. "See if you can use your influence," Abigail had said. "We'd love to have her join our little group." Lily agreed to try, but she knew it would be for naught. Her mother-in-law was not a joiner. Mother Sherman only participated in groups she'd either founded or headed.

*The Century Club—what a thrill*, Lily thought as she

climbed the front steps of the brick and limestone building, an example of Colonial Revival architecture, as Abigail had explained. Although Lily was not yet a member of this particular women's group, she hoped to soon be asked. Meantime, since the Christian Ladies' Society had rented out the ballroom for the afternoon talk, she would momentarily experience the pleasure of belonging.

Lily stepped inside and paused, slack-jawed at the beauty of the reception area. Crystal chandeliers, elaborate crown moldings, a winding staircase, huge vases overflowing with flowers in November. And the mirror, an octagonal beauty with beveled glass inside a black and silver frame trimmed with gilt. Her mother-in-law had tried to describe it to Lily days earlier, but nothing could prepare her for such splendor. According to Mother Sherman, the mirror had once hung in a French castle, and seeing it now, Lily believed it.

"Welcome," a gloved girl said, taking Lily's coat and handing her a program. "Enjoy the presentation." Lily thanked her and stepped into the ballroom, another breathtaking sight with its polished wood floors and impossibly high ceilings. A colored man finished setting up the last line of white folding chairs along the back and excused himself as he stepped around Lily.

Abigail needn't have worried, Lily thought as she made her way up the center aisle to an empty seat in the middle of the second row. The ballroom was already three-quarters full, and women were still milling about in the foyer. Once settled, Lily looked around and examined the fashions. Nothing made a woman feel worse about herself than standing out for the wrong reasons. Lily noted with relief that her jade silk jacket dress seemed appropriate for the occasion, stylish but simple. According to the salesclerk who'd waited on her a few days earlier at the Globe Store, simplicity suggested an understated confidence, and Lily needed any kind of confidence she could muster in this new moneyed world. The clerk had also suggested a simple felt hat with a short high-line brim to complete the outfit. Looking around at all the heads, Lily realized the woman had been right. Only a few ladies had something large and fussy on their heads, and they looked out of place compared to the simpler styles most of the women wore.

Directly in front, Irene Silkman, Abigail's mother, stood behind the podium, frantically scribbling notes and occasionally glancing at the empty speaker's chair. Lily hadn't seen Mrs. Silkman for some time, and noticed she'd added at least twenty more pounds to her already taxed five-foot frame. Lily's father had always said, "Look at the mother if you want to know how the daughter will turn out." Lily wondered if that would be true for Abigail. She started to pity the girl, then thought of her own mother, fairly fit for a woman her age. *Better Abigail than me*, Lily concluded.

Mrs. Silkman glanced once more at the empty chair in front of the room before resting her hefty arms on top of the podium and clearing her throat. "Good afternoon." She waited for a few seconds, allowing a couple of stragglers to take seats in the last row. When everyone had settled, she continued: "Welcome to this month's lecture presentation," she squinted at her program, "entitled, 'Social Hygiene: Worthy Women and Their Health.'"

Lily looked around for her own program and realized it had dropped under the seat in front. With the rows squeezed so closely together, she decided she'd wait and retrieve it at the end. "Unfortunately, our guest speaker has been unavoidably detained," she glimpsed her notes, "so we'll adjust the schedule accordingly. First, I'd like to introduce Mrs. Trethaway, secretary for the Christian Ladies' Society. She was my right hand in organizing this event. Mrs. Trethaway."

When a rather tall woman stood up in the front row and bowed her head slightly, the audience applauded.

"Fortunately, Mrs. Trethaway is a trained pianist and has agreed to lead us in a hymn-sing until our guest arrives."

Mrs. Trethaway stepped over to a piano at the front of the room, smoothed her dress, adjusted her feathered hat, and sat down on the bench. Mrs. Silkman remained at the podium and announced the first song, "The Old Rugged Cross."

At Mrs. Silkman's direction, everyone waited until Mrs. Trethaway played the refrain as an introduction. As soon as she finished, the singing began: *"On a hill far away stood an old rugged cross, an emblem of suffering and shame . . ."*

This was such a familiar song that the whole crowd joined in. Their voices rose, many holding to the melody, while the trained among them broke off into complementary harmonies.

Just as Mrs. Trethaway launched into the second verse, the door at the back of the room slowly opened. A bearded man with a bruised left eye quietly stepped into the room. He folded his hands across his broad stomach and waited. Relief washed over Mrs. Silkman's face, and she signaled Mrs. Trethway to finish up after that verse. As soon as the singing ended, the gentleman addressed the crowd from the back of the ballroom, startling more than a few of the women who hadn't noticed him enter. "Don't stop on my account, ladies. You sing like angels."

Lily craned her neck at the familiar voice and watched in horror as Dr. Peters headed toward the front of the room.

# CHAPTER TWENTY-FIVE

AS THE NOON WHISTLE SOUNDED at the Lace Works, Violet pinned her last shirt to the clothesline. In less time than it would take for the wash to dry, she could get to town on the streetcar and back again. In another hour it would be Daisy's nap time, so it wouldn't put Mother Davies out too much to watch the child. And if it did, there was always her own mother, though if Violet asked her to mind Daisy, she might suggest they all go to town together, and that would not do. God forgive her, but Violet didn't have the patience for her mother's bad legs or her daughter's penchant for standing outside the Globe Store's windows, admiring every item on display. Violet had spent the last five weeks recovering from the accident with everyone buzzing around her, and though her ribs were still tender, she wanted to be on her own this afternoon.

And it had nothing to do with the fact that Stanley worked and lived downtown. Violet could easily steer clear of the courthouse and the room he rented, and she intended to do just that. She had no interest in such distractions. She'd even turned down Lily's invitation to the Century Club. Any other time, she would have been eager to see such a grand building, but not today. She'd been grappling with guilt ever since she'd had marital relations with Tommy a week earlier, and she needed to be alone to sort out her feelings.

Violet stood in the yard thinking about that night. Because of her ribs Tommy had been careful with her. Attentive. Deliberate. "Does this hurt?" he'd asked at first, gently caressing her breasts with his calloused fingers. When she shivered her response, he continued his unhurried exploration at the nape of her neck, the crook of her arm, the inside of her thighs. The lips in between. After a while, he stopped asking questions and heeded her body as it rose and fell, shuddering with a fire she'd never known before. Just at the moment when she thought she might get lost forever in the delicious blur of euphoria and pain, he pulled her on top, guiding her hips as she drew him inside, deeper and deeper, until they both exploded into brilliant flames.

It wasn't until the next morning, when Daisy came into the kitchen carrying Stanley's elephant, that Violet was struck with an ugly truth: she'd encouraged Tommy to stoke a fire ignited by another man.

"Mama!" Daisy yelled from the back porch, startling Violet at the clothesline. "Grandma Davies says to say . . ." She paused to poke her head inside the door and turned back to her mother. "She says to say—it's quittin' time, let's eat!"

Violet swallowed hard and worked up a smile. "Well, thank you for that kind invitation. Please tell your grandmother I'll be right in."

"She'll be right in!" Daisy stayed put, running her foot back and forth along the spindles on the porch railing.

Violet bent forward and dabbed the corners of her eyes with her sleeve before calling out, "Let's eat!" She crossed the yard and took Daisy's hand. "I don't know about you, but I'm as hungry as a bear." She pretended to take a bite out of her daughter's arm.

"I'm a hungry horse," Daisy replied, galloping past the screen door and into the kitchen.

* * *

"I'll do those," Tommy's mother said as Violet gathered the dirty lunch dishes. When Violet started to object, Mother Davies waved her away with a dish towel. "I mean it. I want you to take it easy with those ribs."

"Nonsense," Violet said. "I'm almost as good as new." Holding her side, she inhaled deeply like a swimmer preparing to go under. "I could use a favor though."

"Name it." Mother Davies scraped the plates, saving the little girl's uneaten bread crusts for the birds.

"Will you mind Daisy for a few hours?" Her well-rehearsed reasons lined up at the starting gate and took off running. "There's a sale. On fabric. At the Globe Store. Fifty percent off." She paused to breathe.

"Can't pass that up." Mother Davies rolled her sleeves and started in on the dishes. "As long as you think you're up to it."

"Daisy's growing up so fast. And she could use a new dress."

"Of course."

"And Tommy has a pair of pants that need mending."

"Uh huh."

"I need some matching thread." The last excuse out.

Mother Davies handed the crusts to Daisy, who threw them off the porch before running back inside. "That's fine, dear."

"Can't afford not to go, really. Fifty percent off. They're practically giving it away."

"Practically."

"Unless you think I should stay close to home today. Maybe I better stick around."

"I'm not thinking anything of the kind, dear. It would do you good, so long as you're up to it. Daisy and I will be just fine, won't we, sweetheart?" She patted the girl's head and turned to the dishes.

Daisy shrugged and draped herself over her mother's arm. "I want to go with you."

Violet mindlessly stroked her daughter's hair. "I'll be there and back before you know it."

"In fact," Mother Davies looked at the pair, "I'll bet today would be a perfect day for cookies. If only I had a helper."

Daisy's head popped up. "Me!"

"You?" Mother Davies eyed the little girl as if sizing her up for a new wardrobe. "Let's give it a whirl," she finally said.

Violet untied her apron and folded it over the chair. "Well, if you're really sure," she said, and headed toward the bedroom to change into something more appropriate for town.

Twenty minutes later, she walked out the door in a black wool coat over the bright red dress she'd worn several Christmases ago. Her hair was freshly brushed, and she had a touch of rouge on each cheek.

As soon as Violet stepped foot on the sidewalk, she noticed the widow waving to her from across the street. "How are you, dear? I was just coming to see you."

"Much better," Violet called back without crossing over. "On my way to town," she glanced at her own mother's house next door, hoping she hadn't heard, "but I'll stop by soon to say hello." She waved her hand as if both women had agreed to this arrangement and started down the hill toward the square.

*How awful*, Violet thought. *Just awful*. The widow had been like a second mother to her all these years, and suddenly Violet couldn't spare ten minutes to talk with her? Shameful, that's what it was. Though ten minutes with the widow would turn into two hours, and that was God's honest truth. Besides, Violet reasoned as she turned the corner onto North Main Avenue, she couldn't be expected to drop everything she needed to do on a moment's notice. Not even for an old friend. In fact, it would be selfish for the woman to think otherwise, and if she had anything to say on the matter, Violet would tell her about it the next time she saw her. Violet had a child to think about and a husband. What responsibilities did the widow have these days?

None, Violet thought as she approached the square. No husband to fuss over. No children to tend to. For as much as Stanley stopped by to see her—and that wasn't often—the widow may as well have been alone in the world. And Violet had just dismissed this poor soul with the wave of a hand. What was wrong with her these days? Violet stopped to consider whether she ought to return and apologize, but just then the streetcar pulled up, and she stepped on. She'd say her sorry tomorrow. The widow would understand.

Violet slipped coins into the box and found an empty seat toward the back. Seeing the widow naturally pulled Violet's mind back to this business with Stanley. It was nonsense, really. All of this silly dwelling on lost love. After all, she'd had a concussion, and that sort of injury was bound to unsettle her, jumble her mind a bit. Stanley was in the past, and that's where he would stay. She should have been honest with him from the start, but that was a long time ago. Too long. Nothing she could do about it now, and even if she could, what good would it do? Tommy knew the truth and that's what mattered. He was her husband. She owed Stanley nothing. Stanley had judged her at the train station as she stood with the baby in her arms before she could even open her mouth.

She stepped off the streetcar in front of the Globe Store, so heated with anger all over again that she thought she might give him a piece of her mind. The day of the accident

Stanley had told her that he loved her. Given that she was
married now, such behavior was inexcusable, and frankly,
too little too late. He'd had five years to say those words,
but instead, he'd thrown away his chance, along with her
heart. If she ran into him today, she might tell him just that.

By the time Violet finished her shopping—four yards
of fabric and a new spool of thread—she was thoroughly
convinced that she needed to set the record straight. She'd
called him "my love" but she'd been in a state, her head
concussed from the accident; she wanted to make sure he
understood that. She didn't love him; not in a way that mattered. In fact, as she carried her packages down Wyoming
Avenue, past several streetcar stops in the direction of Hunold's somewhere in the Alleys, she almost laughed at the
thought—such foolishness, and from a married woman. No,
she simply needed to lay the whole matter to rest with Stanley. And since she was already downtown, it was as good
a day as any. Even Tommy would understand, though she
doubted she would ever tell him. No need to stir that pot.

Lost in thought, Violet didn't realize she'd found Stanley's alley until she looked up and saw the *Hunold's Beer
Garden* sign hanging on a post in the yard. A notice on the
front door read, *Rooms to Let*. She transferred her packages
to one hand and finger-combed her hair. *What now?* She
peered around the side of the building and saw a sign reading, *Ladies' Entrance*, but Violet hadn't been in a bar since
she was a child looking for her father.

She walked up to the window, hoping to catch a glimpse
of the patrons inside, but all she saw was her own image.
The red dress under the open coat looked garish in the afternoon sun. Suddenly consumed with shame, she said out
loud, "What am I doing?" Several blocks away, the clock at
the courthouse rang three p.m.

Panic set in as Violet looked up and down the alley to

find her bearings. The houses tried too hard and not at all. They'd been drenched in colors loud enough to clobber the eyes, but that had been years earlier, long before glimpses of weathered boards had muddied the palette. Women, just as loud and weathered, posed in doorways and windows, luring men inside the iron fences and past the occasional dog.

Across the way, a woman called over, "Honey, you lost?"

Now trembling, Violet turned toward the voice, trying to determine where it came from. "Over here!" the woman called again from the first floor of a bright green house which looked like an evening gown that had sat too long in a dirty attic. She waved her fingers through a partially opened window and laughed. "I knowed you didn't belong here soon as I seen you."

Violet pulled her packages tightly to her chest and willed her feet to move, but they remained fixed on the sidewalk.

"Go back the way you come!" the woman yelled over. "You'll see a yellow house on the corner with a red door. Streetcar'll pick you up on the other side."

Knowing which direction to take seemed to liberate Violet's legs. She managed a hushed "Thank you" and hurried down the alley as fast as her ribs would allow. A yellow house with a red door stood on the corner, and across the road, a sign on an electric pole marked a streetcar stop.

Relief washed over her as she settled onto a bench near the sign and waited. If the streetcar came along in the next quarter hour, she'd have plenty of time to get home and start dinner. No one would be the wiser except Violet herself who promised never, God as her witness, to succumb to such foolishness again.

She glanced up at the alley and realized she could not see Hunold's from that distance. Just as well. Violet shook her head, and her eye caught hold of something familiar—

Stanley, of all people, climbing the front porch steps of the yellow house, kneading his handless arm. *Must be getting ready to rain,* she thought. *He always does that when it's going to rain.*

Impulsively and without regard to sense or propriety, Violet shot up from the bench, holding her rib cage and darted across the street. When she reached the other side, she opened her mouth to call Stanley's name but caught herself just as the red door squeaked open.

"Don't just stand there," a voice said from the threshold. "Give Ruby a big kiss."

"*Concedentibus ad victorem per pertinent spolia.*" Stanley pulled the woman onto the front porch. The kiss was fervent, wild. "To the victor belong the spoils," he said, and started dancing her around.

Violet tried to back away but something held her in place.

"My reward," Stanley said, dipping the woman who was laughing, her long red hair dangling behind her, "for winning the case."

Violet watched in stunned disbelief as Stanley buried his face in Muriel Hartwell's fiery red curls.

# C HAPTER TWENTY-SIX

AT THE SOUND OF DR. PETERS'S VOICE, Lily tugged on her hat, but the shortened brim offered little in the way of concealment. She dropped her hands onto her lap and lowered her eyes. *Dear Lord,* she thought, slouching in her seat, *I'm about to be exposed in front of the whole town.* Her breath caught in her throat and stayed there, as if it too needed to hide.

Dr. Peters finally reached the front of the ballroom, his heavy footsteps a counterpoint to the rustle of skirts on either side. "A fine group of virtuous women," he said, looking around the crowd.

Mrs. Silkman smiled, adjusted the podium, and began to speak. "On behalf of the Christian Ladies' Society, I'd like to welcome Dr. Edward Peters to the Century Club." The doctor mindlessly stroked his beard while muffled applause rose from the gloved audience.

Lily held up her hands reflexively, as if to clap, but they simply remained aloft, frozen like a frame around her horrified expression.

"We're honored to have such an esteemed gentleman in our presence." Mrs. Silkman reached for the pair of eyeglasses that dangled from a chain at her bosom and curled them over her ears. "Let me see," she said, thumbing through note cards. "I had his credentials here a minute ago."

"Please don't go to any trouble," Dr. Peters said to Mrs. Silkman. "I'll be happy to introduce myself." The left side of his mouth started a smile that stalled out before it ever got going.

"There it is!" Mrs. Silkman picked a wayward note card off the top of the piano and waved it at Mrs. Trethaway whose fingers rested gently on the keys. "Someone must have moved it on me." The pianist bristled, stood, and returned to her seat in the first row.

Mrs. Silkman started again: "Dr. Peters received his medical degree from the University of Pennsylvania. He dedicated the first twelve years of his career to serving the poor unfortunates at Philadelphia's Good Shepherd Infant Asylum, where he delivered countless illegitimate children into this world. He currently practices medicine at Hahnemann Hospital and is a founding member of the American Eugenics Society. It is indeed an honor to welcome Dr. Peters as today's guest lecturer."

After another round of gloved applause, Dr. Peters took his place behind the podium, and Mrs. Silkman sat down next to Mrs. Trethaway. "Thank you, Mrs. Silkman. I'm humbled by your generous introduction. Good afternoon, ladies, and thank you for your kind attention." He worked at a smile and had better luck this time.

Lily kept her head down but allowed her eyes to mark the distance from her chair to the aisle, and the aisle to the door. Why had she insisted on sitting in the middle of the second row? Pride, she thought. And if Violet had accompanied her, as she should have, she would have said as much. And they surely would have taken less prominent seats. Lily counted—five pairs of stockinged legs including the two tree trunks next to her poking out from under Mrs. Jordan's skirt. Even if she could press past them, then what? March back up the aisle and out the door as if she were ill? That sort of behavior would draw all sorts of attention.

"Today's lecture," Dr. Peters pulled several rolled sheets of paper from his vest pocket and smoothed them out on the podium, "is entitled, 'Creating Heaven on Earth,' but I must confess, as I look over this crowd, I feel as though I've already arrived in God's Kingdom. It's a privilege to stand before such wholesome ladies. The bloodlines in Scranton are strong: the Watresses, the Lynotts, the Silkmans, and all the God-fearing families that are represented before me."

Mrs. Silkman nodded at Mrs. Trethaway as if to acknowledge the inclusion of her own surname and the absence of the pianist's.

"It's refreshing to see such strong bodies, minds, and characters." He abandoned his notes on the podium and stepped into the aisle.

Lily hooked an index finger over her nose, draping the rest of her hand over her mouth and chin. She glanced once more at Mrs. Jordan's thick legs, and determined that she definitely could not push past without creating a scene.

"Before I go any further, I must apologize for my lateness," he pointed to his bruised left eye, "and in the process, explain my unsightly injury. As is my habit, I arrived a day in advance of my speaking engagement. After settling into the Mayfair Hotel, I walked the streets of Scranton in an effort to get to know her better."

The Mayfair? Lily's Mayfair? The hotel where George proposed? Where Lily and George had their marriage supper and for the first time shared a bed as man and wife? Lily didn't dare look into Dr. Peters's face, but she lifted her eyes to his hands. Those liver-spotted hands. They'd soiled everything she loved. Daisy. The Christian Ladies' Society. And now the Mayfair.

"May I say," Dr. Peters took a few steps back and returned to the podium, "your Masonic Temple is a marvel that can rival any of the best architecture in Philadelphia. A testament to the human spirit in these difficult times."

A murmur of agreement passed through the crowd like a rumor.

"But as I meandered back to the hotel, I happened upon such a shameful sight that I could not believe my eyes." He paused as if to prepare his audience for the shock to come. "Houses of ill repute—full city blocks of them."

Most of the ladies nodded in agreement, but a few of them gasped at the nature of the speaker's words. Lily used this opportunity to cover her face with both hands, as if overcome with emotion.

"I found this to be as upsetting as you do, young lady." Dr. Peters stepped out from behind the podium, pulled a handkerchief from of his breast pocket, and handed it to Lily. When she reached out to receive it, their eyes met briefly, but he showed no sign of recognition.

Was it possible that he didn't remember her? Did she dare to hope? He'd delivered hundreds, if not thousands, of babies at the Good Shepherd. And that was years ago. Maybe he had forgotten her. She touched a hand to her permanently waved hair and glanced once more at her silk dress. She was a different person altogether. He'd briefly known an awkward sixteen-year-old girl named Lily Morgan, but now she was a prominent member of society, Mrs. George Sherman.

"In fact," he continued, remaining in place, "so distressed was I by this corruption, I foolishly went out to one of these bawdy houses this morning, hoping to convince some of the women to repent. Instead, I received a blow to the face," he fingered his bruise, "from one of those so-called Johns."

A sharp cry of sympathy rose up from the audience.

"I'll be fine." The doctor smiled and patted his heart. "But I wish I could say the same for your fair city. After my

assault, I made my way to a police station and filed a report."
He stepped back and addressed the entire audience. "It was
there that I learned of the other Scranton, a city where lar-
ceny, games of chance, prostitution, and even cold-blooded
murder have increased two-fold in the last few years. Your
policemen are so overwhelmed by the volume of crime it's a
wonder women feel safe in their homes anymore, let alone
on the streets."

"Amen to that!" someone shouted from the back row.
Probably Pentecostal. Most likely there by invitation rather
than as a member, Lily thought, without turning around.

"Amen indeed," Dr. Peters went on. "For although I'm
not here to preach, what I have to offer today are God-
inspired solutions for these troubling times. And may I say
this moral crisis is not limited to Scranton, Pennsylvania.
Indeed, crime is running rampant across our great nation,
and in order to stop its advance, in order to create a heaven
on earth, people with moral fortitude must take up the
mantle."

Lily folded the handkerchief and slowly raised her head.
Hiding, she decided, made her more of a spectacle. She'd try
for a semblance of interest, though she wouldn't dare meet
the doctor's eyes again, and she'd slip out with the rest of
the crowd as soon as he was finished. She hated the plan but
could see no other way. And she hated this man in front of
her because he had the power to ruin her.

"*But Dr. Peters, you say, we're only women. What can
we possibly do for the cause?* More than you know, ladies. According to the American Philosophical Society," he
glanced at his notes, "eighty-nine percent of crime is due to
heredity. Eighty-nine percent! I've seen what happens when
the feebleminded reproduce—generation after generation of
imbeciles. The same holds true for the depraved. Defects, be
they physical, mental, or spiritual, are perpetuated through

procreation. The Apostle Mark writes of Judas, *It would be better for him if he had not been born,* and the same can be said of any man or woman who is defective."

About half of the audience nodded in agreement. The rest appeared to be giving the matter serious consideration. Trapped in her seat, Lily half-listened to the doctor, wondering how it was she'd never prepared for the possibility of being exposed. Would George honor his marriage vows if she were found out? Her immoral past would certainly give him grounds for divorce.

"God never intended for defectives to survive. Before medical advances, nature used to dispense of them in the womb or upon birth. Careful breeding is God's design. Would a farmer mate a two-headed cow? I hardly think so."

"He'd be drummed out of town if he tried!" someone shouted—another nonmember, to be sure.

"No doubt," Dr. Peters chuckled. "And when your husband buys a horse, what is his first question? *Can you tell me about the bloodline?* He'd be a fool not to ask. I hate to say it, ladies, but we put more thought into the bloodlines of livestock than babies."

A sea of hatted heads nodded.

"Bloodlines matter. Science proves me out on this point, but more importantly, so does the Bible. That's why Matthew tells us that Abraham begat Isaac, who begat Jacob, who begat Judas, who begat Phares, who begat Esrom, who begat Aram. Need a few more? Aminadab begat Naasson, who begat Salmon, who begat Booz of Rachab, who begat Obed, who begat Jesse, who begat David the King, who begat—" He stopped and offered the women a turn.

"Solomon," they said in unison.

"I can always count on good Christian women to know their Bible. And fourteen more begats after that one gets you all the way to Jesus Christ, our Lord and Savior, God's only begotten son. Bloodlines matter. So when someone says to me, *Dr. Peters, Christ's beginnings were humble. He was born in a stable, after all,* I simply say what every eugenicist says, *His ancestors were kings."*

Several women pulled fans from their purses as if this were an old-fashioned, put-some-color-in-your-cheeks revival.

Lily's fear took a step back to make room for indignation. This should never be happening. The widow had arranged for Lily to go to Philadelphia so she could leave her secret behind. Instead, Violet insisted on bringing that secret home, raising her as her own. But in spite of Violet's selfishness, Lily had made a life for herself, a good life, an enviable life, though not a perfect one. She hadn't given George a child yet, but she was young. God might still give her a baby. Then all would be complete. She had that hope. At least she'd had that hope until Dr. Peters showed up and threatened to destroy everything she'd built.

"Bloodlines matter." Dr. Peters paused to smooth out his notes again. "And it's up to you, fair women of Scranton, to take up the cause in your own homes. As the good book says, *Be fruitful and multiply.* It's your duty as wholesome women to populate this city with the best and brightest of our race. *Our* race," he repeated, punctuating that first word with a nod. "Keep our strongest bloodlines going. Help create heaven on earth."

"Heaven on earth," the Pentecostal woman repeated, and at least half of the ladies, many of them members, shouted, "Amen!"

"But this is not our only step. In order to rid our communities of the criminal element—a criminal element that I've witnessed personally in Scranton this very day—dear ladies, you must spread the word. No one but the physically, mentally, and spiritually fit should be allowed to marry and procreate, giving us offspring worthy of our attention."

*What rubbish,* Lily thought, picturing her beautiful Daisy. In spite of her inauspicious beginnings, she was as worthy as any child. So perfect. So pure. And not only Daisy. Lily thought about the other babies she'd seen at the Good Shepherd. Who was Dr. Peters to say they weren't decent just because they'd been conceived in sin? That was a burden for the mothers, not the children. And what about the mothers? It was up to God to judge, not Dr. Peters.

"Keep in mind," the doctor continued, "many states already place limitations on the marriage rite. They recognize the evils of race-crossing and the poor mulatto children born of those unholy unions. They understand the dangers of first cousins reproducing. How is what I'm proposing any different? It is not. Therefore, we need to render all defectives sterile, for our sake and theirs."

*Render them sterile? Ridiculous,* Lily thought. No man in his right mind would propose such an outlandish idea. Yet something about Dr. Peters had never sat right with her, even back at the Good Shepherd. She'd thought it was simply because she associated him with such a dark time, but now she wondered if there was more to it. Maybe the man was truly crazy.

"I have a pamphlet here from the Human Betterment Foundation entitled, 'The Effects of Sterilization As Practiced in California,' listing the benefits of what I'm suggesting. According to the foundation, sterilization prevents parenthood while allowing the defective patient to still perform matrimonial duties." Dr. Peters picked up his glasses and read word for word: *"Sterilization is a protection, not a punishment. It is approved by the patients, their families, medical staff, social workers, and probation officers. Sterilization protects children from being brought up by mentally deficient parents, and takes a great burden off the taxpayers. It has been followed by a marked decrease in sex of-*

*fenses. It is a practical and necessary step to prevent racial deterioration."*

*This man is deranged,* Lily thought. She turned toward Mrs. Jordan to say just that, and discovered that she was listening to Dr. Peters as if he were announcing the Second Coming. In fact, as Lily glanced around, most of the women near her seemed to be taking his words to heart.

Dr. Peters laid his glasses on the podium and lowered his voice. The audience leaned forward. "I need you to spread this message, ladies. I need you to talk to your husbands. Encourage them to speak to their legislators. Scranton is a common-sense city, and I'm here to offer a common-sense solution to its growing troubles."

Lily shifted in her seat, appalled by the doctor's message and the crowd's response.

"And be assured, sterilization is quite simple. Very effective methods have been developed specifically for women who are wanton or feebleminded. Surgical sterilization renders a woman 100 percent infertile."

"No woman in her right mind would agree to that!" As soon as the words flew out of Lily's mouth, all eyes were on her.

"You hit the nail on the head, my dear. No woman in her *right* mind." He smiled. "There are times when sterilization needs to occur without a patient's consent. That's why our counterparts in Europe have developed less conspicuous methods to be performed immediately after labor, for those times when it's impractical to put a nonconsenting woman to sleep."

Lily couldn't help herself; the words kept overruling her good judgment. "And are these methods legal?"

"Not in all states. Not yet." He paused and smiled, giving that last word its full weight. "Presently, it's inadvisable to engage in such practices without the weight of the law for protection. That said, I'm confident that any doctor brave enough to take up this fight has God's law behind him."

Perspiration glossed Lily's brow as the truth worked its way to the surface of her mind. "And have you, Dr. Peters, been brave enough to perform these less-conspicuous methods?"

"Many times," the doctor nodded confidently, "many times."

# CHAPTER TWENTY-SEVEN

ANOTHER STREETCAR HESITATED IN FRONT OF VIOLET, the third one in the hour since Stanley had disappeared inside the yellow house. When she made no attempt to board, the conductor accelerated toward a better neighborhood. The courthouse clock chimed four, but Violet seemed indifferent. She sat on the bench, her eyes fixed on the red door, unable to go home. Not yet. *Give Ruby a big kiss.* Ruby, not Muriel. But Muriel all the same.

In a brothel.

Violet wondered at the improbability of it. Had they only just met? Had he known her in Philadelphia? What was waiting for Muriel back home, after she'd given birth at the Good Shepherd, that made running away and selling herself a better option? Violet pitied the girl and hated her just the same.

Stanley in the arms of a whore.

Violet recoiled, as if she'd just fired a hard-kicking rifle. Both the ugliness of that word and the ease with which she'd conjured it sickened her. "Forgive me my sins, Lord." She thought about Muriel standing on the porch. "And forgive Muriel hers."

As for Stanley, he didn't deserve one more minute of Violet's attention. Not the way he was carrying on. He looked so happy in Muriel's arms.

Had Violet ever made him that happy?

She thought about their courtship, so innocent, so long ago. She remembered the day she'd looked out the window at Walsh's Portrait Studio and saw Stanley across the street. *Could it be?* she had thought. Was he on his way over to see her? She scrubbed the blue and yellow dye off her fingers, casualties of a grassy green she'd mixed for a photograph she was coloring, and made it to the door just in time to see him eating the peanuts Mr. Walsh had left for customers to give to Queenie. How that had made her laugh. She smiled at the memory. And cried.

She hated Stanley. And she loved him.

No longer one or the other, but some altogether new emotion, a grassy green mixed from blue and yellow jars.

The clock at the courthouse rang once to mark the quarter hour. Fifteen minutes after four o'clock. Tommy would be home by six and hungry for a hot supper. Tommy Davies, the boy next door who'd always loved her, who'd stood with her at Stanley's bedside when he'd lost his hand in the mine. The one who'd asked her to marry him, in spite of the ugly rumors. The man who loved her child as his own. No one else had ever had such faith in her, shown her so much devotion. So why was she sitting on a bench waiting for another man?

Stanley Adamski knew every secret she'd ever had— except one. The first time they'd met, he saved her from that bully Evan Evans, or more precisely, from the elderberry bush where Evan had pushed her at the start of third grade. From that moment on, Stanley was always by her side, whether they were playing hooky or selling apples. And when they fell in love, he promised her the world. A house to call her own. A comfortable way of life. A position of respect in the community. "Just name it," he'd said, "and it's yours." She'd never want for anything, if only she'd wait for him. So many promises, and all so long ago.

Stanley made promises. But Tommy kept them. Stanley had judged her without mercy before he'd had the facts. Tommy had forgiven her.

Violet gathered her packages and watched for the next streetcar to take her home where she belonged.

The red door opened. Stanley walked out of the house, alone at first, but Ruby caught up with him before he'd reached the steps, her cherry kimono fluttering, exposing a creamy chemise. "Forget something?" She laughed, holding out his wallet. "Lucky for you I'm mostly honest."

Stanley seemed not to hear her. Rather, he stood frozen at the edge of the porch, staring. Muriel tracked his gaze to the other side of the street. "Violet Morgan?" The surprise in Ruby's voice softened: "I always wondered if our paths would cross again." She waved once before pulling her kimono closed.

Violet raised her hand, but her fingers buckled. She remained seated on the bench.

Stanley looked back and forth between the two women. "You know her?" he said to Ruby.

"I did." Ruby's face grew pensive as she shivered in the cold November air. "When we were both passing through Philly."

"Oh," Stanley said, his voice dropping. "The baby."

"You know?"

"Yes." He nodded toward Violet. "They live in my old neighborhood. I see the girl in the yard sometimes."

"A girl?"

"Yes. Daisy." Stanley maintained his vigil near the railing.

"So she kept it after all." Ruby smiled. "Good for her." She tucked Stanley's wallet into his jacket pocket. "I didn't think Lily had it in her. A nice girl though."

Stanley turned and looked at Ruby, then back to Violet. "*Lily?* You mean Violet," he said.

"I mean Lily. The one who got knocked up."

"Lily?" Stanley turned around and faced Ruby.

Her hand flew to her mouth. "You said you knew."

"I knew *Violet* came home with a baby. And everything changed between us."

"Violet?"

"Yes."

"And what did she tell you?" Ruby walked up to the railing and looked across the street.

"I never asked." His words came out in a choked whisper.

Ruby nudged Stanley's arm. "Maybe it's time you did," she said, and sauntered back inside the house.

Stanley crossed the street and sat down on the bench next to Violet. Without saying a word, he took her hand, then let it go for propriety's sake as another streetcar rolled by. "Why didn't you tell me that Daisy isn't yours?"

"Bite your tongue." Color rushed to Violet's cheeks.

"You know what I mean."

"She's every bit my daughter."

"I'm sorry. I just . . ." Stanley's face twisted with frustration. "It should have come from you, not Ruby."

"What difference would it have made?" Violet stood up and rubbed her arms for warmth.

"All the difference." Stanley looked around. "I don't want to do this here." He waved for Violet to follow him as he headed over to Hunold's. "No one will see us," he said, pointing out a back staircase that led to his room above the gin mill. "I promise. I'd never risk your reputation."

The reputation he'd come to value again in the last half hour, Violet thought, as she followed him upstairs without a word. As soon as she stepped inside his room, she was saddened by the loneliness it radiated. A bed, two dressers, a table and chairs in the corner. All serviceable, but where was the warmth? Stanley pulled a chair to the center of the room for Violet to sit, and from that vantage point, she could see his artificial hand peeking out from a partially opened closet. In all the years he'd owned it, Violet had never seen him wear it, and yet, he could never let it go.

Stanley dragged a second chair out and sat down. "I love you. I've always loved you." He took her hand. "Even when I hated you, I loved you."

"What about Muriel?" Violet asked, pulling her hand away and resting it on her lap.

"Who?"

"Ruby." She said the name slowly, trying to reconcile it and the person she'd seen today with the girl she'd known at the Good Shepherd. "I saw the two of you together." Violet dropped her eyes.

"Ruby's a friend, but that's it." He looked confused for a moment. "She's not the kind of girl you fall in love with."

Violet looked at his face and realized he meant it. She said the first words that came to mind: "I'm sorry to hear that." Saints and sinners—that's how Stanley viewed women. She could see that now. Violet was back to being a saint, but for how long?

"I love you," Stanley said again. "It's always been you."

Violet folded her hands. "Not enough to get past Daisy."

"How do you know?" Stanley's voice cracked. "You never gave me a chance."

"The chance was yours to give the moment I stepped off that train." She saw his face again that day, the disappointment in his expression.

"With a baby in your arms. Honestly, what did you expect?"

"I expected you to hear me out. To not pass judgment."

She looked at him and realized they were both reliving the past: The shock of her return. The argument. Their parting. They would relive it for the rest of their lives.

"You should have made me listen."

Violet considered this for a moment. Perhaps she had allowed her pride to get the best of her. "Maybe."

"And now?"

"And now I have Daisy."

"We'll take her with us." Stanley shot up and started pacing between the half-open closet with his prosthetic hand and a dresser with a half-empty bottle of whiskey on top. "We'll move to Philadelphia like we always said we would."

"And Tommy?" She twisted the gold band on her finger.

"Say that you love me." He stopped and kissed the top of her head. "No one else matters as long as you love me."

"He loves Daisy." Violet's eyes glistened.

"*I* can love Daisy." Stanley nodded as he said the words.

"Tommy already does."

"So that's it?" He sat back down and looked directly at Violet. "You give up everything for her?"

Violet kept her eyes lowered. "That's what mothers do."

"Not Lily."

"She's not a mother." Although Violet had said the words out of anger, she heard their sadness when they hit the air.

"No." Stanley kicked back his chair, punctuating his sentiment. "Because you never let that happen."

"What are you saying?"

"I'm saying, why hold Lily responsible for her behavior when you can play the martyr? You've sacrificed everything for that child. It's what you do. First Lily, now Daisy. Look at Violet Morgan," he singsonged, "putting everyone else's needs before her own."

"Davies." Her back and her tone stiffened.

"Yes, Davies." He pushed his words through gritted teeth. "Leave it to you to marry the only other living saint in Scranton."

"I'm going." Violet stood up and buttoned her coat.

"Wait. I'm sorry." Stanley lowered his voice: "I just want to make you happy. It's all I've ever wanted."

Violet remained standing but didn't move. "We don't always get what we want."

"Not always, but sometimes. You just can't see it. You're too busy punishing yourself like you always do. And we both know why."

Violet's hands flew to her ears. "Stop it right now."

"You've spent your whole life trying to make up for your sister's death, but it wasn't your fault." Stanley stood up and circled the floor as he spoke. "You have nothing to make up for. For God's sake, stop paying for other people's sins. Follow your heart for once in your life."

"Daisy is my heart." Violet glared at Stanley.

"That can't be enough."

"So I should wash my hands of her? Give her back to Lily?" Violet's voice rose in pitch. "Here you go." She lifted her hands as if tossing something in the air.

"You don't have the right to get angry!" Stanley was shouting now. "I'm the one who never knew the truth!"

Violet continued her own conversation: "I'm off to follow my heart."

"You threw everything away and for what?" Stanley said, glancing sidelong at the bottle of whiskey.

"Or better yet, maybe I can turn back time and leave her at the Good Shepherd. That way you and Lily and everyone else in town can pretend she was never born. Wash away the sin, or at least hide it in another city. That would certainly make life easier for everyone, wouldn't it?" When Stanley didn't answer, Violet pressed: "Well, wouldn't it? Be honest. It's what you're thinking. It's what everyone thinks. Life would be a cinch if Daisy weren't here. Love would be easy. Just say it. Say it!"

"Yes."

Any pity Violet might have felt for Stanley evaporated. She knew she'd wrung that syllable out of him, but he'd uttered it nonetheless, and that was his doing. "So that's how you feel."

"I didn't mean—"

"You listen to me, Stanley Adamski. Taking a drink is easy. Paying a . . ." Muriel's face flashed in Violet's head, and the word *whore* dried up and blew away. "Paying someone like Ruby is easy. Love is not easy. Love is patience and sacrifice. Love is taking another man's child into your heart with a fierceness that can't be contained. It's worshipping a woman, in spite of the fact that the whole town calls her a sinner. It's standing up to people every single day without regard for your own reputation. It's . . ." Violet hesitated. "It's Tommy." Astounded by that truth, she took a few steps back and leaned against the wall.

It was Tommy who loved Daisy without question, and Violet without judgment. Tommy, who always put their needs first. Who built a porch swing in the hopes of courting her, long before she'd ever thought of saying yes. Who carried Daisy on his shoulders every night so she could be closer to the stars. Who shoveled the coal and took out the ashes from his own cellar and the one next door when her father could no longer do it for himself. Who woke her with a single kiss. Who trembled in front of her nakedness. Who considered himself to be the luckiest man in Scranton, long before he knew the real the circumstances of Daisy's birth.

All at once Violet knew: she loved Tommy.

"I'm sorry," she said to Stanley. She wanted to run out of there and into the arms of her husband. She had to tell him that she loved him, and that this truth mattered more than any other. The courthouse clock rang out half past five. "I have to get home to Tommy," she said, and walked out the door.

# C HAPTER TWENTY-EIGHT

WHEN THE DOCTOR CONCLUDED HIS LECTURE, Irene Silkman pushed herself up and led the audience in a final round of applause. "Dr. Peters will be returning to his hotel room shortly. He has another speaking engagement later this evening and needs his rest. If you'd like to offer your personal thanks for his edifying message, he's agreed to spend a few minutes greeting people out in the vestibule."

Several women stood up, but they didn't dare exit their rows until Mrs. Silkman, Mrs. Trethaway, and the good doctor passed through. *It's like a wedding procession,* thought Lily.

Once the dignitaries reached the door, women poured up the aisle.

Lily remained seated long after Mrs. Jordan and the other ladies from the second row had vacated their chairs. She didn't know if she could trust her legs. Her whole body had gone to jelly. He couldn't have. It wasn't possible. For one thing, that sort of procedure was against the law. For another, Mother Mary Joseph would never have allowed it to happen under her roof. She was strict, yes, but she loved her girls. And she never judged them. That was God's business, not hers.

And yet . . . Lily recalled a year's worth of monthly heartaches. What natural reason could there be? She was

certainly capable of conceiving a child. Daisy was proof of
that. Had Dr. Peters taken matters into his own hands? She
closed her eyes and recalled the day she'd given birth. He'd
numbed her after she'd delivered Daisy, not before. And she
smelled something burning when he was supposed to be
cleaning her up. *She needs a few stitches,* he'd said to Violet
and Sadie. *You two run along and tend to the baby.*

When Lily's legs finally calmed down, she walked up the
aisle and found Dr. Peters, still in the vestibule, surrounded
by several ladies. A cornered grandfather clock struck the four
o'clock hour. She slipped past the little group, out the door,
and into George's LaSalle. Much to her surprise, the motor
turned over on her first try.

Lily pulled out and drove down Jefferson Avenue. When
she reached the corner, she pointed the car toward the
Mayfair Hotel.

Lily parked the LaSalle in front, so she'd be able to see Dr.
Peters when he arrived.

*What if it's true?*

*It's true.*

*Sterilization*—as soon as she'd digested the word, her
life seemed to end. She slid across the seat, pulled George's
pistol out of the glove compartment, tucked it into her
purse, and shuddered. The clock at the courthouse chimed
the quarter hour. Lily looked around and noted that there
weren't as many people out as one might expect. *Just as
well,* she thought, though she really wasn't worried. A reasonable woman would have been concerned, one who had
everything to lose. What might Lily lose? A man who didn't
love her? Children she could never conceive?

Waiting. She was never very good at it. Every month
she'd wait, and every month the blood flowed, and she'd
have to wait again. A thought struck her. She glanced across

the street at the Electric City Lunch to see if Little Frankie was around. A couple of policemen stood at the entrance, trading stories. No matter. She was beyond help now, even the kind of help Frankie could offer. She thought back to that fall afternoon on the blanket in the woods. As much as she regretted her actions, it suddenly occurred to her that George *never* really loved her. Not even at the beginning. Frankie was her protector, always Frankie. If only she could have fallen for him.

Enough *if only*'s. They never got a person anywhere, and besides, she needed to give her full attention to the Mayfair.

Just as she turned back, Dr. Peters entered the hotel.

Lily got out of the car and trailed behind the doctor. She watched as he lumbered across the lobby and entered the elevator. The operator asked him for his floor, but she couldn't hear the answer. As soon as the doors closed, she stepped forward to watch the brass arrow sweeping across the numbers. It stopped on 3. She took the stairs, and arrived on the third floor just as Dr. Peters turned the key and entered his room. She pressed herself against the wall to find her breath. *Dear Lord*, she started, but when couldn't think what to ask for, she abandoned the prayer. It took Lily another couple of minutes to gather her courage, and then she knocked at room 315.

"The door's unlocked," Dr. Peters called out. "Money's on the bed." His back was to Lily as he poured himself a drink. "Catherine promised me her best girl." He wore only an undershirt and trousers with a pair of suspenders. "Would you like a snort?" he asked, and turned. Lily noticed that his fly was open. "I beg your pardon," he said, grabbing his shirt from the bed. "I was expecting . . ." He paused and turned his back to fasten his pants. "May I help you?"

Lily remained in the doorway, waiting for him to face her again, wondering what she would say.

"You're the woman from the lecture," he finally said when he'd finished dressing. "Please, excuse my appearance. I was just going to retire for a bit." He motioned for Lily to take a seat but she stayed standing. "Is there something I can help you with? A donation for your ladies' group?" He picked the five-dollar bill off the bed and offered it to her.

"I don't want your money," she said.

His expression hardened. "Then what is it you want?" He sat down in a chair near the window and took a sip of his drink.

"You don't recognize me?"

He tipped his head and squinted at the face before lingering over her body. "I'm afraid not."

A fist of boiling pain shot up from Lily's stomach and landed in her throat. "You ruined my life," she said, "and you don't even know my name?"

Dr. Peters stood up, squeezed past Lily, and shut the door. "I'm sorry, Miss . . ." He waited for her to offer a name.

"*Mrs.* Mrs. Sherman."

"And exactly how did I ruin your life, Mrs. Sherman?"

"Five years ago. The Good Shepherd."

"Ah." He smirked. "I'll need more to go on than that. Lots of girls passed through those doors. In any case," he pulled at the skirt of her dress and fingered the fabric, "your situation seems to have improved." He walked over to the bed but remained standing. "I'm surprised. That rarely happens. Were you a Sherman back then?"

"Morgan," she said. "Lily Morgan."

He pinched his forehead, seemingly on the verge of something. "You brought that sister of yours with you. Of course. An unusual arrangement. How could I forget?"

"Is it true?"

He laughed. "When I think about it now, it was rather reckless of me, with her always hovering. It's a wonder I didn't get caught."

Lily unclasped the buckle on the front of her purse and slid her right hand inside. The gun's metal barrel was cool and refreshing to her touch. She cradled the wooden handle in her palm and looped her index finger onto the trigger. "So it's true."

"Honestly, I wasn't sure that particular method would be effective. It's still somewhat experimental." He eyed Lily. "But you're here. That tells me what I need to know."

"Who are you to play God?"

Dr. Peters laughed. "Come now. Don't be so dramatic. It's nothing. Such a small procedure, really. And no one's the wiser. Well," he said, stroking his beard, "almost no one."

"I'll have you arrested."

"An interesting choice. And legally, you have every right. But tell me, Mrs. Sherman, does Mr. Sherman know you gave birth to a bastard?"

"Say one more word about my daughter and I'll kill you." Lily pulled the pistol out of her purse and pointed it at the doctor. She cupped her left hand under her right for a steadier aim.

"People rarely surprise me, Mrs. Sherman, but you," he took a step back and raised his hands, "twice in one day."

"Do you really think you can get away with it?" Lily's hands started to shake.

"Truthfully, yes." He lowered his arms and smiled.

Tears ran down Lily's face but the gun remained fixed on her target. "You monster."

"Blame me if you must," he took a step forward, holding his arms out as if to comfort her, "but if you'd remained pure—" Dr. Peters lunged forward, pulled the pistol from Lily's hand, and tossed it on the floor.

She tried to run, but he grabbed her by the hair and threw her onto the bed, facedown. He yanked up the skirt of her dress and held her in place with his knee. "Stupid slut," he snarled as he unbuttoned his pants. Lily bucked up, trying to throw him off, but the weight of him proved too much. "Still think you can kill me?"

Behind them, a shot rang out, and Dr. Peters collapsed on top of her.

"Try to roll him off," a woman urged. "I'll pull."

A moment later, Lily broke free.

Muriel Hartwell stood over her with George's pistol in her hand.

# C HAPTER TWENTY-NINE

LILY FOLLOWED MURIEL DOWN A STAIRCASE at the end
of the hallway that led out to an alley behind the Mayfair's
laundry room. A last bit of sun clung to the rooftops before
letting go to make room for the dark. How long had she
been gone? Lily wondered. She and Muriel pressed into
the shadows as a paperboy walked by, his bag bulging with
the evening edition. It couldn't be much past five o'clock.
Two hours. That's all it had taken for the most unimagina-
ble combination of people and events to destroy her life—
and save her, she thought as she glanced at Muriel Hartwell.

"You can't be seen with me," Muriel said, watching for the alley to clear. "Cops'll be here any minute."
Lily shuddered, as if throwing off the weight of the man
who lay dead in a room three floors above them. She took
Muriel's hand and pulled her toward the street. "I know
someone who can help," she said, blending in with the
passersby as they crossed over to the Electric City Lunch.

The tabletop cigarette lighter on Frankie's desk was shiny,
solid, its smooth surface an untroubled lake. For a moment,
Lily lost herself in the lamplight reflected along the gold-
plated side. Whatever nerve had prompted her to seek out
Frankie had slipped away. "I didn't know where else to go,"
she said after she'd filled him in on the main details—from

the Good Shepherd Infant Asylum to Dr. Peters's death. She curled her legs up onto the club chair and shivered.

Frankie bent down and lifted her chin. "You did the right thing." He turned and looked at Muriel, who had posted herself near the window. "You're one of Catherine's girls."

Muriel nodded and lifted a slat in the blinds. Across the street, two officers dismounted and tied their horses to a hitching post in front of the hotel. A beat cop guarded the main entrance as a black police car made its way through the crowd toward the scene.

"Can you take care of this?" Muriel pulled the pistol from inside her blouse and passed it to Frankie.

Lily looked at the gun. She turned her right palm up and tried to remember the heft of it, how powerful it had made her feel. But that strength was gone now—like everything else. "It's George's," she said.

"Not anymore," Muriel said.

Frankie set the gun on the desk. "First," he turned to Muriel as he walked to a safe in the corner of the room and opened the heavy door, "we have to get you out of town." He reached inside, retrieved a string-tied bundle of cash, and shuffled through it with his thumb. "Did anybody see you?"

"No," Muriel said.

They both looked at Lily, but she gave no indication of whether or not she'd been seen going into the hotel.

Frankie passed the money to Muriel. "Just to be safe, Gino is going to drive you to the train station in Reading. Too many cops here." He glanced at the window but resisted the urge to peek through. "You have more than enough dough to get you to Florida. Set yourself up in a little apartment. All the oranges you can eat." He tried for a smile.

"You don't have to do this," Muriel said.

"Consider it payment for a job well done." Frankie glanced at Lily. "I just wish I'd pulled that trigger myself."

Muriel finally tucked the bills inside the waistband of her skirt. Gino appeared in the doorway, his stained apron stretched across his stomach. "Car's ready out back, boss."

Muriel gave Lily a light hug. "You're stronger than you think," she said.

Lily reached into her purse, pulled out the cash she had in a pouch, and folded it into Muriel's hand. "Thank you," she said.

Muriel looked at Frankie. "Take good care of her," she said, and walked out of the office.

"I will." Frankie's half-smile slipped from his face. "Muriel," he called out when she was halfway across the gambling parlor, "how long ago were you and Lily at the Good Shepherd?"

"More than five years, now," Muriel answered, flattening her palms against her belly.

Frankie turned back to Lily, confusion registering on his face. "Did you have a baby?"

"*Violet* has a baby." Lily leaned forward and pressed the square button on the side of the lighter. The top slid open, igniting the wick. "I don't have babies," Lily said, running her finger back and forth through the flame. "Not anymore."

Frankie pushed the lighter back, the kind of automatic gesture used around children. He knelt down and took her in his arms just as she broke into sobs.

Twenty minutes later, Frankie lowered Lily onto a bed in the room adjacent to his office. Her trembling body sank into the mattress. He grabbed a feathered quilt from a caned chair, draped it over her, and poured them both a generous drink from a bottle of whiskey on the night table. "Here," he said, lifting her head and holding the glass to her lips.

Now that Lily's crying had subsided, she took a good sip. When the whiskey burned its way through her, she pushed herself up and leaned against the oak headboard. Without meeting Frankie's eyes, she said, "I had a baby. *We* had a baby. A girl."

"I have a daughter?"

"No," she said, her tone somehow apologetic and emphatic at the same time. "Violet has a daughter. That won't change."

"Just as well," he said, pulling the chair toward her and dropping into it. "This is no life for a child."

They sat without speaking for several minutes, only the buzz from a dangling lightbulb disturbing the silence.

"The husband," he said at last, "is he a good man?"

"Yes."

"And he makes a decent living? She shouldn't want for anything."

"She'll never want for love."

Frankie leaned forward and took Lily's hand in both of his. "And what about you? Do you want for love?"

She pulled her hand back and began to pick at a knotted piece of yarn on the quilt. Her fingers were still too shaky to take hold of it. "Is he really dead?"

"Who? Oh, yes. He can't hurt anyone now."

Tears welled up in Lily's eyes. "I never knew it would be my only chance."

"At what?"

"I didn't even know enough to grieve." She wiped her face with the back of her hand. "He took everything away from me."

"I'm sorry."

"I know."

Frankie looked at Lily and smiled. "I remember holding you in my arms after the hayride. I think of that day often."

After a lengthy pause, he found his courage: "Do you?"

"No."

Silence filled the widening gap between them.

"George is probably looking for you by now," Frankie finally said, standing up to leave. "He must be worried."

Lily closed her eyes for a moment. When she opened them, she said, "I don't like to think about those days. I was in such a hurry to grow up, and now, look at the mess I've made. What I wouldn't give to go back and do it all differently."

"We can't change the past." Frankie sat down on the side of the bed and pushed wisps of hair off Lily's face. "But we can do something about the future." He leaned forward and kissed her lightly on the forehead. "George doesn't deserve someone as beautiful as you."

"George doesn't even know I'm alive." Lily reached for her whiskey and drank it down.

"Leave him." Frankie kissed her on the lips this time. "I have money. As much as George Sherman. Maybe more. I can give you everything you've ever wanted."

"I want a baby," she said, finishing the whiskey in Frankie's glass.

"We don't need babies." He pulled Lily into his arms and whispered in her ear, "Just each other."

"People would talk," Lily said, curling into Frankie's embrace, allowing him to bear her weight.

"Let them." He dropped down on the bed, pulling her with him, and kissed her again, lingering this time. "I don't give a damn."

"I do."

"I know," Frankie said, the flush of color draining from his face.

A minute of silence passed, and then Lily kissed Frankie's cheek. "Take me away, Frankie. Far away."

"Sure. Where to?" He ran his finger along the curve of her jaw and down her neck. "Coney Island? Atlantic City?"

"I mean for good, Frankie. There's nothing left for me here."

"For good?" He looked at her in his arms and saw the tears starting again. "Sure," he said. "Anything you want." His face lit up. "I have an uncle in California. Says it's different out there. Everyone has a past and no one asks questions." He kissed her neck, unbuttoned the top of her dress, and slipped his hand inside. "I'd have to work my way up again," his voice became a whisper, "but with you in my arms, I can do anything." He pulled her dress up past her gartered thigh. "Anything to make you happy."

Lily stared at the ceiling, neither resisting nor engaging Frankie's advances. "I'll never be happy again."

"Sure you will." This time he didn't notice the tears as he thumbed the flesh at the top of her thigh where the stocking ended. "I'll make sure of it."

"I can't go, Frankie." Lily shook her head and pushed him away. "I can't go. I need to be close to Daisy."

"Then we'll take her with us," Frankie said. "Whatever you want. We'll even get married."

Lily froze, as much from the horror of the idea as the possibility. Her tears stopped flowing and for an instant she forgot to breathe. "I can't. It wouldn't be fair to Violet."

"She's your kid. Your sister knows that." He kissed her again, slid his hand back inside the dress, and caressed her breast.

Lily tried to object but the words refused to pass her lips.

# WHO MAY AND MAY NOT MARRY

*"[T]he only way to guard the race against pollution with feeble-minded stock is either to segregate or to sterilize them. Society could have no objection against the feebleminded marrying or indulging in sexual relations, provided it could be assured that they will not bring any feebleminded stock into the world."*
—*Woman: Her Sex and Love Life,*
William J. Robinson, MD, 1929

Last Sunday's luncheon went off without a hitch. Roast pork, cranberry sauce, root vegetables, and apple pie. We like to send the men off on the "every member canvass" with full stomachs as a thank you for their efforts. Visiting every con-gregant on the rolls in a week's time is hard work, but we need to collect those pledge cards so we know what we can count on for expenses and benevolences in the coming year.

The committee will give its report during next week's ser-vice. Of course, with so much belt tightening, we may fall short, but no sense dwelling on that. Folks can't give what they don't have. And one way or another, the Lord always provides.

Take those miners from the Von Storch Colliery. We thought they were out of work for sure, but all sixty men have been reinstated thanks to Stanley Adamski. And we're happy for them, though with so many owners cutting back, we can't help wondering how long those jobs will last. Now there's talk of layoffs at the Sherman Mine. Such a shame. And hard to understand, given that people will always need coal. Still, we're happy Stanley won his case. Now if he'd only stop his drinking.

# C HAPTER THIRTY

STIFF SLICES OF TWO-DAY-OLD BREAD LANDED among the dried biscuits, broken crackers, and cast-off crusts from Daisy's lunches. Violet plunged her hands into the bowl and worked its contents between her palms. With Christmas only five weeks out, she was already behind on her plum puddings. Adequate aging took a good two months, but she'd make do. The accident had put her behind this year. Even now, it hurt to breathe when she exerted herself. "Another couple of weeks," Doc Rodham had said, but at least he'd given her permission to remove the binder. It made moving easier, she thought, as she combed through the crumbs for errant chunks. Finding none, she set the dish aside.

A gray sky broke above the slag horizon—another biting November morning. Violet pushed the kitchen window's curtain down the length of the rod, so she could easily look up from her task and judge the time of day. Mother Davies and Daisy would be asleep for another two hours, giving Violet enough time to ready her ingredients. She'd hold off on the final mixing, so they could each take a turn at making a wish while stirring the batter, but that meant she'd be steaming her puddings well past noon. Her previous day's trip into town had put her behind on chores, but once she'd gotten over the shock of seeing Muriel in Stanley's arms, the outing had turned out to be a blessing.

She'd finally realized she'd fallen in love with Tommy. Violet's cheeks flushed as if he were standing before her, listening to her say those words for the first time all over again. "I love you."

She walked over to the cupboard. Flour, baking powder, salt, and sugar. She measured and sifted each ingredient into a second, much larger bowl.

Recognizing her feelings had turned out to be the easy part. Telling him about them, saying those three simple words, took all of her nerve. The memory raised bumps on her forearms. She'd stood alongside the bed, wearing that nightgown again. Aware of her modesty, Tommy had reached to turn out the light, but Violet took his hand. She'd wanted him to see her face.

Now Violet picked up a butter knife and slipped it into the jar of dates, coaxing the sticky skins away from the glass. She turned the container upside down and thumped its bottom with the heel of her hand. The clumped fruit belched into a waiting colander.

It shouldn't have been so difficult. He was her husband, after all, the man she'd promised to love, honor, and cherish. Only she hadn't loved him then. Not the way a bride was supposed to love her groom. There were things she'd loved *about* him. He was a man of integrity like her father. Someone who lived the best parts of his faith—compassion, generosity, forgiveness. And, of course, he loved Daisy. And could protect her. Though Violet was ashamed to admit it, once Lily had married George, Violet lived in fear he'd find out about Daisy and try to claim her. Daisy needed a protector, and Violet could think of no one better than Tommy Davies.

At the sink, she rinsed the dates and peeled them apart with her fingers. The walnuts came next. Tommy had cracked every one and scooped out their meats the previous night, to lighten her load. She tossed them into a sack, tied it off, and ran her rolling pin over it to break the nuts into pieces.

When she'd finally said the words, he pulled her into his arms and whispered, "I've always loved you." Standing in the kitchen now, she shivered all over again at the memory.

She clamped the meat grinder to the table and fed strips of suet into its mouth. Each crank of the handle sucked the slices into the hopper, past the blades, and through the plate. Once the fat had been ground, she added the dates, nuts, and bread crumbs to the bowl and stirred them through. The baking soda and buttermilk still had to be added to make a batter, but she'd wait until the others woke up. She washed the few dishes she'd dirtied, and made herself some tea.

As she stood at the stove, Violet couldn't help but think about last night. How she'd craved her husband's touch, the gentle touch he'd come to understand would bring her pleasure.

*Go and be happy*—her father's words. She'd finally done just that.

The sun sat up higher in the sky, as if trying for a better impression. Maybe the frost would burn off after all. Violet put her cup on the table and pulled out a chair. A pair of shoe-button eyes stared up at her from the caned seat. Queenie. How had Daisy gone to sleep the night before without her? Noticing a torn ear, Violet set the elephant on the table and went in search of her sewing basket.

When she returned, she found Lily sitting at the table.

"What's wrong?" Violet grabbed the back of a chair for balance. "Is it Father?"

Lily mumbled her words into a handkerchief: "I didn't know where else to go."

"Is it George?" Violet sat down across from Lily and

lowered her voice. "Does he know about Daisy?" All the air emptied from her lungs, and for a moment she couldn't breathe.

"What?" Lily screwed up her eyes and shook her head. "He's dead."

Violet's hand flew to her chest. "George?"

"Dr. Peters."

It took a moment for confusion to overtake Violet's fear. "Dr. Peters?" She scanned the kitchen, making sure they were still alone. "From the Good Shepherd?"

Lily's hands started to tremble; she picked up the elephant to steady them. "I was there—in his room."

"What room? Where?" Violet eyed her sister and noticed her rumpled dress, the mussed hair. "What happened to you?"

Like a churning river after a sudden thaw, Lily's story spewed forth in a flood of anger and heartache. The Century Club. Sterilization. The Mayfair. George's gun. Muriel's arrival. Swelling, spilling, surging out of her. All of it.

Everything except Frankie.

"What about George?" Violet asked when Lily's sobs faded into whimpers.

"I haven't been home." Lily tucked Queenie under her arm, went to the sink, and washed her face.

"I don't understand," was all Violet managed to say before Daisy pounded down the steps and into the kitchen. "Where did you find her?" she squealed as she pulled Queenie from Lily's hold.

Lily dried her face, turned around, and stretched out her arms. "There's my girl."

"I thought I lost her for good this time." Daisy squeezed her elephant with one hand and her aunt's neck with the other.

Violet put her finger to her lips in an effort to quiet the child. "Grandma Davies," she whispered.

"Wide awake," Mother Davies called out from upstairs. "I'll be down as soon as I'm decent."

"Show Aunt Lily what a big girl you are," Violet said, "and get yourself dressed while I make breakfast."

"Are you here to stir the pudding?" Daisy surveyed all the ingredients on the table.

"I wouldn't miss it for the world," Lily said.

"Good." Daisy gave her aunt another hug and headed for the stairs.

"There's more to this story," Violet said when the two women were alone again. "What aren't you telling me?" She stood up, grabbed the kettle off the stove, and started to fill it at the sink.

Lily said nothing.

"Have you talked to the police?" She struck a match and lit the burner. "What are you going to say to George?"

Mother Davies started down the stairs. "Company at this hour?"

"Lily came by to stir the pudding." Violet put on a smile and looked through to the parlor at her mother-in-law.

"Not Lily." Mother Davies pointed to the front door just as someone started knocking. "Mrs. Lankowski," she said as she opened the door. "You'll catch your death of cold out there."

The widow stepped inside, her face ashen in spite of the frigid air.

"What's wrong?" Violet asked, glancing back and forth between the widow and Lily.

"It's Stanley," the widow said. "He's been arrested for murder."

# C HAPTER THIRTY-ONE

THE WIDOW PERCHED HERSELF at the edge of a high-backed chair offered to her by Tommy's mother. "Warm yourself," Mother Davies said, rubbing her hands together before the Heatrola, as if demonstrating how to get started.

The widow ignored the advice and turned to Violet. "Stanley's in trouble." Her voice broke. "They took him away this morning. Dragged him to the police station like a common thief. Said he killed a man. A Dr. Peters from Philadelphia. Can you imagine? He has his faults, my Stanley, but he's not a murderer."

Violet gasped. How had Stanley gotten caught up in Lily's mess? Violet cast a glance toward her sister who stood on the other side of the doorframe between the kitchen and the parlor, her head cocked to better hear the conversation. Violet turned back to the widow. "Tell me everything."

"Myrtle Evans dialed me up not half an hour ago," the widow said.

"Myrtle Evans?" Mother Davies patted the widow's leg. "And you believed her? I wouldn't give a plug nickel for anything that passed through that woman's lips."

"Neither would I," the widow said, "which is why I called police headquarters as soon as I hung up."

"And?" Violet's question sounded high-pitched to her own ear.

"He's down there now. And Lord knows what they're doing to him while we're sitting here." The widow pushed herself up, pulled a babushka out of her pocket, and tied it around her head. "I need you, Violet. Stanley needs you."

"I'm not sure what help she'll be at a police station." Mother Davies nodded toward the stairs leading to the bedrooms. Daisy's feet pattered over their heads. "And besides," she said to Violet, "you're needed here."

"Wait." Violet clasped her hands together and faced the widow. "Just give me a minute," she said and walked into the kitchen.

"You can't go with her." Lily's words may have been whispered, but that did not dilute the gravity of her message.

Violet pulled her sister into the farthest corner of the room. "How'd Stanley get involved in this?" she fired back, her voice hushed as well.

"I mean it. You'll ruin everything."

"He's trying to spare Muriel. Is that it? Does he know what she did?"

"Frankie said to stay away from this mess." Lily paused for a moment to get the wording right. "Not to incriminate myself," she said at last.

"Stanley shouldn't have to pay for . . ." Bafflement twisted Violet's expression. "Frankie? Frankie who?"

Lily immediately realized her mistake. Since she couldn't take back what she'd said, she lifted her chin and dressed her response in bravado. "Never you mind. I don't have to answer to you or anyone else for that matter." She tried to push past her sister, but Violet refused to budge.

"Little Frankie? He's bad news, Lily. Tell me you're not tied up with him."

From the other room, the widow called out, "I have to go."

Violet raised her finger and pointed it in Lily's face. She

looked toward the parlor. "Coming!" Turning back to Lily she said, "Tell me."

"I'm not tied up with him." Lily dropped into a seat at the table and folded her arms across her chest. "Just forget it."

"Stay here till I get back," Violet said. "Do you hear me?"

Lily shrugged.

"And watch after Daisy."

"No." Lily shook her head rapidly. "I can't." Tears filled her eyes. "I shouldn't be alone with her." She paused for a moment as if searching for a reason. "My nerves. It's all I can do not to run into the street screaming."

Violet kissed the top of Lily's head. "Then take her next door. Mother can watch her. And she can keep an eye on you too."

Lily nodded but said nothing.

Violet walked back into the parlor and grabbed her coat from the closet. "I have to go," she said to Mother Davies, "Stanley needs me." And then she added as much for herself as for her mother-in-law, "He's a brother to me. Tommy will understand."

Lily remained at the kitchen table long after Violet and the widow had run off to save Stanley and Mrs. Davies had gone upstairs to get Daisy washed and dressed. Finally alone, the silence amplified the thoughts she dared not think. Just for a moment Lily was back in Frankie's arms. Suddenly she understood that he was the only man in the world who could give her back her child. *Her* child. And everything else she deserved. But who would suffer? George? Certainly not. His heart was as hard and black as the coal extracted from his mine. A little humiliation might teach him a well-deserved lesson. But what about Violet? She'd be hurt, no doubt, and that was reason enough to dismiss the idea of out hand.

Then again, Lily wondered, should one sister be expected to trade her happiness for the other? Besides, it wasn't as if Violet were alone in the world. She had Tommy now. And soon enough, they'd have children of their own. And how would Violet's little family feel about Daisy then? Could they ever love her like she was one of them? Taking Daisy could be the best thing for her. And what mother wouldn't want what was best for her child?

Perish the thought—her own mother's advice whenever Lily's selfish side took over. Lily shook her head. Claiming Daisy was out of the question. Of course, as her aunt, she could start spending more time with the child. No one would fault her for that. She might even like to introduce her to Frankie someday. He deserved that much.

Lily went to the sink, splashed water on her face, and tried to smooth out her hair and dress. She needed to look presentable. She'd drop Daisy off next door and find someplace to be alone for more than just a few moments. Violet had told her not to go anywhere, but Lily needed time to think without having to answer to anyone. Maybe she'd take a walk or go to a movie. As soon as Violet returned, she'd start in on Frankie again. That was her way. Like a dog with a bone. It never mattered what Lily wanted or how desperately she wanted it. And she did want, desperately. So what? Desire meant nothing without courage, and everyone knew Violet was the strong one. By the same token, it had taken courage to confront Dr. Peters, but courage is easy when you're fingering a trigger. Still, gun or no gun, she'd taken control of her life in his hotel room. That was something.

"All ready." Daisy stood in the doorway wearing a green smocked dress, her hair done up in sausage curls, with Queenie under her arm.

"Tell your grandmother I'll be over for you as soon as I finish these puddings," Mrs. Davies said as she helped the little girl into her coat. "I'm going to need you to stir them."

Daisy smiled. "I will!" She grabbed Lily's hand and headed out the door and down the steps.

As soon as they reached the Morgan house, Lily paused and looked down at her daughter. "How would you like to ride on a train?" When Daisy shrugged, Lily added, "We can have lunch in the dining car."

This caught the child's attention. "Do they have chocolate pudding?"

"In silver goblets, with whipped cream if you like."

"I like." Daisy giggled at her joke long after the Morgan house was out of view.

# CHAPTER THIRTY-TWO

"I'M NOT DEAF!" the streetcar conductor barked as the signal bell rang repeatedly next to his ear. The widow tugged on the cord one more time before surrendering her grip, but remained standing. Violet slid across the seat so she could slip into the aisle as soon as the widow started forward. Half a block later, the conductor brought the car to a stop, braking harder than necessary.

"Lucky for you," the widow said as she disembarked, "I have bigger fish to fry today."

Unable to determine whether the man deserved to be admonished or pitied, Violet exited the streetcar without a word.

On the other side of the street, Scranton's Municipal Building graced the southwest corner of Washington and Mulberry, its 160-foot bell tower punctuating the left-hand side of the three-story edifice. Stained-glass windows blushed between even rows of wheat-colored stone. This sun-kissed beauty was the kind of building that put Scranton's best foot forward. Inside, the mayor and the men associated with the office conducted the city's important business.

The women crossed North Washington Avenue and started up Mulberry Street, past the building's main entrance. "You do anything for your children no matter how

they come to you," the widow said, taking Violet's arm.
"But I don't have to tell you that."

A shiver ran the length of Violet's spine, and at that moment, she wanted nothing more than to be at home with
Daisy.

After a few more yards, the women turned right into an
alley and found themselves facing the back of the building.
Police headquarters. No rose-colored windows on this side.
No southern exposure to bleach the soot from the stones.

A policeman came along, and when he saw where the
women were headed, he scooted around them and opened
the heavy door.

"Officer Fowler," the man said by way of introduction.
"Can I point you ladies in a direction?"

"I'm here to see about my son Stanley."

"Adamski?"

The widow nodded.

"Salt of the earth." Officer Fowler took off his hat and
leaned toward the women. "Helped my own dear father out
of a bind last year. Wouldn't take a dime. Just made him
promise to get off the drink—which he did, thank the good
Lord." He crossed himself, took a step back, and called,
"Sergeant," over to a man at the front desk. "These are
Stanley's people."

"Uh huh." The desk sergeant looked over the pair before
turning his attention to Fowler. "Don't you have a report to
file?" He tipped his head and spit a stream of tobacco juice
into a cup.

"Yes sir." Officer Fowler slicked back his curls, put on
his hat, and nodded to the women. "The good Lord won't
forget your boy," he said and headed to another corner of
the room.

The desk sergeant picked up a telephone and hid his face
behind a clipboard as he spoke. Violet made out the name

"Adamski" before steam whistled up from the radiators, thwarting her attempt at eavesdropping. The sudden rush of heat closed in on her, raising beads of sweat on the back of her neck. If only she'd brought a few hairpins with her. She started unbuttoning her coat, but thought better of it when she noticed a couple of miscreants who were chained together, licking their lips and winking in her direction.

"Knock it off, the pair of you!" the sergeant yelled as he came out from behind his desk. "This ain't the Alleys." The metal cleats on the toes and heels of his shoes click-clacked across the wooden floor. With his billy club in hand, he feinted left, causing the closest man to flinch, lose his balance, and pull the other one off his feet. Both men tumbled to the ground, just as Violet yanked the widow out of their way.

"Fowler!" the sergeant shouted as he started toward an office door. "Put these clowns in a cell."

"What about Stanley?" the widow called out. "I want to see him."

The desk sergeant turned around. "If I was you, ma'am, I'd go home." He smiled thinly. "Your boy's been arrested for murder. He ain't seeing anybody anytime soon."

"Well, you're not me, and I'm not leaving till I see him." The widow took a seat on a bench.

"I see where he learned his rabble-rousing ways." The sergeant eyed the widow then turned to Violet. "If I was you," he said, "I'd take her home before she gets herself in trouble."

"I can see the headline now," Judson Woodberry announced as he entered the building. "'Frail Mother Handcuffed by Police.'"

"Nothing frail about that woman," the sergeant snarled.

"There will be when I write the article."

The sergeant paused as if reconsidering his tack. "And

no one said anything about arresting anybody." He glanced at the widow. "Wait here," he said as he entered the office in front of him. "I'll see what I can do."

Once the sergeant was out of earshot, the reporter introduced himself. "Yes, he's under arrest," Judd explained when the widow asked what he knew about Stanley. "The alderman issued a body warrant last night on suspicion of a felony. Because it's a high-profile case, the preliminary arraignment is being rushed. They've already taken his mug shot and fingerprints. And he's been interrogated at least once."

"What can we do?" Violet asked as she took the widow's hand.

"Find him an alibi. According to my sources, he won't say where he was at the time of the murder."

"And what time was that?" the widow asked.

The reporter looked at his notebook. "Just before five o'clock."

"The DA says to bring you back to the interrogation room," the sergeant said as he came out of the office. "Some kind of 'courtesy.' Who ever heard of giving courtesy to jailbirds?"

"I'll be around if you need anything," Judd said.

Violet trailed the widow and the sergeant. Five o'clock. She'd been in Stanley's room at five o'clock. She was his alibi. He was trying to protect her. Inhale. Exhale. *Click. Clack. Click. Clack.* Heel. Toe. Heel. Toe. She tried to breathe in time with the human metronome ahead of them.

A moment later, the clicking stopped and laughter started, solid and self-satisfying. When Violet looked up, she saw the sergeant standing in the hallway, cackling with George Sherman.

If only Lily had an automobile. On Frankie's advice, she'd

left George's LaSalle in front of the Mayfair and let Gino take her to Violet's with Frankie alongside her in the backseat. Too many cops still swarming around, he'd said. Gino would drop the car off later today. She'd understood Frankie's logic, but she also knew that her nervous state had figured in his decision not to have her drive.

"Where's the train?" Daisy asked as they exited the streetcar. The smell of hot dogs wafted past them, awakening the child's hunger. "They have chocolate pudding on the train."

"With whipped cream," Lily added. "But first," she stood on the corner looking up at the Electric City Lunch, "we have to make a stop." She peered inside the restaurant, empty except for Gino who stood behind the counter, preparing for the noon crowd. She tapped her diamond ring against the glass, but when Gino didn't look up, she knocked with more urgency.

"Hold your horses!" Gino wiped his beefy hands across his apron and opened the door. "Oh," he said when he saw Lily standing in front of him. "Is the boss expecting you?"

Gino knew perfectly well that Frankie was not expecting Lily to show up that morning, and certainly not with a child in tow. When they dropped her off, Frankie had made it clear that he'd contact her after the whole Peters mess blew over. "Shouldn't be more than a day or two," he'd assured her with a substantial kiss, the kind Gino had obviously trained himself to ignore from the driver's seat.

"He'll see me." Lily grasped Daisy's hand and started for the steps.

"I can't let you do that, ma'am." Gino pushed past the pair, blocking the entrance to the second floor.

"It's all right," Frankie called out from the top of the stairs. "Send her up."

* * *

Daisy started fussing. First she was too hot, then too hungry. Frankie had Gino make her a milkshake, and that seemed to satisfy her momentarily.

"This ain't no place for a kid," Frankie said, nodding toward the gambling parlor. Even at that early hour, a few of the regulars scratched notes on their betting sheets as Black Mike worked the board.

Frankie sat on the edge of his desk, studying the child before him—her lips pursed around the straw, her nose chapped at the edges from a recent cold, her eyes . . . those eyes, those sea-blue eyes of Lily's. He glanced at Lily, seated alongside the girl. "Looks like you spit her out."

Daisy's head popped up as if she were trying to make sense of the words.

"You look like your mother. That's a good thing." Frankie tousled the girl's hair, but she shooed his hand away.

"Aunt Lily says I look like her. Grandma Morgan says it too. Mommy doesn't like when she says it, though." Daisy slurped the last of her drink, giggled to herself, and made the noise again. "Will Mommy be on the train?"

Frankie turned to Lily. "What train?"

"That's what I wanted to talk to you about." Lily pulled a handkerchief out of her pocketbook, handed it to Daisy, and motioned for her to wipe her mouth. "Let's leave today. Go far away. There's nothing left for me here."

"Leave?" Frankie squinted as if trying to make sense of the word. "Today?" He looked from Lily to Daisy and back again. "It's not time yet. Not with what's happened."

"It's too late." Lily tipped her head toward Daisy who was using the hanky to shine Queenie's button eyes. "I can't go back now."

"It's not a good time," Frankie said. "It's too soon. Too fast."

"I'll never ask for anything else." Lily looked at Daisy.

"Sit still," she said as the child swung her feet into the air and back against the legs of the chair. "You'll scuff your shoes."

Daisy sighed loudly but did as she was told. "I want to go home."

"But Frankie here's taking us for a train ride any minute. You'll like that."

Frankie stepped behind his desk, reached for the telephone, and dialed. "Hiya, doll. No," he laughed, "I'm afraid it's business. Yes. Two tickets to Sandy Hook. One adult, one child," he said, writing the information on a pad. "Uh huh. My account. Thanks, Sally." He hung the receiver back on the cradle. "Train leaves at two o'clock. That should give you plenty of time to get down to the station. I'd have Gino drive you, but I think you better take a cab so nobody puts two and two together." He lifted the corner of his blotter and pulled out a ten-dollar bill. When he turned back, Lily was on her feet.

"Two tickets?" Lily asked anxiously.

"You can't just expect me to pack up and leave," Frankie said. "I have a business to run." He leaned in to kiss Lily, but stopped when he noticed Daisy staring up at him.

"This was your idea, Frankie." Lily stood up and glared at him. "You said we'd go away. You said we should take her with us."

"I don't want to go for a train ride." Daisy started to cry. "I want to go home." She pulled at Lily's skirt.

"Now look what you've done," Lily said to Frankie. Her eyes welled with tears as she bent down and picked up the child.

"I don't want chocolate pudding," Daisy said, pressing her head against Lily's shoulder.

Frankie surveyed the scene. He leaned toward Daisy and wiped her tears with the back of his hand. "You'll love the train." He peered up at Lily. "I'll come see you soon. This weekend."

"I don't like this, Frankie." Lily patted Daisy's head. "You promised we'd do this together."

"We will. Just not yet." He smiled at Daisy. "You'll love the ocean. It's so big. And you can swim in the waves."

As Daisy seemed to consider this point, her crying stopped. "Will Mommy and Daddy Tommy be there?"

"Sure, kid," Frankie said. "Anybody you want." He looked at Lily. "It's right on the Jersey Shore. When you get there, ask for Bertha. She'll set you up real nice."

"You said you'd marry me." The tears started to run down Lily's cheeks.

"And I will. Soon as your divorce comes through." He glanced at Daisy. "And maybe an annulment. Do Protestants get annulments? I want her raised Catholic," he said. "Meantime, I'll visit as often as I can. We'll have dinner, take in a show. You'll like that, won't you? We'll get Bertha to watch the kid." He gently pinched the tears away between his thumb and forefinger. "And here's a few bucks." He reached into his pocket, pulled out a wad of cash, and peeled off several one hundred–dollar bills. "This should be enough to get you started. Set yourselves up. Buy some new clothes." He lifted her left hand and fingered the diamond that George had given her. "And track down a jewelry store. When I get to town, I'm putting my ring on this finger."

Lily's sniffling abated somewhat. "Better be the biggest one in the store, Frankie Colangelo."

"I wouldn't have it any other way."

AS VIOLET AND THE WIDOW approached the two men standing at the end of the hall, their laughter stopped abruptly. George glanced in their direction, walked into a dark-paneled meeting room, and took a seat on the far side of a rectangular table. The desk sergeant motioned for the women to follow. Dumbfounded, Violet wondered at the odds of George Sherman being at the station on a different matter altogether. And if he was there about the murder, how much did he know? Had Lily called him? That hardly seemed likely, given her state this morning. Stanley? Not for any reason Violet could imagine. Unable to discern any cause for her brother-in-law's presence and not yet willing to divulge the little she knew, Violet walked into the room and asked the obvious question: "What are you doing here?"

"My civic duty." George eyed Violet for a moment and said, "I might ask you the same question."

"They've arrested my Stanley." The widow sat down at the table, her back facing the door. "Violet's my rock. I can always count on her in a crisis." She motioned for Violet to take the seat beside her. "I don't suppose you're here to assist us, Mr. Sherman. I'm not too proud to accept a hand."

"I'm afraid not, Mrs. Lankowski. We seem to be at cross purposes today. I've been asked to give a statement that will no doubt add fuel to your son's fire." George looked at Violet. "I'm surprised your husband allowed you down here. I thought he had better sense."

"And your wife," Violet said, "does she know what you're up to this morning?"

"She will soon enough, I suspect." He jingled the loose change in his pocket and half-smiled. "Don't worry about Lily. She understands a woman's role in a marriage. Honor thy husband and all the rest of it."

"It's *Honor thy father and thy mother*. The only Commandment that pertains to marriage is the one about adultery," replied Violet.

"I have to hand it to you, you still know your Bible. Even after all those years out of the church."

The desk sergeant nodded as a tall man in a brown wool suit entered the room. "I'll be at my post if you need me," the man said, clicking his way back down the hallway.

"George Sherman."

"Jonesy. Good to see you." George stood up, slapped the man on the back with one arm, and shook hands with the other. "I haven't seen you since the election."

"What a night," Jonesy said. "the wife couldn't have been too pleased when she saw the shape you were in."

"Just celebrating my investment," George replied. "It's always good to have a friend in the DA's office."

"Well, someone has to clean up this town."

George laughed and the DA joined in. After a moment, George scratched his head. "Someone must've set the courthouse on fire. How else could they get you down here?"

"When the mayor asks for a favor . . ." The DA finished his sentence with a shrug.

"The mayor?" The widow refused to be excluded from the conversation any longer.

"Sorry, ma'am. Sam Jones, district attorney."

The man looked over and smiled at the women. "And you are?"

Violet answered: "Mrs. Davies and Mrs. Lankowski."

"You're Stanley's mother." Jonesy nodded. "The desk sergeant said you were here. What can I do for you?"

"Why is the mayor involved?" the widow asked again.

"He wants to expedite matters. This Peters fellow was some kind of favorite son in Philadelphia." The DA looked at his notes and nodded. "The same city where Mr. Adamski studied law."

"Excuse me, gentlemen, ladies." A strawberry-blonde whose ample cleavage strained the buttons on her dress appeared in the doorway. "Miss Merino, stenographer."

The desk sergeant walked in behind Miss Merino, carrying a heavy black stenotype machine. "Where do you want it?"

Miss Merino nodded toward a small table in the corner. "Set it down gentle. Otherwise the keys'll stick."

"Well, ladies, looks like it's time to get the wheels of justice moving," the DA said. "I'll have someone from my office keep you posted on your son's situation." He extended his hand to the widow. "A pleasure to meet you." When she did not return the gesture, he rubbed his palms together as if that had been his intention all along. He turned to the policeman who was a little too interested in a lesson from Miss Merino on QWERTY keyboards. "Sergeant?"

"Yes sir." The man shot to attention.

"Arrange to have an officer drive these ladies home."

"Yes sir."

The widow looked at the district attorney. "We're not leaving without Stanley."

"Mrs. Lankowski," the DA said, walking to the door, "I'm afraid that's not possible. Your son is in serious trouble. He won't be released anytime soon." When she didn't budge, he addressed Violet: "This is no place for her."

Violet did not say anything and remained seated.

"Mrs. Lankowski, I must insist." Jonesy pointed to George. "Mr. Sherman is here to give his statement, and you can't interfere with that."

"Off the record," George said quietly, winking at the DA.

Jonesy nodded at Miss Merino, who looked at her stenotype machine with uncertainty. "Take a long lunch. I'll keep an eye on it for you." He watched as she exited.

"Mr. Sherman won't mind indulging an old woman." The widow pulled out her rosary beads.

"Mrs. Davies," the DA said, "a little help?"

"I'd like to hear Mr. Sherman's statement." Violet stared at George, and all other eyes followed hers. "Off the record, of course."

"I'll have you removed if I must," the DA said.

Violet continued staring at George.

He smiled, lit his cigarette, and inhaled deeply. "Let them stay. If that's what it takes to move this process along, so be it." He blew a line of smoke into the air and watched as it disappeared.

The DA's mouth dropped open. "This case is highly sensitive. The mayor would not approve."

"Relax, Jonesy. I have nothing to hide."

"Still, I must object. This request is highly unorthodox."

"So are these proceedings," said Violet.

George waved off the DA's continued protest. "Let's get started." He looked directly into Violet's eyes. "It might do her some good to see what St. Stanley is really made of."

"According to the officer you spoke to earlier this morning," DA Jones thumbed through the folder containing notes and photographs, "you witnessed the events at Hunold's Beer

Garden on the evening of Monday the eighteenth, the night before the murder."

"That I did." George pushed his chair back from the table, grabbed hold of his left wrist, and stretched his arms overhead.

"And you witnessed Mr. Adamski, and I'm using your word here, 'slug' Dr. Peters in the eye and threaten to kill him?"

"I'd say it was more of a sucker-punch, but yes. The poor fellow never saw it coming. Seemed like a decent sort too."

"Any idea what caused the altercation?"

"The usual." When the DA looked confused, George added, "A girl . . . a woman of questionable character." He stared across the table at Violet. "Are you sure you want to hear this?"

She nodded. "I'd like to know how a married man like yourself, a deacon in the church, ended up at a beer garden."

"Had some mine business to take care of." George smiled. "Takes you into some pretty unsavory places."

The widow gave George a sidelong look. "You conduct mine business in the Alleys?"

The two men glanced at each other at the mention of the Alleys. They'd probably never heard the expression pass the lips of a decent woman.

"Mrs. Lankowski," the DA said, "if you continue to interrupt these proceedings, I'll have to ask you to leave."

"I go where my men go," George explained. "Try to help them reform."

The DA stifled a chuckle. "Of course." He glanced at his notes again. "And did Mr. Adamski appear to know the woman in question?"

"She's a firecracker, that one. Ruby." George closed his eyes and smiled.

The DA scattered several photographs on the table and pushed the top one in front of George. "That her?"

Violet resisted the urge to gasp when she saw the picture of Muriel.

"Mug shot's about a year old," the DA said.

George opened his eyes. "She's better looking than most of the girls at Catherine's."

"And you've seen this woman in Mr. Adamski's company?"

"Sure have. Stanley's one of her regulars. I see them at Hunold's from time to time." George laughed. "I suppose catting around is thirsty work."

"And on that evening?"

"I guess you could say the good doctor showed a little too much interest in her."

So they knew about Muriel, Violet thought. But did they know she'd been at the hotel that night? She glanced at the DA's folder. And did they know about Lily? A photograph of the hotel lay on top. It had obviously been taken last night, after the murder. A police wagon was parked in front, and several policemen stood at the entrance. "But how would Stanley know where he was staying?" Violet asked.

"Announced it at Hunold's. Said something about bringing company back to the Mayfair."

"None of this makes Stanley guilty of murder," the widow said.

The DA looked at the woman as if wondering whether to reprimand her. "Your son threatened to kill the good doctor, and unfortunately, he has no alibi for five o'clock yesterday when witnesses heard the gunshot."

"I know where he was." All eyes turned to Violet.

"You do?" George smirked.

"Yes." Looking down at her hands, Violet twirled her gold wedding band. "I went down to Hunold's yesterday. I needed to talk to him."

"So you went to Mr. Adamski's room?" The DA took out his notebook and started to write.

"Yes. So we could speak in private." She looked at the widow. "Nothing happened. We just talked."

"That's quite a story," George said, "but I don't buy it." He looked at Jonesy. "Stanley and Violet go way back. She's lying to help him."

"Let me get this straight," the DA said. "You're saying that you're willing to swear that you were with Stanley Adamski at the time of Dr. Peters's murder?"

"I am."

"And were there any witnesses?" the DA asked.

She shook her head.

"Violet, don't." Stanley stood in the door, his lip split, a bruise forming over his left eye.

"What happened?" The widow started up from her seat but the DA motioned her to sit down. "What did you do to my boy?"

"What is Mr. Adamski doing here?" the DA asked the officer standing alongside Stanley.

"Sorry, sir. We're on our way from processing. I took the back way to avoid that fellow from the newspaper."

"You can't get yourself involved in this." Stanley started toward Violet, but the officer gripped his shoulder and pulled him into the hall.

"Too late," Violet said.

"Are we supposed to believe this malarkey?" George pushed his chair back, away from the table.

"I've never known her to lie," the widow said and patted Violet's hand.

The DA excused himself, went out into the hallway, and proceeded to reprimand the officer loudly.

Violet caught George's eye. She peeled a photograph of the hotel off the pile and pushed it over to him, pointing

at the bottom. The front of his LaSalle, including its torpedo hood ornament and part of his license plate, had made
it into the picture. Violet whispered, "I'd hate to see your
good name dragged through the mud."

George lowered his face, squinted at the photo, and
turned pale. "What the hell?" he mumbled. "You know who
had my car."

"I don't know anything of the kind," Violet said.

"How is Lily mixed up in this?"

"Maybe if you spent less time on 'mine business' and
more time with your wife, you'd know what she was doing."

The DA came back in the room and sat down. "Where
were we?"

George peered at Violet and gritted his teeth. "We're
finished."

The DA turned his attention to George. "Excuse me?"

"Violet's word is good enough for me," George said,
slapping the table and standing.

"But you said . . ."

"I said he'd had a fight with the good doctor the night
before, nothing more. Now that I think about it, the guy
probably had it coming."

"He was an evil man," Violet said. "Look into the
matter, you'll find he did unspeakable things to women."

"So you knew the victim?" The DA settled back in his
seat. "How?"

"From the infant asylum." Violet dropped her head.

"I'm inclined to believe Mrs. Davies." George looked
at the DA. "If I were a gambling man, I'd bet you're going to find out that his wound was self-inflicted. Probably
couldn't live with his sins anymore. This investigation is
closed."

"I don't understand . . ." the DA started.

"Well, Jonesy," George looked menacingly at the man,

"you don't have to. You just have to go along. That's the deal. That was always the deal."

"Looks like my Stanley is free to go," the widow said.

Jonesy ignored the woman and continued his conversation with George. "So I'm supposed to set that communist loose, just like that?"

George thought for a moment. "Where did you pick him up?"

Jonesy looked at his notes. "Hunold's Beer Garden."

"And I assume public drunkenness is still a crime in Scranton?" George glared at Violet as if daring her to object.

"So it is," Jonesy said.

"Then let him cool his heels inside for a day or two." George looked at Violet and mouthed the words, *You'll pay for this*, and headed out of the interrogation room.

With the murder charges dropped, the district attorney allowed Officer Fowler to take the women back to see Stanley in his cell. The widow hugged him as best she could, through the iron bars. "Thanks be to God," she said. "And to this one." She looked back at Violet, standing against the bars of the empty cell across from him.

Stanley kissed the widow's cheek and nodded at Violet. "Can I talk to her, Babcia? Alone?"

The widow looked from one to the other. "Two souls," she shook her head, "burdened with love." She squeezed Violet's hand. "Take your time," she said. "Come find me at St. Peter's. I'm going to walk over to offer up a prayer for thanks."

"Fowler," Stanley tipped his head toward Violet, "can we have a minute?"

The officer glanced at the locked door to Stanley's cell. "I'll go make myself useful," he said.

Stanley stood at the front corner of his cell, straining to see down the hallway. "Is he gone?"

Violet stepped closer and watched as the officer disappeared from her sight. "Yes."

When she turned back around, Stanley looked at her straight on and broke into a smile. "You still love me."

"You didn't kill him." She lowered her voice and her eyes, hoping Stanley would do the same. "That's all there is to it."

"I love you too." Stanley threaded his hand through the bars, toward Violet's face, bending his fingers to mimic the curve of her reddening cheek.

She swallowed her breath and remained still. "I couldn't let you go to prison for something you didn't do."

"We were meant to be together." He pressed his fingers lightly into the pillow of her cheek.

Violet took a step back, where Stanley could no longer reach her. "No," she said. "I came here because of the widow. And because I knew you were innocent. That's all."

"Say that you love me." Stanley extended his arm again, but Violet remained out of reach.

"I love Tommy, and that's the truth."

"Tell me you don't love me," Stanley said.

Violet remained silent.

"You love me." Stanley's face brightened. "Another truth."

"Some truths matter more than others," Violet said. "I'm sorry."

"So that's it?" Stanley ran his foot along the bars of his cell.

"Yes."

"Does he make you happy?"

"Yes." Violet stepped forward and took his hand in both of hers. "I'm sorry."

Stanley eyed her for a moment. "Be happy, then." He dropped his head and Violet stood there, holding his hand a moment longer. When she finally let go, she turned and saw Tommy heading toward her. "I can explain," she said, letting go of Stanley's hand.

"Something's happened." He pulled Violet by the shoulders, his voice cracking. "Daisy's gone."

# C HAPTER THIRTY-FOUR

VIOLET FELT AS IF SHE'D MISSED NOT ONE STEP, but a thousand. Her heart stopped; the blood drained from her head. Her hands and feet prickled, then numbed. Her breath caught at the back of her throat and choked her.

*Daisy's gone.*

Her thoughts, like wild dogs, pounded forward without regard for reason. *Is she warm enough?* Think. *Where can she be?* Falling. Falling. Lily. Something about Lily. And Mother. Was Daisy next door with her? Concentrate. She caught the end of a "No" on Tommy's oval lips. Had she asked that question aloud? And Frankie. What was it Lily had said about Frankie? His name charged ahead briefly, then settled back into the pack. *Daisy's gone.* Her coat sleeves need to be let down. All arms and legs lately. Her arms and legs would get so cold. Falling. Falling. Must look for her. Grab hold of something. Anything.

Tommy pulled Violet into him. "I'll find her. Don't you worry." His embrace absorbed her tears.

Violet buried her face in the front of his red and black–plaid hunting coat, catching a whiff of tobacco from the breast pocket. Tommy's Chesterfields. Familiarity pinned her in place. "Lily," she finally said, the name landing as an accusation.

"Yes." Tommy spoke as calmly as he would to a child,

but the veins and arteries in his neck bulged red and blue. He nodded. "Lily. We have to find her. Them." Still holding on, he took a step back and studied Violet's expression. "Where could they be?"

"Do you think she's scared?" Violet struggled to order her mind.

"I think she needs her mother," Tommy said with gentle firmness. "Someone has to know something. What about George? A friend?" When Violet didn't answer, he held her at arm's length. "I'm going to talk to the police."

"Won't do any good." Stanley walked to the front of his cell. "Sherman's got the chief in his pocket.

"Then I won't go to the chief," Tommy said, not taking his eyes off Violet. "There are a dozen other men out there who will help us."

"They're all beholden to your brother-in-law," Stanley said. "Even the honest ones have wives and kids to support."

Tommy's head snapped toward Stanley. "I'm not afraid of Sherman."

"You should be. What do you think will happen if you go off half-cocked," Stanley lowered his volume to a whisper, "and accuse his wife of kidnapping?"

"He doesn't give a damn about Lily," Tommy said.

"But he does give a damn about his reputation. And his pride." Stanley paused for a moment as if considering whether or not to speak what he was thinking. He finally said, "He's already licking his wounds over that alibi your wife gave me."

A quick twitch pinched Tommy's cheek. "I'm sure Violet has her reasons, whatever they are. But Daisy is the only thing that matters right now."

"And what if he figures out what happened and decides he has a right to her?"

Violet shuddered. Stanley had just given voice to her greatest fear.

"I can't worry about that now," Tommy said. "We have to find Daisy."

"So he can take her away?" Stanley started to pace back and forth in his cell. "Keep him in the dark. Find her without the police." He charged forward. "Think, Violet. Think. Where could she be?"

*This is all my fault,* Violet thought. *I should have known.* "Don't let him take her away."

"I'll never let that happen." The tone of Tommy's words left no room for doubt.

The lawyer in Stanley took over. He turned to Violet. "You know Lily better than anyone. Where would she take her? Where could they be?"

*What if I never see her again?* Violet shuddered.

"We're wasting time here." Tommy pulled at Violet's arm, but she didn't move.

"I know you know." Stanley rattled the bars. "Think!"

*I'm her mother,* she thought.

"Officer!" Tommy yelled toward the front of the station.

"You're the only one who can do this," Stanley said.

*I'm the one who made the sacrifices. I'm the one who saved her.*

"I need to talk to an officer!" Tommy's voice echoed down the hallway.

"You can do this," Stanley's voice softened. "Daisy needs you now."

*This morning. Muriel. Plum puddings. Lily. The sunrise.*

"Think," Stanley murmured as Fowler turned the corner at the top of the hall. "Think!"

*Dr. Peters. Ruby. The widow.* "Frankie," Violet spoke the name aloud.

"What's the problem here?" Fowler called out from halfway down the hallway.

Violet looked at Tommy and shook her head. "I know," she whispered. "Don't involve the police."

"No problem," Tommy said but he sounded unconvinced. "We're finished here, is all."

By half past two, the lunch crowd at the Electric City Lunch had dwindled to a couple of fruit vendors from the wholesale district and a shopgirl from Woolworth's. Gino stood behind the counter, scraping the grease from his grill into a bucket. "Be with you in a minute," he said without turning around.

"We're here to see Franco." Tommy kept hold of Violet's arm as he spoke.

When Gino didn't answer, Violet added, "I'm Lily's sister."

At this piece of news, Gino swung around, wiping his hands on a nearby towel. "Don't know no Lily." He looked at Tommy. "And as you can see," he waved his hand around the room, "Mr. Colangelo," he paused as he spoke the name, "is not in." Gino reached under the counter, pulled out a Luger, and started polishing the barrel with his apron.

Violet gasped at the sight of the gun and Tommy pushed her behind him.

The shopgirl scooped up her hot dog and hurried out the door.

"I'll let him know you stopped by, though," Gino said.

Tommy whispered to Violet, "Go back and get Fowler."

"Please," Violet said to Gino, "we're not here to cause trouble. I just need to ask him about my sister."

"Like I said," Gino continued to polish the gun, "don't know no Lily."

"But Mr. Colangelo does," she said. "They've known

each other for years. Can't you just see if he's here?"

Gino studied Violet for a moment, then waved over his son who was manning the shoeshine station near the entrance. The boy dropped a brush into his kit and ran upstairs. A minute later, he returned and nodded to his father.

"You can't be too careful," Gino said, giving Tommy a quick pat-down before watching the boy escort the pair to Frankie's office.

"Violet Morgan," Frankie greeted the visitors at the door. "And Tommy Davies, if my memory serves me."

"It does," Tommy said.

Violet eyed the man, looking for signs of that young boy who used to pick Lily up at the house, instead of the mobster who stood before her in an expensive suit.

Once they were inside, Frankie leaned against his desk and motioned for the pair to sit, but they all remained standing. "What brings you downtown?"

"Where are they?" Violet pleaded, grabbing Frankie's lapels.

Frankie shot a look at Tommy, who pulled Violet away. "Get your wife under control," he muttered. "Or I'll have Gino do it."

Tommy stood toe-to-toe with Frankie. "Don't you ever threaten her again," he said, "or I'll kill you before Gino hits the first step."

"I'm going to excuse that comment, since you're both from the old neighborhood." Frankie smoothed his lapels and walked around to the other side of his desk. "But I wouldn't make that mistake again," he said to Tommy. "If you do, it'll be your last one." Frankie smiled.

"I know you know," Violet said, undeterred. "Where are they?"

"I'm afraid I don't know what you're talking about."

Frankie put a hand on his hip, exposing the gun holstered at his waist.

"My daughter is out there." Violet started to cry. "And I know you know where she is."

"Your daughter?" Frankie pushed his lips forward as if giving the matter serious consideration. "Are you sure?"

Tommy stepped closer, glanced at the piles of paper on the desk, flattened his hands on top of them, and leaned forward. "Very sure," he said. "Violet is the one who changed her diapers. Fed and clothed her. Took the brunt of this town's blame while Lily chased after George. Hell, they deserve each other. Violet is Daisy's mother and I'll do everything in my power to keep it that way." He curled his fingers into fists and his knuckles turned white.

Frankie grimaced and glanced at the clock. They followed his gaze. Eight minutes to two. "Well, I'm not sure what you think I can do about the situation."

"Help us," Violet moaned. "She's just a little girl."

"A real beauty," Frankie replied. "I would imagine."

"Let's go," Tommy said. "This is a dead end."

"If you won't help us, help Lily." Violet folded her hands together. "She's making a terrible mistake."

"If only I could." Frankie checked the clock once more, sat down, and pulled the phone toward him. "Now, if you'll excuse me."

"Come on," Tommy pressed, grabbing Violet's arm.

"But I wouldn't worry," Frankie said, picking up the receiver. "That sister of yours has a good head. I'll bet she's sitting at home right now, waiting for you with Daisy." He looked at Tommy. "Take her home before she gets herself into trouble."

Tommy sneered at Frankie as he led Violet out of the room.

* * *

"How could you do that?" Violet said when they stepped out into the street. "He knows something. I'm sure of it."

"Track one." Tommy opened his hand and showed her the scrap of paper he'd palmed from Frankie's desk. "Two o'clock."

"The station is ten minutes away, we'll never make it."

"We have to," Tommy said, and they started to run.

# CHAPTER THIRTY-FIVE

VIOLET GRABBED TOMMY'S HAND as they ran up Linden Street. The wind pushed her skirt past her knees. Ahead of them on Wyoming Avenue, St. Peter's Cathedral towered, its golden crosses shining in the gray sky. Catholic or not, Violet offered a quick prayer as they sprinted by.

By the time they reached the post office on the corner of North Washington, Violet's injured ribs seemed to be pressing in, stabbing at her lungs. Every gulp of air felt like a knife wound. She held onto Tommy with one hand and clutched her chest with the other. Washington, Adams, Jefferson: avenues named for the presidents. Her father had taught her that when she was no older than Daisy.

Violet's legs and lungs burned, separate fires blazing at the same time. Ahead, the courthouse occupied a full city block that now seemed never-ending. With Violet in tow, Tommy pushed his way across the crowded sidewalk, Moses in this Red Sea of strangers. The automobile traffic at the intersection slowed them long enough for Violet's calves to clench, and when she started to run again, they refused to slacken. *Just make it to the next corner, and the next.* Alleys conspired to lengthen the distance between each block, squeezing themselves into tight spaces like children cutting ahead in line.

Halfway up the steepest part of the hill, Tommy yanked

Violet to the right, pulling her in the direction of the Elm
Park Church, just a few blocks from the station. In spite of
her desperation, her lungs gave out. *Run,* she mouthed on
the end of a breath before doubling over. She let go of Tommy's hand with the Lackawanna Railway Station in sight.
Without turning back, Tommy pounded toward it.

Violet bowed her head. *Dear Lord* . . . The courthouse
clock chimed twice, snuffing out her prayer. Tears rolled
down her cheeks. She looked up and waited. A few seconds
later, two short blasts of a whistle sounded as a train pulled
away along the tracks.

Passersby turned up their collars and shoved their hands
in their pockets to protect against the November winds. Not
Violet. She welcomed the numbing cold. Such bitter air pre-
vented thought. She barely felt the spots on her feet where
her blisters broke as she limped the last two blocks. Another
whistle blew, this one three times, indicating the approach
of a train. Violet imagined throngs of people standing at the
track to greet their loved ones, and wondered what awaited
her as she now stood in front of the station.

*No need to hurry. Stay outside and savor the unknow-
ing. Imagine a world where trains depart late, and sisters
change their minds, and husbands arrive in time to spare
your heart.* Time. Violet glanced five stories up at the station's ornate clock, nestled in the center of the limestone
façade. The longer of the two bronzed hands pointed at the
Roman numeral *I.* Five minutes after the hour. If only that
hand could reverse its rotation. If only she could take back
her decision to rush to Stanley's side that morning. The
eagles flanking the clock seemed to agree.

Violet dropped her eyes and let them settle on the cast-
iron canopy bolted over the front entrance. Elaborate scroll-
work graced the gently arched frame. Protection from the
elements was only a few steps away. And Tommy. Violet

started forward. Whatever she had yet to face, Tommy was on the other side, already facing it.

Her wrecked feet dragged heavily in contrast to the unremitting patter in her chest. A few more steps. A hundred heartbeats. She staggered toward the entrance and watched as a uniformed man peered through the beveled glass, opened a shiny shellacked door, and waved her inside.

"The man in blue now helps her through!" he said, offering up a generous smile. "And tells her when her train is due." The doorman's words seemed at once familiar and absurd. Seeming to recognize Violet's confusion, he pointed to an old Lackawanna Railway poster on the wall with the slogan he'd just recited and a picture of the fictional Phoebe Snow, traveling in her immaculate white dress.

Violet stared at the man for a moment, unable to process his words.

"Are you all right, lady?"

She looked at him and tried for an answer. When the words refused to come, her knees began to buckle. She was still unable to catch her breath.

"You better sit down," he said, taking her arm.

Violet allowed herself to be led into the grand lobby with its marbled walls, and she took a seat on a bench that faced away from the main entrance. She bent her head toward her lap and fixed her eyes on the geometric pattern in the mosaic floor.

"I'll get you some water," the doorman said and hurried off.

When she lifted her head, the sun winked through the clouds, lighting up the vaulted stained-glass ceiling.

"Mommy!" a voice shouted from the far end of the lobby.

Violet cried out, then opened her arms as Daisy wiggled out of Tommy's embrace and ran toward her.

# C HAPTER THIRTY-SIX

LILY SAT WAITING at the back of the railway station, but for what, she didn't know. Hot air blew through a grate on the bottom half of the bench, warming her legs. To her right, a silhouetted hand, painted on a shingle, pointed to the newsstand inside the lobby. A little farther down the track, a clock jutted from the wall, displaying the time on a simple face—quarter to three. Overhead, a canopy spanned the length of the platform, its cast-iron design echoing the one out front, in the same way a plain girl resembles her pretty sister.

"All aboard!" the conductor called out from the 2:45 to Buffalo. When no other passengers came forward, the porters lifted up the footstools and closed the doors.

Two whistle blasts, and the engine pulled out of the station. Lily watched as the last car followed its coupled companions down the track and disappeared around a bend. Her eyes lingered on the empty space, as if to conjure up another train.

"I'm only here because Tommy insisted." Violet approached the bench, took a seat, and faced forward.

"I know." Not daring to look at her sister, Lily stared straight ahead as well. "He's a good man."

"And a good father."

Lily nodded. "You'll get no argument from me."

"And it stays that way." Violet's tone did not allow for compromise. "I refuse to worry about George Sherman any longer."

"George has no say in the matter." Lily's words were matter-of-fact. "Never did."

"Well, if he's not the . . ." Violet's brow furrowed as she worked out the answer. "Frankie?" she said with a start.

"He won't give you any trouble."

Violet pressed into the corner of the bench as she turned toward her sister. "How can you be so sure?"

"He's not here, is he?" said Lily, not bothering to look around. "The last thing he needs is a kid. Oh, he was willing, for my sake, but his heart isn't in it." She stiffened. "Besides, no child of mine is going to be Catholic. *Stand up. Sit down. Kneel.* And so much penance." Dropping her eyes she added, "The sin is mine, not hers."

"Frankie is bad news, Lily. Promise me you'll stay away from him."

"Not all bad," Lily smiled. "Maybe I'll give him a chance once I'm finished being mad at him."

"I don't want to hear that kind of talk, not even in jest."

"Can you imagine what George would say if I divorced him for an Italian?" Lily's laugh was joyless and short-lived.

"Enough," Violet said, as a trio of cigar smokers sauntered past on their way to the newsstand, exhaling pungent clouds. Violet fanned the air away from her still-aching lungs. "I don't know if I can ever trust you again."

"I understand." Lily nodded as if she'd already considered this and drawn the same conclusion. "If it means anything, I was out of my mind with grief."

"You can't be alone with her. Not for a long time. Maybe not ever."

"I know."

"Not without me by her side. Or Tommy." Violet shook her head.

"I couldn't do it. Did Tommy tell you?"

"It doesn't change anything."

"He found me here," she rubbed her hand across the back of the bench, "after the train pulled away. I never got on. I couldn't do that to you." She glanced at the space between them and patted the seat. "Or to her."

"It's not enough."

"It's something, though, isn't it?" The hopeful note in Lily's voice faltered. "It's all I have."

Violet needed to be angry, so she ignored the spark of pity in her heart. "They're waiting for me out front." She stood, but couldn't leave. "What are you going to do now?"

Lily considered the question for a long moment. "I don't know."

To Violet's surprise, the uncertainty appeared to engage Lily, not trouble her.

"I'm sorry," Lily said, looking Violet in the eye for the first time since she'd sat down.

"I know."

"I've made a mess of things. I'm not like you."

"You never had to be."

"Maybe."

Violet patted Lily's shoulder. "They're waiting for us."

Lily hesitated before standing up. "But you said . . ."

"You have to sort this out someplace. And Mother can use the extra pair of hands."

"Thank you." Lily looped her arm through Violet's and kissed her cheek. "I hope for Daisy's sake you and Tommy have another girl one day." She smiled. "There's nothing in the world like a sister."

# CONCLUDING WORDS

*The author trusts that* Woman: Her Sex and Love Life *will help,
in some slight degree, in spreading healthy, sane, and honest
ideas about sex among the men and women of America.*
—Woman: Her Sex and Love Life,
William J. Robinson, MD, 1929

Marriage seems to suit Violet. With Tommy by her side, she's lighter somehow. Proof of the old saying, *A burden shared is a burden halved.* Of course, welcoming her back to Providence Christian did her some good as well. We always said it was the decent thing to do.

Wish we could be as optimistic about that sister of hers, though. Not sure what's going on with Lily Sherman and her devil-may-care attitude. When she's not helping out at Grace and Owen's, she's running around making plans for a new orphanage, of all things. Doesn't leave much time for that husband of hers. And just where does she think she's going to get the money for that sort of undertaking? The Sherman family is certainly not known for its charitable works. When Myrtle was within earshot, Lily mentioned something to Abigail about a benefactor downtown, but try as we may, we can't imagine who that might be.

Stanley Adamski still lives down there, but he already gives most of his money away to the widowed and crippled. Now that the United Anthracite Miners joined back up with the United Mine Workers of America, Stanley is putting his energy into fighting for those with black lung. He says he'll make his case all the way to the Supreme Court, and we think he's fool enough to do it. That's what happens when you're raised without limits.

Like little Daisy Morgan. Or is it Davies now? Either way, Violet is going to have her hands full with that one. Why, just the other day, when Mrs. Trethaway was telling Reverend Sheets how it's a sin to marry out of your faith, Daisy interrupted with some story about an elephant married to a donkey up at Nay Aug Zoo. She may well get away with that sort of cheekiness now, but it's bound to catch up with her later in life. No man will want that kind of wife. Some lessons need to be taught in childhood if they're going to stick. Not every opinion is worth airing. The sooner she learns that, the better off she'll be.

# ACKNOWLEDGMENTS

"It is well to remember a good turn," as the Welsh proverb goes. I owe a debt of thanks to those who assisted me with the historical research for this book: Jane and James Widenor from the First Christian Church of Scranton; Mary Ann Moran-Savakinus and everyone at the Lackawanna Historical Society; Brian Fulton, staff librarian at the *Scranton Times-Tribune*; the employees at the Albright Memorial Library; and P. Casey Telesk who taught himself all about 1934 LaSalle automobiles, so he could teach me.

Also, many thanks and lots of love to my nephew, Jimmy McGraw, who answered all my questions about broken bones with his characteristic patience.

Thank you to my fellow "workshoppers"—those who were there from the beginning and those who joined us along the way: Tom Borthwick, Laurie Loewenstein, Nina Solomon, Theasa Tuohy, Liz Dalton, Kevin Heisler, Monique Lewis, Matthew McGevna, Deidre Sinnott, and Wendy Sheanin.

To Teresa Beattie, thank you for getting me through that last set of rewrites. You're an amazing life coach (truly!) and a wonderful friend.

Speaking of friends, thank you to Chris Tomasino. You read an early draft of *Sing in the Morning, Cry at Night* long before you became my agent. Over coffee, you talked to me about my next project and suggested my characters might have more to say. *All Waiting Is Long* was born out of that conversation, and I'm grateful for your insight.

And thanks to publisher Johnny Temple and everyone else at Akashic Books for giving me a chance to tell my stories. I'm proud to publish with Akashic and Kaylie Jones Books.

Special thanks to Kaylie Jones—mentor, editor, publisher, friend. Quite simply, everything I am as a writer is because of your patience, tenacity, talent, and passion for writing. Your generous spirit is boundless, and I love you.

And finally, although my dad passed away in 2013, I'd be remiss if I didn't acknowledge his contribution to this novel. He answered every question I had from pistols to prostitution. (Just to be clear, he had firsthand knowledge of the former, not the latter.) One night my sister and I took my dad out to dinner, and on the way home he noticed some overhead cables and started explaining streetcars to me. When he finished, he turned to my sister and said, "You know we're writing a book." And we were. However this novel is received, it's far better than it would have been without my dad's input, and I am a far better person for having known him.